GENTLEMEN OF THE NORTH

This is the Story

A STORY of the north and of the rivalries of the great fur companies. "Medicine Hair" the Indians called her, because of her golden-red locks. By another sort of "medicine" she charmed young Franklin to a new life. It starts a series of adventures that will keep the reader thrilled to the last page; the breaking of a bully, a journey through Indian country when the braves are on the warpath, a journey which comes to a surprising and breath-taking end.

GENTLEMEN OF THE NORTH

by
HUGH PENDEXTER

THE LITERARY PRESS LTD
LONDON

TO
HUGH PENDEXTER, Jr.
GOOD PAL, GOOD SON,
THIS BOOK IS AFFECTIONATELY
DEDICATED

PREFACE

In building this story I have made use of the following books for colour and historical facts: Alexander Henry's Journal, edited by the late Dr. Elliott Coues; "Lewis and Clark's Expedition," Chittenden's "American Fur Trade," H. H. Brackenridge's journal of his Missouri trip in 1811. Almost all the Indians named in the story were real characters. Old Tabashaw was killed by a Sioux war-party at Wild Rice River in the winter of 1807. Eshkebugecoshe, or Flat Mouth, chief of the Pillager Chippewas, was about thirty years old at the time of the story, and was one of Henry's hunters on Red River. He is credited with influencing the Chippewas to cease their practice of poisoning, and he refused to fight against the United States in 1812. Le Borgne is drawn after descriptions given by Brackenridge, members of the Lewis and Clark Expedition, Henry and others. For the sake of speeding up the action I have forced the coalition of the N. W. and the X. Y. companies by a few months. The merger was completed on November 5, 1804, and the winter express brought the news to Henry at the Pembina post on January 1, 1805.

Hugh Pendexter.

CONTENTS

CHAPTER I

THE ICE GOES OUT

A BROWN river rolling up from the south between banks of oak and willow and bois blanc, surrounded by the wet, steaming woods of April and flanked on the west by plains which climb higher and higher until they find the Rockies. A brown river bearing the trunks of mighty trees; a silent, sullen flood carpeted with dead buffaloes. This is the most persistent of all my pictures of the Red River of the North.

It is long since I have gazed upon it. Yet there is scarcely a day my thoughts do not travel back to some phase of it; to the time when the rivalry was at its height between the North West Company and our opponents, the X. Y. Company.

Sir Alexander MacKenzie's vehicle in fighting our arrogant Simon McTavish for the fur trade—and the indomitable Hudson's Bay Company, which was to swallow us all. Of all my recollections of cruel hardships and wild freedom, that view of the river in early April, 1804, left the deepest impress on me. This, partly because it was a symbol of the country's desolation and loneliness and savage hostility to us Northmen, partly because that April day proved to be the threshold to remarkable experiences, wherein I was to suffer much and find the great happiness.

When the spell is on me, which is often, the civilised horizon of the Northwest films over and again I behold the brown expanse of freshet waters hurrying with their gruesome toil to mingle with the Assiniboin at the Forks. No other river linked us Northmen so closely with the Sioux country in the South, that source of perpetual menace. The danger that might come down the river at any minute kept alive my interest in it and stimulated my imagination as I watched its muddy tide, choked with innumerable shaggy victims, sweeping by the Pembina River post of the N. W. Company. It was a bridge between the known perils of the Pembina country and the barbarity of the Adder People.

It was tingling to young blood to know a fate worse than death might be descending the river at any time. Let the Sioux war-parties range ever so wide of our domain, and yet, night and day, we felt their presence, we few Northmen and our Chippewas.

The slamming of a door to one of the men's huts outside the stockade at night became the discharge of a Sioux gun; a frightened mob would come hammering at the gate and frantically demanding admittance, old Tabashaw, the chief and thorough scoundrel, in the lead. A buffalo bull with a broken leg had been wounded by a Sioux; for days the hunters would hug the fort. Or the buffaloes stampeded, or large flocks of swans rose in alarm from the river above us; it was break open the gun cases and serve out powder and ball. The wind from the south brought smoke; only a Sioux fire could have made it. An old woman dreamed a Sioux warrior stuck his head in her hut and counted the men there; the children and women are hurried inside the stockade. Horsemen riding and raising a cloud of snow can only be Sioux warriors on a winter path. Even Flat Mouth, chief of the Pillager band of Chippewas, young like myself, a very brave man and much travelled, has galloped to the fort after mistaking red deer in August for enemy horsemen.

Thus it went from day to night and then repeated. Always omens and signs to remind us of those ferocious people who gave no quarter and who would never forget it was the Chippewa Nation that prevented their holding a clear title to the headwaters of the Mississippi. Summer and winter, with the new leaf and with the yellow, tobacco was passing between the Chippewas, Crees, and Assiniboins for war against the Sioux. Never while I was in the country did the Northern Indians accomplish anything lasting. A sudden foray, a few scalps danced; that was about all.

Undoubtedly a subconscious fear of the Sioux was also responsible for the picture of the brown river in April. Some imaginative quality of reasoning, perhaps, interpreted the herds of drowned buffaloes as a symbol of the Sioux's power and remorselessness. When Nature has an opportunity for unlimited slaughter, she turns Sioux and kills on a tremendous scale.

Three seasons I heard the ice give and go out with the noise of many guns, wrenching earth and trees from the banks like some aquatic behemoth with claws many fathoms wide. The first time was at the Park River post above the Pembina; once from our outpost at the mouth of Reed River, ten miles below the Pembina. But never was I filled with such longing to follow the ice through the Forks and down the trail of lake and river to Superior as on that mild April day of 1804. It wasn't homesickness, for I was completing my third season as company clerk and had no ties back East to draw me. It was "Black" Chabot, *bourgeois,* or postmaster, who was serving in place of Mr. Alexander Henry, the man I came out with, who was now up the Saskatchewan on important business for the gentlemen of the North.

It's not boasting to say I felt no physical fear of Chabot, although he was an overgrown hulk of a man with an immense black beard. His savage ways left nothing for our Chippewas to teach him. But I did not fear him, for I could kill him as a last resort. It was the daily grind of having to associate with the brute that got on my nerves. The best of friends wear on each other at times when cooped up for a long winter in close quarters; at his best Chabot was intolerable. For two months I had kept my hand on my skinning-knife whenever he approached me.

I hoped he would keep his beastly temper in check and never lay hands on me; for, did he do that, the

Pembina would need a new master or a new clerk. The danger lay in his growing love for alcohol, thinly mixed with water—"high wine" the trade called it. When in drink, which was his normal condition, he was very variable in his moods, ranging from the caressing to the ferocious and always foul-mouthed. If he ever attacked me, I was determined not to cower like a sheep and be murdered, as I've known Chippewa squaws to die when their husbands were in a drunken fury. And, did one resist him, it must be to the limit; kill or be broken.

The post was well situated at the mouth of the Pembina, and opposite Peter Grant's old fort on the east bank of the Red, now in ruins, the first North West Company post established on the river. Below us grew large bois blanc, or whitewood, which we used for floorings. Between us and the western plains were the big oaks we had drawn on in constructing the buildings. From the Pembina to the Park the country was level and open, the only timber being along the banks of the Red. The Pembina site was discouraging enough when Mr. Henry and I looked it over. It was heaped high with fallen trees and the underbrush was so rank one couldn't see a dozen feet in any direction.

We soon remedied that, however. But the fairest spot on earth would become detestable if it had to contain Chabot and his drunken humours. He may have done big things for the N. W. when he was on the Assiniboin. Give the devil his due; he must have accomplished much to be appointed master at Pembina. It must have been that he traded his high wine instead of giving so much of it to himself. He had held himself in during the fall, but the winter had broken down all self-restraint. So I was keen to return East and ask for another position. I had committed myself to furthering the interests of Simon McTavish, of McTavish, Frobisher & Company.

The breath of the fur company had filled my lungs, and, although well educated for those days, I had no dreams of ever doing anything except to trade for buffalo robes and beaver. I had nursed ambitions. I desired to become a notable Northman. So the wild fowl, filling the sky, were no more eager to make their Northern homes than was I to make the Grand Portage and hasten on to Montreal and obtain a transfer.

Now that the time was near for starting the skin canoes down the river it did not seem I could compose my soul in patience to await the great day. Strangely enough this approach of freedom suddenly caused me to fear that I and not Black Chabot might precipitate a tragedy. As I gazed on the woeful waste of hides swirling by the post, I repeatedly vowed I would watch myself every minute and keep away from Chabot as much as possible. I even planned to leave ahead of him and the brigade, on the excuse it would be well for me to visit our station on the Scratching, where the X. Y. opposition also was established.

"Red" Dearness was the new master there, having arrived late in the winter with Madame, his woman. He was a surly sort, I heard, something of a recluse. Fragments of gossip about his woman had her full-blood and quarter. It would never do for me to suggest the trip. Black Chabot must think it was his own idea and something of a hardship for me. I fancied I was intelligent enough to bring this about.

I thought of several different methods for planting the notion in his thick head as I idly watched the Indian women drag buffaloes to the bank. They were lifting the back fat and removing the tongues, leaving the rest to rot except for one or two which they cut up for their own use. We white men would not eat drowned buffalo, but the Chippewas were fond of it. The meat did appear to be all right, fresh and firm. Of course the women could secure only one or two out of each hundred huge bodies floating by. There were literally herds of the big brutes. Above and below our post every river was contributing its ghastly cargo. Thousands and thousands perished each season in crossing the ice. And this terrific waste had been going on for hundreds and probably thousands of years. In addition to the carcasses floating downstream there were countless bodies lodged along the banks of the many rivers. Soon there would arise an awful stench, for there were not enough scavengers to cheat the hot sun.

On the plains as far as the eye could reach were living and dead buffalo. Bald eagles and crows and wolves were battening on the fallen. Our dogs chased those afoot that wandered near the fort. Many a scabby old bull carried a crow on his back and displayed a furious temper under the implacable and continuous pecking. The beasts were a sad sight to look at now, lean and showing huge patches where their winter coats had fallen out.

Back in February one of the hunters said he had found a calf frozen to death and declared it was a positive sign of an early spring. At that time we were finishing two hundred cords in our four chimneys and were sceptical of such prophecies. Still, the season did break early, although for the life of me I never could understand why abnormally cold weather in February should forecast an early breaking up of the ice. For that matter the strong timber Indians have many signs and omens which come to nothing.

The town-bred would have found nothing but grim severity in the panorama. But I knew the ash-leaf maples were running and that the women were making sugar, and I felt the wind mild and mellow as it blew up from the south, promising a clear passage home even if it brought the reek of smoke which might mean the Sioux. The summer birds and frogs unqualifiedly insisted it was springtime and high time for one to desire to go somewhere.

In and outside the stockade the hunters were preparing their traps for the spring hunt. Already the racoons were beginning to leave their hollow trees during the daytime, and quite a few were being taken. That morning one of the Indians had brought in several wolf pups, tame and playful as kittens. He intended raising them for sled dogs. An important event was the arrival of two men with the winter express from Portage La Prairie, bringing orders to Chabot and bearing other matters which must be taken without delay to Grand Portage.

How I longed to carry the express! With the season so early I knew I could make Sault Ste. Marie before June. Unfortunately Chabot was the master, and after reading his orders he had stuffed them in his leather coat and lavishly treated the messengers to rum before sending them on their way. They were half drunk when they left, and he continued drinking alone.

Short Arms came in howling over the death of a child, and he must have a keg of liquor to drive away his sorrow and some red cloth and vermilion to cover the body. Chabot had no excuse for getting the express drunk and thereby delaying the business of the gentlemen of the North, but of course it was necessary to give the rum to the Indian. With the English, as with the French before them and as it would be with the Americans in the South, liquor was the backbone of the fur trade.

It made it beastly disagreeable at times for any one inclined to be fastidious, but only high wine would bring in furs and skins for a surety. Even in Montreal, the heart of the Northern fur trade, I have heard people complain about the universal practice of trading rum for pelts. Substitute something else for rum and see how many packs of beaver go down the St. Lawrence.

I do not suppose that that particular morning differed greatly from those that preceded it, yet it sticks in my memory like a burr to a bull because it was the beginning of a wonderful experience for me, the coming of something which was to affect my whole life and bring contentment out of a welter of great dangers. The details, even the trivial things, stand very clear-cut. All things counted, it had been a busy morning. Old Tabashaw was drunk early and bawling some new medicine songs in an attempt to cure a young woman whose jealous husband had shot an arrow through her body. Those not employed in making their traps fit were playing their game of platter and pestering me for liquor.

Before pausing to watch the river I had overseen the making of the last of the pemmican, ninety pounds to a bag, fifty of beef and the rest in grease. I also had supervised the repairing and the gumming of the canoes. These had rested all winter under thick covering of hay, their frames loosened, and they needed careful attention. I had pursued and caught Little Crane and made him give up pelts due for his debt. He was taking his hunt to the X. Y. post, angry because I had refused him an extra ration of rum.

When I halted him and insisted on his squaring his debt, the scoundrel tried to knife me, but a clout over the head with my strong club quickly brought him to his senses, or, rather, knocked him senseless. My duty to my employers demanded I prevent the Crane from cheating us out of the debt and enriching "Red" Dearness, of the opposition.

I had small stomach for what immediately followed. Some women came in from the Pembina Mountains, bringing a pack of prime beaver which they were taking to the X. Y. post on the Scratching to pay their men's debt. We had a hut in the mountains and a small assortment of goods to catch the Cree and Assiniboin as well as the Chippewa trade. Had there been any chance of honourably trading for the pack, our men would have done so. But the furs were already owed to the opposition. When Chabot learned of the women's presence and their intention of carrying their pack down-river, he raged and cursed the hill men for fools for ever letting the beaver get by them. Then he demanded the women give the furs to him, and when they refused he fought them. They fought like wildcats, but he got the trade.

Such work was bound to make bad business for us, for the devil had been to pay ever since the X. Y. and the H. B. opposition came to the Red. During my three seasons there I had seen the Chippewas, Crees, and Assinibois spoiled. Each season they grew worse.

If a man killed a few skins, we treated him as if he were a big chief. Almost all of them had scarlet coats. It was bad enough when we had to cater to old Tabashaw, the drunken nuisance, but when we had to coddle every hunter who made an ordinary hunt it was not only tedious but dangerous. If I punished a man for stealing supplies, he would go down to the Scratching to be petted up by Dearness. And we made much of those who came to us after being corrected at the X. Y. Of course, such conditions couldn't continually grow worse without our dead bodies being thrown into the Red to vary the monotony of drowned buffalo. And, having created such an evil situation, it was madness for Black Chabot to take skins from the native women by brute force.

All this and a dozen other tag ends of trouble were swimming through my mind as I watched the women drag the buffaloes ashore and tried to perfect my scheme for being sent on ahead to the Scratching.

When a great hubbub inside the stockade attracted my attention I took it for granted another jealous buck had knifed his wife or bitten off her nose, but a glance showed me Chabot's huge form and black whiskers, and the air seemed to be filled with wolf pups. The owner of the pups looked bad about the eyes but contented himself with grunting as he gathered his pets in a corner. Chabot, from sheer brutality, had halted on entering the gate to kick the little creatures out of his path. Now he swaggered up to me, looking very nasty. I dropped my hand over my knife and braced my feet.

His first words, bawled out so the whole post could hear, were—

"Found out yet who cut that hole through the back of the storehouse?"

This stock question was the barometer of his drams. Nearly three months before some Indian had cut a hole through the logs of the storehouse and by means of a gun-screw on the end of a stick had attempted to fish out some of our trade goods. Fortunately the screw had broken off at the first trial and had dropped inside, and we had lost nothing. When at the fighting peak of his drinking Chabot always brought this matter up, treating it as if it were a fresh crime and peculiarly within my province to solve. There was scarcely anything outside of personal abuse which he could have said that would have irritated as did this query.

In my exasperation I answered—

"I'll get a *wabeno* drum and go into a trance and maybe find out all about it."

Instantly I was sorry to have said it, for I remembered my fears of a flare-up at the last minute and my firm resolve to avoid it. And now I had invited a tragedy by my sarcasm.

"Franklin, that ain't the way to talk to me," he murmured. "As clerk you're supposed to keep track of the goods."

Once more my good intentions flew away and I angrily rejoined:

"I can't keep track of anything stolen unless I steal it myself. Please remember that nothing was taken."

"I do remember," he snorted. "This post would go to——if I didn't do most of the remembering. Why didn't you look for tracks?"

This was a fair sample of his drunken unreasonableness when he was primed to pick a quarrel. Now I was determined to hold myself in check and politely observed—

"Pardon me, but the dogs had raced back and forth through the snow and destroyed all signs before you and I could look the round over."

"You've always got a good reason for not doing things," he murmured.

Once he lowered his voice it was time to look out for trouble. Twice within a minute he had spoken gently. I stepped back, pretending to be watching the sturgeon jumping in the river, but in reality to get elbow room as I toyed with the haft of my knife.

"When you going to finish that pemmican?" he softly asked.

"It's all finished," I said, gripping the knife-handle.

"Well, for God's sake, try to find something to do besides sight-seeing," he bellowed. The danger was past for the time and my hand dropped to my side. In his bull of Bashan voice he continued, "One of the men is just down from up-river with twenty beaver, six still in the meat, and you ought to be on hand to trade them. Give him a quart of that West Indies rum that's spoiled. The fools think it's French brandy. Tell him it's a present for getting skins while those other skunks do nothing but loaf. Shows what they can do if they want to. He's only been gone two days."

His idea of teaching the idlers the profits of industry caused me to smile, try as I would to keep a straight face, for the loafers were all drunk. He caught the smile, although I swallowed it fast enough, and added—

"After you've traded the skins I want to see you in my room." Low tone again, the danger signal.

I believe we had reached a point where something radical must happen. I could no longer gain anything by trying to avoid him, to dodge his vicious moods. The man who found the wolf pups and several others were watching us and listening. They furnished me my cue and, jerking my head toward them, I warned:

"You're spoiling your own trade when you talk this way to me. They're ready for mischief. The X. Y. has spoiled them."

My reference to the opposition caused him to forget me. With a howl of rage he began cursing "Red" Dearness and his woman. He had never seen the latter, yet he included her in his volley of invectives. He had met "Red" Dearness once at the mouth of Reed River and came within an inch of locking canoes and having it out to the death.

"I kicked White Partridge nearly to death after he stole my horse and went over there. When Dearness heard about it he made a chief out of the skunk. As soon as I can get the Indians off for the summer hunt and the brigade under way I'm going to have a settlement with that red hound."

"That will mean the two posts will fight it out with the Indians waiting to kill off the survivors. Then the H. B. will have a clear field. Dearness is new down here, but from what I hear you don't want to start blazing a trail toward him unless you're willing to finish it. I don't see as he has done any worse than you have. He'll probably have something to say about your taking the skins from the women."

Instead of increasing his rage this frank speech set him to chuckling heavily. He was remembering his coup against the X. Y.

"The Arrer's woman tried to cut my throat," he guffawed. "He'd sell her to me for a nine-gallon keg."

"If he does, she'll cut your throat in earnest," I warned. "But to get back to me; when the Indians see I am treated with disrespect, they'll decide you can be treated the same way."

"Pooh! I'll break the back of the first dirty buck that looks at me squint-eyed," he bellowed.

"Hurt one and you hurt every Chippewa in the Northwest. Next fall we'll find they've been passing tobacco to wipe us out."

This statement jolted him and he stared at me steadily for half a minute and began plucking at his long beard. He was half drunk and wanted to deride my warning. However, there was a streak of fear in his make-up. He tried to laugh and carried it off poorly, for in the midst of a guffaw he happened to catch the scowling gaze of the wolf-hunter and grew very sober.

"Never mind about the beaver pelts. I'll go down and trade them," he mumbled. "Old Tabashaw has been telling the men he has a new medicine and can make rum and iron arrers."

"He's bad," I gravely agreed. "The year I was at

the Park post we gave him a New Year's treat of rum,
flour and sugar, and he paid us by trying to bribe our
hunter to leave us, so we would have to pay more for
our meat. We were giving the hunter sixty skins, cloth
for his wife and all his ammunition too. Trouble with
him is our giving his men too many red coats. When
he alone had a red coat and a red feather for his hair,
he felt he was chief. Now all his men feel as big as
he does. He knows his power over the tribe is slipping
and he wants to get it back. He's making ready for
the Grand Medicine ceremony. After that's over and
they begin making the *wabeno*, he'll spring some new
tricks. That's why he plays his new drum so much.
Black Robe told his woman yesterday that the chief can
kill any man, red or white, by just wishing him to die."

"The poisoners!" grunted Chabot, winding up with
a little shiver. "He's at it now, the murderer!"

He referred to the monotonous thudding of the new
drum, accompanying the chief's yowling voice in more
wabeno songs. The chief had pretended to extract a
piece of metal from the wounded woman's side and had
collected a big kettle and two blankets from the husband. Now he was seeking another piece of metal in
her neck, for which he would be generously paid.

The fact that the arrow had left no foreign substance
in the wound did not impair the husband's credulity.
The more fragments of iron the old rascal would pretend
to draw from the poor body the greater his reputation
as a medicine man. His voice rose above the noise
made by the dogs, the women and the children. Chabot
had heard him throughout the morning without paying
any heed. Indian howling and drumming and fighting
was a background we were used to, just as we were
used to the song of the river and never heard it unless
we stopped and deliberately listened.

Now, because of my words, the chief's song had a new
significance. In it Chabot was finding a threat against
his life. Although I was glad to have diverted his attention from me, I began to regret having mentioned poison.

It would never do for him to show he was afraid. We were but a handful of white men possessing treasure the natives yearned for—rum. We were surrounded by one of the largest tribes on the continent, a people numerous and brave enough to drive the Sioux south. We held our place at the top of the heap only by holding our heads high and forcing the impression that we belonged there.

I had often travelled alone to the Pembina Mountains and all through the Reed and Red Lake Rivers districts and up the Red far beyond Grandes Fourches, in seeking Indian families to kill skins for us. But with the exception of eccentric attacks by drunken men I had never been in actual danger. There had been many times, however, when my scalp would have dried in smoke over a tent-pole had I shown the white feather. There was only one Indian along the whole river in whom I put any trust. It was a whimsical truth that this exception should be Flat Mouth, a chief of the greatest band of robbers in the whole Chippewa Nation. So it was with lively concern that I watched the changing expression in Chabot's eyes and feared that his face under the heavy beard was developing lines of weakness.

"The only thing to do is to be firm with them," I remarked.

"Yes, yes. Of course. We must be firm," he muttered, trying to frown at the wolf-hunter. Then with a shrug of his powerful shoulders he said, "We'll be getting out pretty soon. Very soon."

"Not for a month at the quickest," I reminded.

"As soon as I can settle their accounts and hire the summer men, the brigade starts," he sullenly replied.

"But the X. Y. and the H. B. canoes won't start till sometime in May," I protested.

"They can start when they please," he growled. "The brigade from this post pulls out when I give the word. I shall have the packs made up very soon."

This was a startling announcement. I was keen enough to go down the river, but a premature departure would cause a commotion among the company heads. However, I did not believe he could complete his arrangements for the summer men as speedily as he intimated.

"If we go out before everything is caught up, the opposition will steal our trade and our hunters," I was reminding, when a shot from the plains side of the stockade, quickly followed by excited whoops, saved me a stinging rebuke and sent him hastening to the window.

It was nothing out of the ordinary. Prior to our conversation Chabot would have thought nothing of it. Now he looked apprehensively from the window, sighed in great relief, and allowed his face to twist with mirth. He shouted boisterously and clapped his hands. One would have thought it a great feat. A scraggy bull that had lost its sight in some recent prairie fire had wandered near the stockade. A hunter had fired a ball into its side.

Now the poor brute was running wildly about, colliding with trees and stumps, pursued and tormented by half a dozen Indians. Blind buffaloes were a very common sight, especially in the late fall when the plains burn in large areas until extinguished by heavy snow or prolonged rains. With all their hair burned off and their skin shrivelled up they prompt a humane man to end their misery with a ball. But this spectacle was sickening and I wasn't over-fastidious. I turned to get my gun and end the miserable sport but was anticipated by a buck, who ran in and leaped on the brute's back, then to his side and despatched him with an axe.

Thrusting his head from the window, Chabot applauded in a stentorian voice.

"Well done, Mauvaise Hache! Good work! Come inside and have some new milk (rum)!"

It was nauseating. Rewarding an idler's attack on a blind bull as if he had penetrated deep beyond the old Sioux war-road and had brought back a dozen packs of prime furs to trade! The unexpected invitation not only brought Bad Axe, proudly flourishing his bloody weapon, but all the others, whom I had refused during the morning while Chabot was drinking with the express. I went down with him and, to make matters worse, he drank with them. The condescension of the fool was disgusting. Once you drink with a man whom you wish to feel your inferior he will proclaim himself your equal. To watch him pour the rum and pat Bad Axe on the shoulder and bellow out praise would make one think the lazy dog had brought in ten tents of his people, all heavily loaded with trade. The owner of the wolf pups edged toward the master and I stepped to his side and made sure his hands were empty and no knife was in his clout.

Chabot no sooner glimpsed him than he eagerly extended a brimming mug. The fellow snatched it, his little eyes flickering like a snake's, and vague wonderment at his luck, at the meaning of it all, showed in his heavy face. While they were guzzling their first dram old Tabashaw sniffed the air and threw aside his drum and staggered into the room, loudly proclaiming:

"New milk! Give it to me! It gives a good taste to the smoke. Let us have plenty of new milk so the children won't cry!"

I wanted to cuff the old vagabond's ears until he couldn't hear the last trump, for his drunken speech contained a most vicious threat. It was the same as if he had said we would all be killed if he was refused a drink, thereby leaving our children to mourn. An hour before Chabot would have kicked him back to his damnable drumming, garnishing his flight with a volley of curses. Now he actually grinned and poured him a mug of "wine."

During our first season on the river we could dilute a quart of river water with a gill of alcohol and trade it for six prime beaver skins. I've traded a three-point blanket and a nine-gallon keg of high wine, highly diluted, for a hundred and twenty-five beaver; less than fifteen dollars' worth of stuff for more than four hundred dollars' worth of skins, Halifax currency. But our Indians would no longer stand so much water and the profits were a bit less. Now their milk must be strong. It was; the effects were speedy.

Old Tabashaw howled out another poorly veiled threat by saying a hunter had found a sign that meant the destruction of the post and all the white men on the river. He referred to a badger that had chased a skunk into a hollow stump and had been caught in a trap hidden there. This prophecy was bound to have an evil effect, yet Chabot made no move to counteract it. So I grabbed the old villain by the throat with one hand and snatched Bad Axe's weapon with the other and, as he crashed over backward with me on top, I loudly promised to leave his hair and brains sticking to the floor unless he explained what he meant by such talk. He wasn't so drunk but what he could be cunning, and he protested:

"The Sioux will come. But the Chippewas will die fighting for their white friends."

I accepted this amendment, having scored my point of showing the men we would stand no nonsense; only it should have been Black Chabot and not a subordinate who took action. A year before, when Mr. Henry was at the post, Tabashaw had started much the same kind of talk as a preface for a general massacre. But Mr. Henry had taken the notion out of him before he could barely begin.

Chabot looked troubled but did not upbraid me; nor did he rebuke the Indians. With the chief silenced the effects of the drink returned to its usual ruts. A young buck decided his woman was unfaithful and stabbed her in the knee as she was stealing a drink out of his mug. And he would have done for her had I not nearly brained him with a stool. It was not my place, however, to keep the men from murdering each other. Even had the master been absent, it would not have been customary

to interfere with their drinking beyond driving them
clear of the fort.

To be rid of the scene I went for my horse to ride
out on the plains to try my new double-barrel gun on
the buffalo. The horse came from the Mandans and
was a noble buffalo horse. He was crazy for the hunt,
but I quickly found my heart was not in the sport. He
repeatedly ran me along beside bull or cow and waited
for me to shoot, while the only ambition I could enter-
tain was to follow the river north, to get clear of Chabot.

The sun was screened off by clouds of pigeons and
the earth was cluttered with buffaloes; I did not fire a
single shot, although I rode several miles from the fort.
I was so absent-minded that I kept but little reckoning
of my wanderings until my mount halted beside a calf.
It was lying down and hiding its head in the grass after
its silly fashion. It had followed its mother until tired
out.

As I was mounted it was not afraid of me but
staggered to its shaky legs and would have followed my
horse back inside the stockade had not its mother at
that moment come tearing back to the rescue. My horse
raced me into a desirable position. But we had buffalo
enough and our stock of frozen meat was thawing and
spoiling. So I galloped away and left the calf to be
consoled by the mother until the river or an arrow
measured out its destiny.

On my return to the fort I found the place in an
uproar, the women now having procured rum and adding
their jealousies and whimsies to the general confusion.
As I entered, Tabashaw, in an exuberance of ferocity,
threw his drum from him and trampled upon it and
smashed it and loudly proclaimed that thus would he
stamp out all white men. The Indians were over-
running the place. A few years before there had been
no stockades about the forts in the Northwest, and the
red nuisances came and went as they would. When
Mr. Henry built the stockade round the Park River post
they had been very wrathy until we made them believe

the barrier was intended to keep out the Sioux. The Lord knows we had gone through enough in teaching them their place without letting down the bars now. Chabot was not to be seen, but the bucks and the women were everywhere and several boys were openly fighting over sugar one of them had filched.

I came just in time to witness the climax of one family row. Old Crow's young wife had resented his trying to disfigure her for life by burning her rather comely features with a brand from the fireplace and was leaving him. The old devil pursued her through the gate to make her leave their boy with him. The child, not more than seven or eight, guarded his mother's retreat with great sportsmanship by shooting several arrows at his father. The bow was small and the arrows were not sent with much force, but one did wound the old sot in the cheek, whereat the youngster claimed a coup and yelled like a young demon.

The sight of the savages swarming over our quarters, handling and appropriating our effects, maddened me. Mr. Henry had been stern in Indian discipline. What I beheld was a prelude to a massacre. Unless the licence was immediately squelched every white man on the river would fight for his life and most likely lose it. I grabbed a tent-pole and began swinging it in a circle, bringing them down in rows, regardless of sex. Those who could not crawl out were thrown out. As Tabashaw beheld his people making this unceremonious exit he reasserted himself and called for volunteers to capture the fort and make an end of the white men.

"We will kill them all and trade the furs at the Scratching post for new milk!" he yelled.

His speech appealed to their drunken minds. One man, who had been dancing wildly before the stockade gate, waving his axe and calling the Sioux "old women" and defying them to come out of the plains and give him battle, turned around and threw the axe at me. I had my gun and my first instinct was to shoot. But the man was crazy, the others were crazy, and the lesson would be lost. An Indian in rum never profits by an object lesson. So I stood on my guard, watching out for axes or arrows, and called over my shoulder to Chabot. Apparently the test had come and the long threatened uprising was about to be a fact. Chabot heard me, or else he happened to be appearing on the scene, for I heard his heavy step behind me as I faced the infuriated Indians.

"Kill them all! Kill old Black Face!" incited Tabashaw.

Chabot's countenance, despite his beard, betrayed a great fear, and yet it was not the Chippewas he feared, for without seeming to sense the climax now thrust upon us he passed by me and descended among the gesticulating figures. Buffeting them aside and walking like a blind man feeling his way, he advanced to the stockade gate and closed it and dropped the bar in place without a hand being raised against him. Whether his bold action took them so by surprise as to leave them incapable of hostile action, or whether they were so drunk as not to realise the master of the post was in their power, I can't say. Anyway, he gained the gate and then turned back, but now he made the mistake of trying to run.

Instantly they became galvanised into venomous activity and only their bloodthirsty eagerness saved him. They crowded so closely about him they could not wield their weapons effectively. Chabot continued oblivious to their purpose. I raised my gun, trying to decide just where the two barrels would do the most good, when the master found his voice. Raising both arms and throwing back his big head, he roared out:

"The Sioux! The Sioux are upon us!"

There was nothing so likely to sober the Chippewas as this alarm. Although remaining very drunk in the body their minds reacted mechanically at the dread words and their hostility to us instantly vanished. Old Tabashaw clawed at Chabot's arm and pleaded for protection. Many times I had believed the Sioux were upon us in force, but never had I betrayed my fears. Let the master show concern and the natives become worthless. They will leave a stout stockade that can defy several hundred Sioux, and scatter helter-skelter to the woods to be run down and slaughtered. Chabot's wild outcry threw them into a terrible panic, and they raised a tremendous clamour. These were the very men who another day would pass war tobacco and penetrate deep into the Sioux country and seek desperate odds.

It was always thus, one side attacking, one giving away; seldom did two forces grow brave at the same time. Therein they differed from white men. They required a show of weakness to arouse their courage; then they could be quite terrific.

Old Crow's runaway wife and child now returned to the gate and began pounding it and screaming to be admitted. They could see no foe, but from their noise one would think the devil was within a rod of them.

Jumping down into the mob, I caught Chabot by the arm and dragged him into the door, demanding—

"What have you seen?"

He eyed me wildly, as if not recognising me. It was not until I had him over the threshold and had shaken him smartly did he find his voice.

"The hills is full of their smokes!" he bellowed.

I ran to a rear window and looked to the west. Only the buffaloes and their ghostly trailers, the grey wolves, were on the plain. Smoke was crawling high in the direction of the Pembina Mountains. But it was nothing unusual at this time of year. Beaver hunters, about to return, invariably made a smoke to announce their coming. I told Chabot as much, but he insisted the smoke was made by our inveterate enemy; and he began breaking open the gun cases. Some of the racoon hunters now arrived from the woods and joined Old Crow's wife and child in demanding admittance, one of them frenziedly trying to chop a hole through the gate. Those inside were crowding and pushing against the gate in an attempt to get out. Hell was loose.

I left Chabot working over the gun cases and fought my way to the gate and removed the bar, then battled until it had space to swing open. In rushed the hunters; outward surged those already inside. The impact of the two opposing bodies brought the entire group to a standstill for a moment. Placing my hands on the shoulders of two bucks, I raised myself above their heads and harangued them, saying:

"What is the matter with you? Are you all old women? Does a little smoke scare you? Where is Flat Mouth? He isn't a coward."

Old Tabashaw began babbling the omen of the skunk chased by the badger. The woman who had dreamed of a Sioux warrior counting the men in the Chippewa tents shrilly added her prophecy. Then, to my relief, Flat Mouth came running from the river. He was the only composed one in the lot. Pointing to the smoke and then to my horse outside the gate, I explained the situation and asked him to ride out on the plains and learn the truth. Without a word he leaped on the horse and dashed away, riding straight for the signal.

His prompt readiness to investigate tended to calm the others, and they intelligently commenced preparations for our defence. In about an hour Flat Mouth came galloping back. We opened the gate, but he dismounted outside and entered leisurely, announcing:

"Beaver smokes. Some Crees and Assiniboins are coming with the hut people from the hills, bringing their trade here instead of leaving it at the hut."

At once the Chippewas were hysterical with joy and they danced and clapped their hands and proclaimed their intentions of exchanging tobacco with the newcomers and arranging for a big war party against the Sioux. As changeable as children, they were now lusting to go seek the enemy.

I took Flat Mouth aside to satisfy myself his information was correct. He was sure, he said. Although he had seen the hill party at a considerable distance he had recognised the carts used by our three men in taking trade goods to the hill hut. Being freed from a Sioux menace did not leave me altogether happy, however. It meant another kind of unpleasantness, that was all. The new trade being brought in would call for more drinking; when the Crees and Assiniboins have a drinking match with their friends the Chippewas it's high time to hide all weapons.

Going inside, I told Chabot what the Pillager had learned. He quit the gun cases and in his usual bluster went to the door and berated the Indians for being cowards. Returning to me, he fumbled inside his leather coat and finally fished out a despatch, brought by the express, and informed:

"I have orders to send you to the X. Y. post on the Scratching. You are to make a bargain with Red Dearness to the effect that neither the X. Y. nor the N. W. shall send out any men to drum up trade. The N. W. is anxious to agree not to accept any trade unless it's brought in to a post. When the brigade goes out, I will see the H. B. factor myself and strike a similar bargain."

"When does the brigade start?"

"I don't know," he evaded, lowering his eyes. "But you are to start to-morrow."

"I shall want a man to go with me."

"Take old Tabashaw and drown him and I'll give you a pack of beaver," he gritted. "I'll give him a hundred drops of laudanum in his next dram and see if that will stop his yawp. Take who you want to."

I picked Flat Mouth. The trip I had secretly planned was now an open path for me without my having said a word. Inwardly I rejoiced and was impatient for the morning to come. Only I wished I knew more about Chabot's plans for going down the river. I was intensely loyal to the N. W. and hoped he had changed his mind about a too early departure.

CHAPTER II

THE BRIGADE GOES OUT

EARLY next morning a Red Sucker band of Indians came in with their families from Turtle River above us, where they had wintered. They brought sixty beaver, a bale of fox, another of wolf, a few fisher and two martens; also a skin canoe loaded with bear fat, melted the fall before and poured into bags of red deerskin. They had quite a quantity of pemmican, which had spoiled because their fear of the Sioux had prevented their taking the ordinary precautions to dry out the skin canoe at least once in each twenty-four hours. The skin canoe is made of raw buffalo hides stretched over a willow frame with the hair inside. It will carry a heavy load but is no good except for floating downstream. Unless emptied and dried over a fire or by the sun once a day, it becomes waterlogged and will sink.

One of the party had found a buffalo with a broken leg. Although their own people frequently wounded buffalo, which escaped, they took it for granted this creature had been hunted by the Sioux. They had precipitately decamped, leaving their sugar making, driven by fear to make the post. They did not dare stop and dry the big canoe until it began to settle. Before they could unload, the pemmican was soaked.

Like excited children telling some tremendous bear story they described the Sioux signs. Had we not already passed through a siege of nerves the day before their recital would have had our Indians badly frightened. As it was, their alarm fell on deaf ears. No one showed any interest in them until one of the band informed Chabot he had killed a big grizzly and must have rum to appease the spirit of the slain monster, also half a yard of red cloth to hang up as an additional conciliation.

This request, like the demand for rum to wash out grief over the dead, was reasonable. There are times when it is imperative the Indian should receive free rum rations, such as when his deepest superstitions are involved. I measured out the drink and the post idlers immediately began begging an allowance from the new-comers. Old Tabashaw, who had withstood a hundred drops of laudanum given in five doses spread over an hour, was very wide awake and urging the Red Suckers to take war tobacco with them to their summer home on the Grand Passage on the Assiniboin for distribution among the Crees. The drinking bout promptly started, but there was no danger of the men repeating yester-day's performance, as they were still afraid of the Sioux, and when the shadow was over them they could be quiet enough in their drams. The Red Sucker band as hunters was worth all the Chippewas on the Lower Red, although Tabashaw's men were keen enough for fur during my first season in the department.

I found Flat Mouth at the river ready to push off my canoe. Chabot came running after me, calling out—

"Stop at the Reed and tell Probos to take his packs to our Scratching post at onoo!"

"Yes, sir. But if there is a chance of the brigade going out at once, I would like to know it, as I have some stuff of my own I want to pack up," I replied.

"Oh, you'll have plenty of time to do that," assured Chabot.

My errand appealed to me aside from affording me a vacation. I was curious to meet Red Dearness. Chabot had given a garbled description of him, likening him to a red ape. But they had met only the once and, as Dearness had accused my superior of sending trap-pers to encroach on the X. Y. line and they had come near to fighting, which must have meant death for one, if not both, I took but little stock in the master's account.

Flat Mouth had seen much of the man when he was on the upper Saskatchewan and I questioned him for details. The Pillager briefly informed me that Dearness's whiskers were fully as long as Chabot's and a vivid red, hence his nickname.

"His woman? What tribe did he take her from?"

He stared ahead at the brown current and did not seem to hear me. I repeated my query and he shook his head. Beyond his description of the man's beard, I could get nothing from him. His silence, however, and his way of speaking gave the impression he stood in awe of Dearness. The colour of the man's beard might account for this, the Indian's love for red amounting to reverence.

Without incident we covered the ten miles to the mouth of the Reed and hunted up his camp on the north bank. Neither he nor any of his Indians was to be seen. Flat Mouth said he was up at Reed Lake after sturgeon. As the lake is surrounded by a half-mile belt of swamp grass and reeds, I had no desire to search for him. Once I had tried to follow an old Indian and French path from this patch of water to Lake of the Woods, but I soon decided the roundabout way was the quickest. For taking out packs it was the only route. Not being disposed to enter the marshy country, I made myself comfortable in the camp and sent the Pillager on discovery. In a short time he returned with Probos and several Indians, the latter clamouring for "milk." I gave them all a few inches of tobacco, delivered Chabot's orders to the clerk, and resumed my journey.

After leaving the Reed we came upon five bears drinking at the river. I nearly broke Flat Mouth's heart by refusing to stop while he shot them. The fur was excellent at this season and a few pelts were not to be despised, but there was something in the back of my mind that impelled me to finish my business and return to the Pembina. Twenty-four hours since I had been desperate to quit the post; now I was keen to return. I couldn't get rid of the notion that the brigade might start before I was ready to accompany it.

However, I cheered my red friend by reminding him that bear was plenty about the Pembina if an Indian would forget the Sioux and go after them. He proclaimed his willingness to go, even to the thickly wooded country of the Cheyenne just south of Devil's Lake, where, he declared, the grizzlies went in vast droves and the region must verily be the abode of the great bear *manito*. The explanation for this abundance of bears was simple enough, as that region was the disputed northern boundary of the Sioux hunting range.

Any Indian venturing there in summer was pretty sure to remain while his hair travelled south. As there was no hunting to prevent the brutes from multiplying rapidly, I suppose they did thrive in enormous numbers. Flat Mouth was pleased with my reasoning, as it gave him a new viewpoint and inflamed him to go there. Heretofore, he said, he had kept away because of the great bear spirit. But if all he had to fear was the Sioux and almost certain death, he was keen for the trip. He measured up higher in courage than any other redskin I ever met.

For miles we swapped bear talk. He entertained me by describing the difference in the habits of grizzlies within so narrow an area as contained between the Red River and the Pembina Mountains. I have no reason for doubting his statement that in the hills, where the soil is dry and sandy, with the frost seldom penetrating more than a foot, the bears, both grizzly and black, den up in the ground. Our Red River bears took to hollow trees. Flat Mouth said they did this because the bear *manito* had taught them how the frost sinks into the muddy banks for more than four feet; therefore they imitated the racoons.

I had never gone after bear in the hills, but before Chabot took over the post one of the men brought me a cub which in a way bore out the Pillager's words. The cub was as tame as a kitten and trotted after me even when I quit the fort and took to the woods. When cold weather came I had the men open up a big hollow tree near the stockade and chop up some boughs and put inside so he might be unusually cosy. The place was almost snug enough for a human being. It measured six feet across, with a two-foot shell to keep out the cold. But the cub promptly showed his hills instinct by refusing the nest and insisting on digging a hole to live in. I never saw him after he retired for the winter, but I suppose he was frozen out and took to the hills.

With stories and wood lore we beguiled the passage down. Flat Mouth talked glibly enough unless you touched upon something that was tabu. Finally we came to the Scratching, where our small post was in charge of a fellow called Desset. On the opposite side, hidden by a grove of strong woods, was the opposition post. When some distance above the post we could catch the din made by the Indians as they swallowed all the profits of their spring hunt; men, women and children all getting drunk as rapidly as possible.

It's nasty work, peddling rum to Indians. But, after theorising and sermonising from Montreal to the Rocky Mountain House on the MacKenzie, let some of the sanctimonious critics give out heavy debts to a race that believes successful thieving is a greater honour even than scalp-taking, and then let them see how they'll get the debts paid without rum.

To rob a trader, kill him if need be, but get his goods at any costs, would be a great coup if not for the knowledge such treatment would cut off the supplies. There was hardly an Indian in the Northwest who would not cheerfully have cut my throat for a keg of rum, if he knew it was the only keg in the world and that there could never be any more. My friend and companion was proud to call himself chief of the Pillagers-Thieves. The name wasn't given him by outsiders but was bestowed by his own people upon themselves.

After all, thievery among the Indians is only another name for looking out for one's best interests; a characteristic of the white man also. A man may take many scalps and count many coups, but the really valuable man in a tribe is he who can fetch home the most stolen horses. If getting what they want above all else—high wine—results in their women being sold and debauched, that is much their own business, not the trader's.

As we drew nearer the rival posts the hooting and singing seemed ot emanate impartially from both banks, and I deduced it had been going on all night. No one was down at the river when we grounded our canoe. Leaving Flat Mouth to stay with the canoe, I went up to the fort to interview Desset, the clerk. I found most of our people sick, as they were every spring when they shifted from meat to fat sturgeon.

The Indians, too, seemed to be badly off, men, women and children coughing, several being far gone with consumption. Desset obviously had been generous with the "milk," as all the Chippewas were drunk. To add to the hubbub was the Indians' excitement at having found that morning a Canada lynx in a sturgeon net some ten feet from the shore.

Desset had endeavoured to explain that the cat broke through while trying to cross the thin ice, which forms every night only to float out at mid-day, and had become tangled in the net and drowned. But nothing so simple as that could content a Chippewa when he could read so many signs from the curious happening. Optimistic from liquor, they read the sign favourably. The sturgeon net was the Chippewa Nation. Some of the hunters at the post were of the sturgeon gens. The lynx, of course, was a symbol for the Sioux. The Chippewas were to exterminate the Sioux. Not a shadow of a doubt about it in their minds, and already plans were perfected for sending the glad news and war-tobacco far up the Assiniboin. Had the Sioux appeared at that time in battle array, the Chippewas, firm in their faith, would have given them a terrible beating.

Desset had no control over them and spent most of his time in keeping out of the way. Several bore bloody wounds. As it wasn't my place to discipline Desset's Indians, I withdrew to a cubby-hole that served as an office and sought information concerning Red Dearness before crossing the river.

"He never comes here. He doesn't want me to go there. I never see him, only when he passes up the river or rides on the plains. Until the snow melted, I saw nothing of him or the Madame."

"What kind of a looking woman is she?" I asked.

He shrugged his shoulders, explaining:

"The few times I've seen her was when she was at a distance. Then she wore a capote. I've heard she's a Slave, also a Cree. I know she isn't Chippewa, or our hunters would be going over there for rum. They're afraid of Dearness and don't bother him after the first time."

We talked for some time and I read the fellow pretty thoroughly. He may have been a good office hand in Montreal, but he was sadly out of tune on the Lower Red. Theoretically he understood the business of buying furs. I could see that if all Indians were exactly alike he could learn the technique. Inasmuch as they were individuals, he was helpless. His babbling revealed that much.

It was Chabot who got him the post, and I should have disliked him because of his patron had he been less inoffensive and helpless. He confessed he had but few furs and that it wouldn't take him long to make up his packs once he knew the brigade was going out. In pity for the poor fool I offered to go over his books and make sure his accounts were straight.

"That's the worst of it," he bitterly took on. "The Indians were all drunk in here a few weeks ago and threw my books on the fire. I haven't even an account showing their debts.''

As he confessed this I detected him slyly watching me to read the effect of his announcement. My pitying contempt suddenly evaporated and in its place I felt a strong aversion to him. He seemed to be so weak, physically and mentally, I might have bothered much to help him out. Now I wondered if it wasn't a part of Chabot's scheme in getting him there to have the books disappear. The Pembina post would show fat returns. The Scratching post would mark up a loss. If Desset was discharged it needn't follow that anything criminal would be suspected. With the books gone and nothing but mismanagement proven it would be possible for him and Chabot to share a fat profit out of the past season, one which would make our gentlemen of the North tear their hair did they guess they were being bilked. These suspicions came to me because I believed Chabot to be a bad one and because of the furtive glances Desset gave me.

I talked some further with him and then went outside to visit the X. Y. On my way to the river I met Joe Pouliot, one of the best men the N. W. employed, and in a bantering way he made the boast he had brought in two hundred prime skins from one *derouin*. This, if true, was the most successful *derouin* ever made on the river.

I encouraged him to give me the details, which he did eagerly; and when he had finished I believed him. Now a *derouin*—the sending of men forth to scare up trade among the Indians instead of having them bring their hunt to the posts—was generally frowned upon by rival companies. It smacked of free trading, the great sin in a company's eyes. It tended to take the control of the fur business out of the companies' hands, besides encouraging the men to do a little sly trading for themselves, or to carry part of the skins to some rival.

Furthermore, it was disastrous because it petted up the Indians until they were too lazy even to send their packs in by their women. Now the point was this: Why, if the N. W. post on the Scratching was securing any such number of skins in this fashion, should Black Chabot be eager to strike a bargain with Red Dearness, of the X. Y., to suppress the practice?

Desset was paid a hundred a year, Halifax currency, five hundred dollars in States' money. I had pitied him for a weakling. I quickly revised my opinion when further questioning brought forth the information from Joe that the season had been a good one.

"You don't seem to have much for the brigade to pick up," I remarked.

"But we sent out twenty-six packages of ninety pounds each right after the express stopped here," said Joe.

"How was the express? Pretty drunk?" I asked.

He smiled gently, caressed his long fair moustaches as if wiping off the dew of a drink and replied:

"They were asleep when our Indians saw their canoe drifting sidewise. They woke up after we got them into the post and held a dram of rum under their noses. We sent two Indians to look after them until they got through the swift water below. After that they'd be all right to look after themselves."

It was transparent. Desset and Chabot had traded for a canoe-load of prime furs and had sent them on ahead of the brigade, consigned to some one other than Simon McTavish's company. Indian troubles, a general failure to pay their debts, the loss of the account books, would be cited to cover the empty shelves.

I wasn't hired to spy on the Scratching River outfit. If Mr. Henry should return, I would tell him what I suspected, give the facts and leave the rest to him. But the N. W. had seen fit to put Chabot in Mr. Henry's place. I would hold my tongue.

Leaving Flat Mouth behind, I took the canoe and paddled into the mouth of the Scratching and crossed over. I landed in a willow growth so thick and stout I would not have attempted to penetrate it if not for a narrow path making down to the water's edge. On the rising ground back of this was a second growth of very big oak, elm and ash. Cutting through the strong timber, I came out on a meadow that reached nearly to the Red. As I entered the meadow I beheld an old acquaintance, and he was having trouble with his horse.

It was the "Rat," French, with a dash of Chippewa. He had worked for us during Mr. Henry's first season on the Red and was thoroughly untrustworthy. After we turned him off he had joined the X. Y. as an interpreter. When we came to the Red, there were practically no horses on the river, although the Chippewas were constantly fighting the Sioux who had many. During the last two years we had increased our number of animals so that it was common enough sight to see the Indians mounted. Besides those we and the opposition brought in were a few the Crees had traded for new medicines.

But I never saw any horses on the river, aside from those owned and cared for by white men, that were not in wretched condition. The crude wooden saddle commonly used by the Indians was largely to blame, as it ripped the hide off a nag's back in no time. I've often seen the poor, tortured beasts turn and bite their sides till the blood streamed, once the saddle was removed. The Indians never paid any attention to their condition nor tried to correct the fault. They would throw the wooden saddle on to the raw flesh and ride them as unconcernedly as a white man would use a canoe.

The Rat's horse was fighting against the saddle. Its back was a ghastly sight. As I came on to the scene the maddened brute managed to break loose and ran for the plains. The Rat, in a whirlwind of rage, raised his gun, then decided the enjoyment would be too dear and started in pursuit afoot. I called out to him, and the moment he recognised me his dark face lighted up and he forgot the runaway and eagerly cried:

"Meester Chabo'? Where he ees?"

I replied that Chabot would come down the river as soon as he had packed up and had sent the Indians off some time within the next thirty days. His manner in asking the question rather puzzled me, for theoretically he should feel no enthusiasm for the head of a post that had discharged him. It was Mr. Henry who had turned the beggar loose, but according to the Red River way of thinking he should nurse resentment against all N. W. representatives.

"What do you want to see Mr. Chabot for?" I asked.

"I go to ride up the reever to see heem, to get heem to hire me," he explained.

"What are you quitting the X. Y. for?"

"Meester Chabo' ees one live man," he grinned. "Meester Dearness maybe a dead man when snow come some more."

"Who has charge of the summer men while he's away?"

"Hees gal, maybe."

"Meaning his wife?"

"When Meester Chabo' hire me I can talk," was the non-committal reply. "I go to ride that horse, now she run away. I paddle up to meet heem."

"You'll be sure to find him at the fort," I said. "But Mr. Dearness's girl? Could she handle the summer men?"

"Han'le summer men? . She can go to han'le the deveel like she want to," he emphatically assured.

Then, as if fearing he had talked too freely, he hurried away.

Now I didn't believe there was a mixed blood in the country capable of handling the Indians. Certainly there wasn't a squaw. Let her be ever so brainy, let her be educated in Quebec and made much of by the English and French, yet her Indian blood would be a terrific handicap when it came to handling her people. Such a woman could have a big influence with her people and swing trade to whatever post she favoured. But as trader, having charge of the debts and advances and the rum, she couldn't do it. The hunters would not respect her commands. If she refused them liquor, they would take it more evilly than if she were a white.

Of course, I understood the Rat had a lively imagination. There was no reason to doubt his statement to the effect that Dearness was ill. We had received reports to the same effect. When his season closed he probably would send some one back to run things until fall, when he, or his successor, would come on. If he were seriously ill, then any bargain I might make with him might be ignored by his successor.

Orders were orders, however, and I hurried on to the fort. The Rat called after me the cheering information that Dearness knew of my stopping Little Crane from taking his furs to the X. Y. and had advised the Indian to kill me. This scarcely primed me for a cordial reception, yet it was part of the game we were playing and worried me none.

The fort presented a scene of industrious activity despite the carousal going on inside the stockade. Men were making carts and fashioning wheels from solid sections from three-foot trees. A smith was turning out nails. Some sick Indians were making a sturgeon net while their women smoked tongues.

On the whole I really felt rather jealous of the discipline. Those drinking were obviously entitled to their liquor and had paid high for it. Red Dearness was like Mr. Henry in that respect; the drams were for those who had earned them. Somehow I gained the impression, probably from Chabot's sneering talk, that things were at sixes and sevens in the X. Y. post. The evidences did not support any such notions.

To be true, all was not harmony, and the master was having his rum troubles. As I entered the stockade I nearly stumbled over one of his hunters who had been stabbed six times in the side and abdomen and whom they were trying to heal with *wabeno* songs.

Entering the big room of the fort, I met a young man with a twisted face, who told me he was Angus, the clerk, and would I state my business.

"I want to speak with Mr. Dearness," I informed.

"You come from the N. W. post upstream?" he asked in a gloomy voice.

I answered in the affirmative and repeated my request. With much reluctance he told me I could not see the master.

"Scurvy treatment even for the X. Y. to give a N. W. man," I hotly retorted. "And I don't know that you have authority to tell me your master won't see me."

He squirmed uneasily, then blurted out: "He's drunk. He can't see any one."

This did not square up with what I had heard about him. He traded high wine for pelts, as did every North-man, but he was exceedingly temperate in his habits. I suspected the clerk wished to hide his master's illness from the N. W.

"I can wait," I said. "Mr. Chabot sent me to see him on business. He will be sobering up some time."

The clerk shook his head discouragingly, saying:

"He sleeps like a dead man. Very, very drunken."

I was electrified, and the clerk fairly jumped from his stool, as a clear voice from an inner room called out in the Chippewa tongue:

"That is not true, Angus. You know he isn't drunk and hasn't been drunk. Tell the young man he is ill from changing from meat to sturgeon."

It was a woman's voice, undoubtedly Madame's, or his "gal's," for I was getting mixed on the relationship. And it was a wonderfully musical voice. I was tempted to advance to the room, but the curtain of rawhide was pulled snug and the woman continued:

"Ask him what he wants here with your master. Have you lost your tongue?"

"I will ask him," Angus meekly replied in Chippewa.

"Let me tell my business without being asked," I fluently spoke up, rather proud of my knowledge of Chippewa. "Mr. Chabot wishes to make a bargain with the X. Y. to the end that neither the X. Y. nor the N. W. send out men to·hunt for trade."

"He is sorry when he hears men are sent out on *derouin*," she mockingly retorted. "What about the *derouin* Pouliot made this winter? Bah! The man is a snake, and I have no trust in a man that goes on his business."

"I am only a clerk," I stiffly replied, glaring at the curtain. "I'm not passing any tobacco to get help for Chabot. I obey orders."

She was silent for nearly a minute, and I was about to take my departure, when she spoke, very softly this time, saying:

"I am ashamed of my words. You are not to blame if Chabot is Chabot. The good God made him, as he did the skunk and white wolf. And only the good God knows why He made him."

"For the fur trade, just as He made the skunk and wolf for the fur trade," I smartly replied.

She ignored me and continued:

"The X. Y. will agree not to send men to trade in the Indian camps. It is a bad way to trade. The N. W. has been doing it on this river. If the N. W. stops it, we won't begin."

"You talk Chippewa like a native," I complimented.

"And French like a Frenchwoman, and English like an Englishwoman," she quickly answered, using the two languages.

"And I don't know which of the three you are," I regretted. "Am I not to see you?"

The rawhide curtain rattled viciously and in Chippewa she commanded:

"Make a writing for him to sign, binding the N. W. and the X. Y. not to make a *derouin*."

Clerk Angus wrote rapidly, making two copies. I signed them and waited while he went to get the X. Y. signature. He did not go behind the closed curtain but to a similar recess at the opposite end of the room. He was absent for a few minutes, and when he returned he was followed by Red Dearness.

The man was tall and very muscular. He was as heavy as Black Chabot, only a more graceful distribution of flesh and brawn did not allow him to look it. My first thought was, what a fight the two would make of it if they ever clashed. My second thought was one of congratulations to Chabot for having avoided a tussle.

Red Dearness's face possessed staying qualities which I knew Chabot lacked. His beard was long and full and as red as the autumn sun when the smoke from prairie fires makes it look like fresh blood. His eyes were large and deep blue but sadly sunken. His general mien was that of great melancholy. My first glance told me it was not sturgeon diet that ailed him. Nor had he been drinking. He impressed me as being marked by Death, and yet there was no falling away of the flesh, no lack of elasticity in his step as he approached me.

"I have heard what you have said and what has been said to you. I have your signature to a paper, which pretends to bind your company together with the X. Y. to post trading entirely. I have signed the agreement. I will send no man to trade among the Indians. They must bring their hunt to the post. I agree, not because Chabot asks it, nor because I expect him to keep his agreement, but because it is the one thing a post must do if it is to exist. Your people have used me foully. You have stolen my skins from my Indians. Little Crane was robbed of a pack belonging to me."

Not even a sick man can accuse me of that without hearing my voice. Had he accused Chabot of robbing the women, I would have admitted the offence; for that was a nasty fact. Evidently he had not learned of that particular coup yet. I contented myself with saying:

"I was the man who took the skins from the Crane. He took a debt and we wanted it paid. The skins belonged to us."

"Damnation! He's taken a debt from us. Now he will never pay," fumed Dearness, his blue eyes blazing.

His anger seemed to tire him, and he more quietly continued, "I am doing you the compliment of taking your word for it."

"You had better," I shortly retorted, "or when you recover your health I should have to have a reckoning with you."

"You young fool!" he contemptuously replied.

The woman behind the curtain laughed derisively. I must have coloured or in some way shown my anger, for in a more decent tone he said:

"There! There! Words are foolish as the pounding of sticks on those cursed medicine drums. If I spoke harshly, it was out of envy for your youth and health. After all, we're but a handful of white men up here and should stick together as much as the trade will allow. You will eat with us."

"Does the young lady who laughed at me eat with us?" I asked.

"She keeps quite by herself," he slowly replied, staring at me in a peculiar manner.

"And I think I will follow her example," I decided. "One word before I go. We'll call it a bonus for signing the paper. You have a man—the Rat—hired as interpreter. He's a scoundrel."

"They all are," he quietly reminded.

"It's not my business to warn the X. Y. against his tricks. I have spoken."

"I shall break his neck for his tricks some day," said Hearne. "However, I thank you for your warning. We're getting ceremonious enough for Quebec when the season is high. Now I must give you what may not set well on your stomach. Your master, Black Chabot, is a rascal."

As he spoke he leaned forward and stared round-eyed, as if expecting a hot denial.

"He's a —— rascal," I corrected.

The ghost of a smile played round his bearded lips. The tinkle of a little laugh came from behind the hide curtain.

"You should be working with honest men, working for the X. Y.," he murmured.

"The N. W. has the best men in the business. Skunks are found everywhere."

"True," he mused; "only a skunk's pelt is worth something. Sir Alexander MacKenzie appreciates young men who can do things."

"So does Simon McTavish," I added.

"It's hopeless for me ever to suggest it, isn't it?"

"Quite. Now that I've done my errand I'll be going."

"You'll not change your mind and eat?"

"I'll eat at our post. It's so close it would be foolish for me not to."

He glanced toward the curtains and I flushed beneath the tan of the April wind. He was amusing himself with thinking I would have stayed gladly enough if the woman had offered to join us.

He rose and followed me to the door, and either he was suddenly in physical agony, or else the sunlight revealed more than I had already noticed, for his eyes were contracted and his lips pressed firmly. We exchanged a courteous farewell and I went to my canoe, already regretting I had not accepted his invitation to eat with him. In all probability I should have seen the woman. And speech with an educated woman, as I knew this woman was educated, would be a heavenly treat after three years of isolation.

Until this day I had known of but one white woman ever being on the river. She had come with some Orkney Islanders, disguised as a boy. She betrayed her secret to one man at the Forks, who debauched her, and her child was born at our fort, the first white child born on the Red River of the North.

To return to the Dearness woman; whether she was a white or a breed I couldn't decide. Rumour and gossip had given me to understand she was mixed blood. But if such she must have been taken East when very young to be educated by the Sisters. I had met French-

Indian and English-Indian girls in Montreal and Quebec who would grace any home.

This incident of calling on Red Dearness, so long in the telling, was a great adventure for me. It gave me a new train of thought. It is the lack of fresh mental food and the eternal chewing over the same thoughts which drive men mad in the lonely places. No one can appreciate the thrill and zest that such a trivial encounter can afford one who has lived in a savage rut month on month.

Accordingly I was in something of a state of mind when I returned to the post and found Desset excitedly superintending the last of the packing. The storehouse was cleared and the Indian women and children were rummaging through it in frantic search for articles overlooked. They had even taken up the whitewood flooring in hope of finding trinkets dropped through the cracks.

Desset's activity astonished me. He was like a man fighting against time.

"Why are you in such a hurry?" I asked.

He grinned sheepishly, hesitated, gave me one of his sly glances, then frankly confessed:

"I'm so keen to get out of this country. It makes me forget if I am busy."

"But it will be days and weeks before the brigade comes down. You've packed all your goods. What will you do if the Indians bring in a hunt?"

"I've got plenty of rum out and ready," he replied with a vacuous laugh.

"The Indians seem to have had enough," I observed as I caught an outburst from the stockade.

"The red beggars won't have any more," he growled.

"You'll have to give them presents when you go away," I reminded. "Ho! When did that rascal come?"

I pointed to the reeling figure of Old Crow.

"Since you came," was the careless reply.

It surprised me the Indian would come alone down

the river, and I knew his wife and child would have none of his company. I couldn't believe Chabot had driven him out of the fort, as Chabot had lost his power as a disciplinarian. I sauntered up to the stockade gate and glanced inside.

It was the usual scene. Old Crow held my interest, however. He not only had had too much liquor, but he was also wearing a red hat with a round red feather in it, usually a gift for a chief. I knew he had not traded a skin for the season. I caught him by the arm as he was dancing by in a drunken line and asked—

"Who sent you here?"

"Black Face," he answered, meaning Chabot.

"What did you bring?"

"The white bark that talks," he grunted, lurching away to join the dancers.

I would have given a prime skin to know what written message Black Chabot had sent to Desset. No doubt but that it concerned some of their schemes for looting the N. W. I found something to eat and heartily wished I had accepted Red Dearness's invitation to eat at the X. Y. Confusion and clamour surrounded me, Desset allowing the Indians to overrun the fort as if it had been abandoned. One fellow boldly tried to take away my sugar, and when I resented it his woman took offence. It was only by an extravagant display of anger that I brought them to their senses. If the day had not been so far advanced, I would have taken to the canoe and returned upstream.

Going to the river, I found Flat Mouth and a man of his band dragging the water for sturgeon by suspending a long net between two canoes and sweeping upstream. Mr. Henry was the first to introduce such a net to the Red. While I watched them, a man came in with eight kegs of new sugar and six beaver skins. Desset came down to the river as the man landed, but he showed no enthusiasm for the trade. He gave the impression of being annoyed and refused to trade anything but high wine, powder, and ball. An idea of how permanent alcohol stood in our trade venture is shown from the fact that, out of twenty-eight "pieces" of assorted goods brought in by each canoe in the early fall, ten were kegs of liquor, each holding nine gallons. Gunpowder, which one might expect to hold first place, furnished only two kegs per canoe.

The fort was so noisy that night, and there was so much fighting going on, that I moved back into the woods where Flat Mouth threw together a shelter and where we built a small fire and roasted some fish and spent the night.

After our morning meal we started for our canoe, eager to be quit of the place. The Indians were quiet, either sick or sleeping, and I saw nothing of Desset. We were near the bank when out of the early shadows upriver shot a canoe, and after a glance Flat Mouth said it was the Rat. He also pulled the casing off his gun and suggested the man was fleeing from an enemy, perhaps the Sioux; this because the Rat gave an excellent exhibition of a man in a great hurry. I poohpoohed the Sioux notion. Even if they came in such force as to take the Pembina post there would have been a few survivors to flee down the river. Instead of crossing the mouth of the Scratching and making the X. Y. post, the Rat drove full speed for our bank and was ashore almost before his canoe found the mud.

Without a word to me he started on the run for the post and I chased after him. Desset had seen him land and was at the stockage gate, his manner nervous.

"Very soon! Met heem coming like ——!" exploded the Rat.

"Did he send any word?" asked Desset, his eyes brightening.

"To be ready. That is all."

Having finished his errand, the Rat ran back to his canoe and set off for the X. Y. establishment.

"Who did he meet? What's up?" I impatiently asked.

"I supposed you knew," innocently answered Desset.

"Nothing's up except what happens every spring. The Pembina post brigade is going out. Mr. Chabot sends word he will be here soon and that I'm to have my packs ready to join him."

"The brigade going out?" I spluttered. "Devil's hoofs! The Rat must have lied. Nothing has been done about the planting, next season's fuel, arranging for the summer men——"

"I should think, Mr. Franklin, those were matters for your superior to worry about," tartly broke in Desset.

"I don't think he will worry about them," I slowly replied. "Maybe his superiors will, though."

He turned away to round up some Indians recovered enough from their spree to carry the packs to the shore. I walked leisurely back to the river. Chabot had told me I would have ample time to return and get together some few belongings; he had intended from the first to make this unusually early start. Mr. Henry usually went out during the last week in May or early in June. The only explanation I could scare up was that Chabot, his nerves shaken by rum, was in a panic lest our Indians rise and massacre us. Perhaps my mentioning old Tabashaw's boast that he could kill a man, white or red, by just wishing him to die was responsible. Anyway, I now knew the nature of the message Old Crow had brought to Desset. The clerk had been ordered to have everything in readiness for an immediate departure.

My personal effects at the post could await my return in the fall or be stolen. They were of not enough value to worry over. I had my double-barrel gun, my dearest possession, and I could arrange with one of the X. Y. people to go after my horse or to care for it after Flat Mouth brought it down. Probos, our clerk at the Reed, would be left in charge of the post during the summer, but I did not wish to trust the horse to him. He was honest but slow-witted. The Crees could steal his moccasins and he would never know it until he went out barefooted and got a blade of porcupine-grass through a toe.

Now a dozen canoes of Indian families turned the bend above, stringing out in a long procession; then came the post's nine canoes and two boats, a man in each, the rest of the space being heaped high with equipage and skins. This would leave twenty-odd Indian canoes unaccounted for, and I was forced to the conclusion that despite his precipitate departure Chabot had found time to make up small assortments of trade goods for the Hills and other outposts and to assign hunting territory to the summer men.

Flat Mouth, who stood beside me watching the brigade, now gave a low grunt. I observed he had shifted his attention downstream. I looked in that direction and beheld the X. Y. brigade of eight canoes was starting down-river. This was my second great surprise of the morning.

Yesterday Red Dearness had shown no symptoms of taking an early departure. Now he was off, and seemingly in great haste to precede our brigade. When Mr. Henry ruled at the Pembina post, rival brigades usually travelled to the Forks each spring in a most neighbourly fashion.

Red Dearness, enveloped in a cloak, was in the first canoe. He turned and looked back only once, and then to wave his hand to the X. Y. Fort. Dearness, I deduced, was in a serious state of health, and some sudden symptoms had forced his departure. Which of the blanketed figures was the woman who talked in English, French, and Chippewa it was impossible to determine. Angus, the clerk, stood clear of the woods on the little point and limply waved a hand in farewell.

Poor devil! I pitied him for the loneliness he must endure as summer keeper of the fort, for the stench of the decaying buffalo, for the possible plague of grasshoppers which would rival the buffalo in stinks. For when these pests came to blight the land they died in millions along the river. I've seen the shores of Winnipeg inches deep with them decaying. Oh, I had room to pity him for many things, even if he did belong to the opposition.

Our brigade swung ashore and the Indians gave a hand in unloading the skin canoes and turning them up to be dried out by the sun. Chabot arrived last, having Probos with him. I greeted him and reported on the agreement signed by me in behalf of the N. W. and by Dearness for the X. Y., by the terms of which neither in the department of the Lower Red River was to drum up trade among the Indians.

He was not interested in my report but stood and grinned ferociously down the river and boasted:

"The red rat wasn't keen to see me. According to your say, he was going to do something about the furs I took from his women. I was loaded for him. He knew it, too. Skun out ahead of me, eh? Well, maybe I'll catch up with him before he makes the Forks."

"He's a sick man," I said.

"He'll be sicker before I get through with him," he bragged.

"If you have any trouble with him, you must kill him. If you don't, he will kill you. I talked enough to know he will go the full distance. While sick, he hasn't lost his strength. Heart, probably."

Chabot lost some of his assurance and his leer changed to a dark scowl. I asked:

"How is it you go out so early? I thought I was to have time to get back and pack up some of my belongings."

"It's likely the affairs of the North West Company will be held up to make things easier for you," he sneered.

"At least tell me when you leave here. I've got to arrange to send for my horse and have him cared for."

"I start just as soon as the skin canoes get dry and Desset is ready."

Now something was amusing him, for as he finished

he commenced chuckling. I suspected it might be the canoeload of furs he and Desset had sent off. With an oath he suddenly began raging:

"That Desset has gone and lost his accounts! Let some drunken Indians burn them up. Pretty Northman he'll make! I'd planned to leave him to look after the summer trade, but now the company will want to shift or ship him."

"He expects to go along with you. He's been busy packing ever since Old Crow brought your message."

He slowly turned and eyed me, to see if my words hid anything.

"He'll go as far as the Forks, where he'll wait for the Assiniboin brigade to come down. I ought to get orders from up country about his case. How did you know anything about my message?" The last savagely.

"I was here when the Crow came," I lied, not wishing to make trouble for the Indian. "Joe Pouliot was pretty lucky to make that *derouin*. Two hundred skins."

"Desset will never make a Northman. He talks too much. The X. Y. will hear of it and then they'll howl."

"He's your man. You brought him here."

"Then it's none of your business, Franklin!" he roared, his beard seeming to bristle. "I don't like your way of talking."

"All right. I'm through. Here's the Rat dancing round to speak to you."

Chabot mumbled under his breath and turned aside. The Rat, with much writhing and gesticulating, poured out a torrent of softly spoken words. Chabot listened with a frown creasing his forehead. When the Rat had finished, he answered him briefly, talking from the corner of his mouth. The Rat fell back.

"Hired him?" I inquired.

"Told him to go to ——!" Chabot growled. Which was surprising to learn after seeing how resignedly the Rat had taken it.

That night Chabot and Desset and Probos and a few

of the men—whites—drank deeply from a ten-gallon keg of brandy and distributed much mixed rum not only to our Indians but also to those eagerly flocking across the river from the X. Y. post. An Indian can scent rum a mile, I believe. Open a keg in any open space with not a redskin in sight, and before you know it they will begin to drop in like crows calling on a dead buffalo.

They gave away fifteen kegs all told and speedily put a fighting edge on the Chippewas. Inside of an hour after the bout began I saw four separate combats going on at the same time. As I was leaving the hall, old Tabashaw stumbled against me in the dark. When I pushed him away he attempted to stab me. I knocked him down and threw him out. Little Shell, imagining him to be a Sioux, grabbed his hair and would have counted coup if my foot hadn't landed under his chin. Desset, under orders from Chabot, had endeavoured to collect all weapons before giving out the rum, but I never saw an Indian drinking match yet when weapons could not be produced. This night the women were largely to blame, as they persisted in smuggling knives to their men.

Early next morning we routed the Indians, but many of them were in no condition to go on. There was no intention of taking any with us except those bound for the Assiniboin, where they proposed to summer. With a hearty shower of curses Chabot assigned families to various locations for the summer hunt.

He told some to go after red deer and bear east of the Red, while others were to go after buffalo on the plains. I noticed that neither Desset nor Probos was taking any notes of these orders. The former, I knew, was booked for a home passage, but Probos would be shifted from the Reed to the Pembina. When he had finished, Chabot wheeled on me and fiercely demanded—

"So you can carry all that in your noddle, eh?"

"In my noddle?" I blankly repeated.

"You heard me say it," he growled.

"But why should your orders interest me? It's for your summer man to prick up his ears."

He grinned maliciously, fished out his orders received from the last express, placed a trembling finger on one paragraph and invited me to read. It was an order for me to remain at the Pembina post during the summer, with Probos staying at the Reed camp and keeping an eye on the Scratching River post, which was to be closed after the brigade departed. Chabot had known this all the time and had allowed me to believe I was going back east.

For fully a minute I stood stiff and motionless, frozen all over with rage and disappointment. His rough voice sounded far off as he explained:

"This post will be closed. The Reed camp will bring their trade to you at Pembina. Just remember my orders to the summer men and you'll have a mighty fine and easy time of it. Before I go, I'll take a long drink to the new master of the Pembina post."

My hand dropped to my knife, but I clenched my hands and walked away, fighting to keep my mouth shut, my fists closed until sure of myself.

My first impulse was to enter my canoe and paddle downstream to the Forks. Gradually reason stole through my black mood. After all, the orders did not originate with him. Some of the gentlemen of the North had picked me to have charge of the Lower Red River department until the brigade returned in the fall. Black Chabot's cruelty was his withholding of the information. There was nothing to compel me to remain there. I was free to refuse if I so wished.

Chabot, not done with his tormenting, came after me, perhaps to spur me into quitting the river, and arrogantly demanded:

"What do you mean? Mean you won't take this high honour—that you won't serve as master at Pembina, per orders?"

The Reed River clerk was watching us with a greedy gleam in his eyes. Chabot had brought him along, intending to promote him to the position after bullying me into refusing it. The master was expecting me to refuse, was hoping I would. Did I refuse, he would treat me well enough all the way to Montreal, satisfied in knowing the N. W. would have no more of me.

"Refuse? God bless you, no!" I cried, forcing a ringing exulting note into my voice. "Refuse promotion from clerk to master? Why, I came out here to make a career, to become a Northman. I shall do everying necessary to keep the post fit. But, so long as I am to be master in your place, I'll make the assignments for the summer hunters."

Which was well within my right to say.

CHAPTER III

THE STOLEN VOICE

THE return up the river was dreary enough for me. Probos and a family of Indians accompanied us as far as the mouth of the Reed. Leaving them, Flat Mouth and I hurried on, with old Tabashaw and several families pursuing in the vain hope of free rum. At least I would be the master until relieved of my trust, and I was determined that neither the chief nor any of his following should have any liquor until they earned it. If they would drink, they must work. As one of the results of the drinking bout at the Scratching post, there was the burning of a summer Indian's tent.

Chabot had just advanced goods to him to the value of a hundred and fifty skins. That is, he was to pay us in skins according to our valuation of that number of pelts. Now the goods were burned, we would get never a pelt from him. Just above the Reed we met the Northwest Annual Winter Express from the Athabasca, making all speed to overtake the brigade. They stopped only long enough to voice their surprise at having found the post closed and to ask if the Indians were on the war-path.

The fort looked very lonely as we drew ashore and hauled up our canoe. The solitude of the place was intense even when we were surrounded by drunken Indians. Now it was deathly. The procession of drowned buffaloes was thinning out, though still the river rolled a daily grist over the southern horizon. Within twenty-four hours after my return I had sixty-five men and women, brigades of children and nearly a hundred dogs camping about the stockade. All were begging for rum except the dogs. I called for Tabashaw, who came on the jump, and explained to him his people should be leaving for the Pembina Mountains to make their summer hunt.

The crafty old villain loudly replied:

"When Tabashaw speaks, they will go. Tabashaw is chief of the Chippewas. It is for him to send his people on the hunt."

Meaning that it was none of James Franklin's business what the Chippewa men should do.

"I have heard you speak," I carelessly answered. "I am very busy. I must write down each word you say, so the gentlemen of the North can see by the talking paper just what kind of a man you are."

He wriggled uneasily. The accounts I worked on each day were a big mystery to him. That I could preserve in writing a verbatim report of every word spoken in my hearing was no harder for him to believe than was any other of the phenomena of the white man's ways.

"A little rum will smooth the road to the hills," he cunningly reminded.

I bowed over my books and pointed to the door. He withdrew and commenced a violent tirade against me. He was concluding with a spirited call for volunteers to rush in and cut my throat and seize the milk when he glimpsed me at the window, apparently taking down his speech. Without comprehending that the written word could never condemn him until delivered, he flew into a panic and with many an explosive "Hough!" bitterly upbraided his people for not departing at once. Yet I did not feel easy until I saw the entire party with their nine horses and many dogs strung out in a mile-long line.

They left just in time to escape a fine fright. Two Indians came tearing down the river, wild with fear. They had been hunting at Grandes Fourches (Grand Forkes, North Dakota) and had found where a man had placed sticks to kneel on in drinking. On the same day they came upon a buffalo bull, and it was wounded. Two positive proofs the Sioux were hiding in that neighbourhood. They packed their hunt into their canoes and wanted me to know they were through with any country above the Pembina fort.

As they brought forty beaver and seven bear, my alarm was tempered with rejoicing. Now that old Tabashaw and his crew were gone I threw in a gallon of mixed wine as a bonus. It came off cold that night with snow. The plains had been clear and dry for several days, but with the storm the buffaloes edged in to find shelter in the timber along the river. By the time we were settled we could hear them crashing about close to the fort and at times scraping against the stockade. The wolves followed them in, looking for an unprotected calf or a sick creature. I've noticed that while wolves can run a herd for short distances the beasts will not stampede because of them. That is why our Indians always suspected the Sioux instead of four-legged wolves when they saw the buffaloes in rapid motion.

The wolves, however, aroused our dogs, and what with the whistling of the storm and the racket made by the brutes one needed to be very tired to sleep.

In the morning we found several inches of snow but with the sun fast melting it. Flat Mouth came to me and gave it as his opinion that the Sioux were above us. Had he been any other Indian, I would have laughed at him. He had fought them many times and was not quick to give the alarm.

"The men saw their own tracks and grew afraid," I insisted, to drive him into giving me some reason.

From under his blanket he drew an arrow, short of shaft and long in feathering, with shallow grooves down the shaft—the "lightning marks" or "blood" grooves.

"Sioux," he quietly said.

"Where did you get it?"

He pointed to the river, where buffaloes were occasionally floating by.

"It was sticking into a bull. The bull was not killed by water but was chased into the river."

If I had had a half dozen whites and some sober Chippewas inside the stout stockade, I would have defied half a thousand Sioux to dig me out. But, being alone, my Indians off in the hills, it might come to pass that I should seek safety in flight down the river to save my skull from serving as a drinking-dish. Such a forced retreat on the part of a white man and a North-man would demean him in the estimation of the Indians.

"If there are Sioux at Grandes Fourches or this side, I must know it at once. I shall start up the river within an hour."

"If the Sioux have come, they will cross the river to steal down on the east side," he said.

"Then I will go up the east side and do two jobs at once. There should be some of the Red Sucker band making sugar at Thief River. I must see them. There should be good beaver at Goose River. I want to look that country over."

"You will find Sioux," he warned, turning away.

I did not ask him to go with me. The sun was warm and the snow was melting fast, and by the time I was ready to start it was gone. I planned to go horseback, as the country was level to Park River. The beast showed an ugly streak when I headed him south along the edge of the timber instead of taking after the buffalo, which were now far out on the plain.

There was a danger that the Sioux might be concealed anywhere along the bank, but that was a risk I must take. Flat Mouth was not in sight when I quit the fort, and I was deciding I must make the trip alone when he overtook me. Without a word he took the lead. Late afternoon brought us to the Park, which we crossed on a log bridge built by Mr. Henry the year before.

Thus far we had seen nothing alarming and made our camp a few miles beyond the river. Before sunrise we were mounted and rejoicing that the weather still held clear with the river dropping rapidly. We crossed to the east bank of the Red, wallowing to our horses' bellies in the mud left by high water.

We went through two miles of strong timber, then struck willow and poplar, filled with red deer. We were continually scaring the creatures into flight and I made a mental note of the place for the benefit of our hunters. The willows were bad enough, but nothing compared with the stretch we next encountered. Now it was long grass concealing holes, and marsh ground, which tired our nags greatly. Not until mid-day did we reach decent footing on an open plain. The deer signs were very thick whenever we struck a little stream.

Plenty of bears was shown by the appearance of the bushes, where they had gathered fruit and berries the season before. That night we camped on Snake River without having discovered any signs of either friendly or hostile Indians.

Flat Mouth lost none of his keen concern. I had been with him enough to know he expected trouble. In the morning we crossed the Snake to follow up its western bank and in a few hours were in sight of the strong woods along Red Lake River.

Now Flat Mouth motioned for me to hold back. Leaving his horse with me, he went on a discovery. A turkey-buzzard was lazily ascending above the tree tops, and it was the presence of this scavenger, leaving his feeding, that had attracted the Pillager Chief's attention. I waited half an hour; then Flat Mouth came into view and beckoned me to approach. I rode ahead, leading his animal, but I could surmise nothing from his face. Therefore, the shock to my nerves was severe when, without a word of warning, he led me to the remains of a bloody tragedy.

An Indian, one of the Red Sucker band, was on the ground, his body feathered with arrows. He had been mutilated beyond all imagining. The Sioux—for there was no mistaking their work—had raised the scalp and removed the skull to use it as a dish. After I recovered my composure Flat Mouth pointed ahead and informed:

"Signs two days old. They followed him from up the river. He came from somewhere near mouth of the Red Lake River. He was carrying a pack of beaver on his back."

Mounting his horse, he again took the lead, and we passed through the woods to the bank of the Red Lake and found ourselves opposite the mouth of the Clearwater. This stream, very rapid where it empties into the Red Lake, was famous for sturgeon. A short distance above the mouth was the ruins of the winter post built several years before by Jean Baptiste Cadotte. His father, of the same name, went to Michilimackinac fifty years back. Flat Mouth told me it was Cadotte senior who prevailed on the Lake Superior Chippewas not to join in Pontiac's conspiracy against the western garrisons. I had visited the ruins the year before and had no desire to go there again, as the woodticks would devour us. I intimated as much when Flat Mouth started up the bush-grown path. He gave a low hiss for silence and pointed to some almost imperceptible marks on the edge of the bank while his lips formed the word—

"Sioux!"

Now I was after Sioux, but I was not a bit anxious to come upon them unexpectedly or while they were in any considerable number. Then again, the sight I had just witnessed rather weakened my fighting spirit. My companion seemed to read my thoughts, for he whispered:

"Hurt."

I plucked up spirit. If the Sioux were hurt, I wasn't much frightened. I nodded, and we dismounted and led our horses along the narrow path.

It was only a short distance to the old Cadotte place, and once more I acted the hostler while the Indian went ahead. This time I was alone only a few minutes, and this time his gestures on returning to me were those of exultation. I hurried forward and beheld another dead Indian. The Red Sucker Indian had struck like a rattlesnake before being killed, and he had bagged a noble victim. For the dead man must have been a great war chief. This was indicated by his feathered head-dress and the beautiful redstone pipe by his side. A buckskin bag, which had held his medicine and mysteries, had been torn to pieces by wolves. The beasts had mauled the body until it was only a bundle of bloody bones and torn leather. By some freak the head-dress had not been disturbed. Altogether, the remnants of the dead man's dignity were in a sad condition.

"They were in a big hurry," explained Flat Mouth. "Some time they will come to get the bones. The Red Sucker was taken by surprise while carrying the pack. He had just time to throw his axe and crack the Sioux's head when the others got him. It was a good trade."

"If they are in a hurry, we can hurry," I urged. "I must know whether they have left this country or are hanging around for more scalps."

"Only a few came up here. Lost their war-chief and ran back to their war-camp near Grandes Fourches. May find them quick if we follow."

Which meant we might find them before we were prepared for the meeting.

The sight of the war-chief revived my fighting courage. Thus far the Chippewa Nation had no reason for hanging its head. Flat Mouth scalped the chief and followed the trail downstream till we struck the main river. There the signs prompted him to cross over to the mouth of the Cottonwood. We struck into a beaten path made by deer and for a bit lost the trail. When Flat Mouth picked it up he showed surprise. Instead of making off southwest to Grandes Fourches, it led us back north, forcing us to recross the Red Lake River, then swerving to the north-east toward Thief River, which empties into the main river below the Clearwater. In short, we were travelling in a rough circle.

Flat Mouth reasoned it out, saying:

"The Sioux were very much afraid when their war-chief was killed. They started to run back to their camp and ride their ponies for home. Then they remembered the beaver pack. If the Chippewa was taking it down the river, he would be in a canoe. They know the maple grows thick along the Thief. Good beaver as well as sugar country. They think the dead Indian came from there. They forget they are afraid at the loss of their chief. They want to take more skulls. So they start to find the dead man's family."

There was no need for hurrying, as either the Sioux had found their victims or hadn't. As it was near sundown, I suggested that we camp. He agreed and, still holding his gun, began picking up dry twigs with one hand, working in nearer the woods very slowly.

"You've got enough wood," I called out, making to dismount and much surprised that he should think of lighting a fire.

He startled me by dropping a handful of twigs and by raising his gun and firing among the trees.

His shot evoked a chorus of fiendish yells and a volley of arrows and the *snick* of a lead ball against a tree. Almost immediately six Sioux warriors, hideous in their paint and howling like demons, burst from cover. Flat Mouth moved back, keeping his face to them, coolly reloading. On sighting me, a white man, they came to a halt, undecided for a few seconds as to what course to pursue. While they were weighing the matter I let drive with the right barrel and scuffed off the top of a man's head; the gun was loaded for buffalo bulls.

With a shriek of rage, fully believing our guns were empty, the remaining five sprang forward. I fired the left barrel, potting another warrior. Had they pressed the attack they would have had us for the killing, but according to their ignorant notions a gun that shoots twice can shoot indefinitely. With yelps of fear they faced about and raced for cover. By this time Flat Mouth had reloaded. He sprang on his horse to get a better view of the bush-grown ground at the edge of the timber and scored his second kill. Then he threw back his head and raised the Pillager Chippewa yell of triumph. And for good measure, being proud of my race, proud of my two shots, and somewhat young withal, I added my voice to his.

I told him he could have my scalps and claim the double kill if he wished to. This, I knew, would stand him such a coup as no Chippewa had counted within the knowledge of their oldest men. I waited until he had finished his ghastly work and selected a beaded buckskin bag which contained some coloured stones and bits of coloured feathers. This, Flat Mouth said, was Cheyenne work and must have belonged to a big chief. The bearer of it had killed his man, as shown by the feather in his hair, but he was no chief.

"The bag held the chief's medicine. It belonged to the dead chief on the Clearwater. One of the Sioux was taking it home, leaving his own in its place. It must be strong medicine to belong to a chief."

And Flat Mouth eyed it with awe.

"It wasn't strong enough to protect him," I reminded, slipping the trophy into my pocket.

"No man knows how strong his medicine is until he fights," was the reply.

Flushed with success, Flat Mouth wanted to chase the Sioux, depending upon my gun to slay another brace. I refused. The Sioux had lost heavily on the expedition. Five men—and one a big chief—killed, and only a Chippewa skull to show for it. Whoever carried the pipe on that raid lost caste once they sighted their village and began throwing themselves to the ground to prepare their people for bad news.

Many a finger on the left hand would lose a joint when the relatives and friends of the dead went into mourning. Then again the Sioux afoot could easily evade us. Once they reached their ponies they would lose no time in retreating. They would believe other whites were near.

Most potent of all was the medicine of my gun, shooting twice without reloading. It would be talked about from the upper waters of the Missouri down to the

Mississippi. This miracle alone should keep them from the river for the whole season. We had done our work well. We had located beaver and maple-sugar country —the real maple, not the ash-leaf which grew near our post.

So we found a suitable spot on the river and camped. Flat Mouth tied his hunting-knife to a sapling and speared a sturgeon. I stumbled on to a small herd of buffalo which were in much better flesh than those on the west side of the river. I shot a calf to get the hind-quarters for steak. While I was acting the cook the Pillager investigated up the river.

He had been unable to locate the dead man's family, but he had found the camp. That the Sioux had not found the camp—or, at any event, had not come upon the family—was evident by Flat Mouth's failure to find any victims. My companion believed the men and women and children at the camp had taken alarm and fled far back into the marsh country. I afterwards learned that this was true.

Flat Mouth regretted exceedingly the absence of his friends from the post, for seldom would the Red River Chippewas have such a glorious collection of hair to dance. I was pleased they were gone, for it saved the cost of a prolonged drinking bout.

Of course I gave Flat Mouth a generous allowance, and he spent the evening in arranging his hair and painting his face and pounding on a drum and chanting songs. After building a song that narrated each move in the fight, and, being thoroughly primed, he let out a terrific yell and danced the scalps.

In the morning Flat Mouth's luck was still with him, as he managed to kill two beaver opposite the fort. I turned gardener. Thanks to the foresight of Mr. Henry on entering the country, we were able to raise many vegetables.

Our harvest was aside from what the Indian women and children stole. This kind of thievery became such a nuisance that we were compelled to enclose the whole potato field with a high stockade. Otherwise it would have been necessary to post a guard by day and night.

I had just traded the two beaver killed by Flat Mouth and was on my way to plan my garden campaign when six Crees and two Assiniboins came in. All told, they had a dozen beaver and a quantity of wild fowl.

I traded and gave them a dram, but while they drank they kept their bows and arrows in their hands and seemed suspicious of something. At first I thought they were afraid of the Sioux pouncing down upon us. To quiet their fears I told them of Flat Mouth's coup. They put no stock in my story till the chief came dancing in and held the scalps up before them.

Now this should have brought them great joy, for according to their beliefs nothing is so wholesome as a Sioux warrior dead. Yet the sight of the scalps seemed to alarm them instead of bringing them any pleasure. Their attitude was sullen as they heard Flat Mouth recite his coups. Finally he made his exit, still dancing and singing the song he had composed.

"What is the matter with my friends? It is time you finished your milk and went to the hills where the Chippewas are hunting," I rebuked.

"The Chippewas have stolen our medicine. We will not go among them," informed White Buffalo, leader of the Crees.

His companions followed the speaker's example of staring after the Pillager, their bows and arrows ready for instant use.

"What do you mean by drinking in my house while you hold strung bows in your hands?" I demanded. "Have you passed war-tobacco against my children, the Chippewas?"

"We have passed no tobacco," grunted White Buffalo. "Do not be afraid, white man, that we shall make a fight. We cannot fight. The Chippewas have stolen our medicine."

No matter how ridiculous I might think this allegation to be, I knew it was the most serious matter on earth to them. If they sincerely believed the Chippewas had stolen their medicine, then good-bye to the hunting on the lower Red River. The accusation might easily create a situation more grave than any spasmodic attack by the Sioux.

"What medicine have they stolen?" I solemnly asked.

White Buffalo pointed after Flat Mouth and gloomily replied:

"It was our stolen medicine that let the Pillager chief count coup against the Sioux. No Chippewa can take four scalps with only Chippewa medicine to help him."

This would have impressed a newcomer as being the silly superstition of an Indian. And yet, unless happily cleared up, it might mean the ruin of the North West Company's fur trade on both the Assiniboin and Red. The story would spread like a malignant disease.

It was fortunate that the Chippewas were in the hills. Flat Mouth was too deeply engrossed with preparing his scalps as permanent trophies to bother us. Realising the uselessness of attempting to force an explanation, or of belittling the accusation, I waited. At last White Buffalo continued:

"The Sioux followed the Voice and it led them to Flat Mouth. The Voice made the Sioux blind and they did not know Flat Mouth was cracking their skulls."

"The Voice?" I repeated, seizing upon this, the first clue to the Cree's meaning.

"The River That Calls has lost its Voice," informed White Buffalo with a little shiver.

Now Riviere Qu'Appelle, as the French knew it, or Catabuysepu, as the Crees named it, was regarded with much awe and fear by the Indians of the Northwest. It being the main fork of the Assiniboin, my travels up that river had made me somewhat familiar with it. It derives its quaint name from an Indian belief that a mighty spirit haunts it, flying along its course and crying aloud in what sounds like a human voice. I had never observed that the Calling spoke differently than any other river. But some one had tagged the superstition to it, and some *manito* lived there.

What I couldn't understand was my visitors' reason for believing the Chippewas had stolen this spirit, or Voice. While the belief persisted, however, it was a very grave matter and very detrimental to our interests.

"When did the Voice go away?" I asked.

"So many sleeps," mumbled White Buffalo, holding up his fingers to indicate a week. "It was the Voice that helped Flat Mouth take his scalps."

"Perhaps the Voice is tired and is resting," I suggested. "It may be asleep, waiting for the mud-water to leave the river." The last was the true solution, I believed. Freshet water had eliminated the little, musical tinkling sounds of the shallows, and perhaps had interfered with the air currents and their murmurings among the trees.

"On the Pembina, above this fort, we have heard the Voice," was the rejoinder.

"You heard a summer bird singing."

Ignoring me as if I had never spoken, White Buffalo continued:

"We have heard the Voice on the Red River. It sounded like women weeping. The Voice wants to go back home. The Chippewas cannot keep it."

The Crees worshipped the Voice because it was big medicine. It was powerful enough to permit Flat Mouth to kill four Sioux warriors. White Buffalo believed that as thoroughly as he believed he liked rum. Yet a stronger Chippewa medicine held it prisoner. It wept and moaned and wanted to go back to the River That Calls and couldn't, and the Crees intended to rescue it by force of their bows and arrows. So I solemnly promised:

"Within a moon I will see that the Voice is back on the Catabuysepu." I believed that inside a month the river would be back to normal conditions. "Let the Chippewa magic be ever so strong, there is no medicine as strong as the white man's. But there must be no fighting with the Chippewas. If any blows are struck, the Voice will refuse to return.''

My bold assurance seemed to put a little heart in them, although White Buffalo was curious to know why it took a moon for my strong medicine to work.

''My medicine can work as quick as that,'' I said, snapping my fingers. ''But it will take a little time to learn if the Crees have done some evil thing and have driven the Voice away.''

All protested their innocence. One of the Assiniboins smacked his lips over the dregs of his rum and informed me—

''No summer trade will go to the Scratching.''

I attached no importance to this remark, thinking the wily fellow was fishing for more rum. I pricked up my ears when he added:

''They will trade no new milk this summer for skins.''

''No rum at the X. Y. post?'' I incredulously asked.

The Indian, in a voice of deep disgust, repeated—

''No rum.''

If this news were true, I would have no rivalry during the summer. To handle the trade without liquor was to fly without wings. I was glad that Red Dearness had gone away without requesting me to sell him a few kegs. Had he asked the favour, I should have granted it—not as a courtesy, but as a protection against a possible time when the N. W. might need a similar favour. And yet, even if Dearness, because of sickness or haste to be gone, had neglected to tap our stock, why had not the clerk Angus come up for a few kegs?

''What were you doing at the X. Y. post?'' I sternly demanded, remembering that they had no business to take their hunt there.

''We took our goods there, as we were afraid of the Chippewas here, who had stolen our medicine,'' defended White Buffalo.

''If you could have traded for rum, you wouldn't be here now?''

They readily admitted this to be true.

"You have heard my promise about the Voice," I said. "You are not to be afraid of my Indians. You are to tell all your people, all the X. Y. summer Indians, that there is plenty of strong milk here."

"We will bring our hunt here—all of it," he promised.

This new promise of trade pleased me immensely and I gave each of the men another dram and left them. I was anxious to have Flat Mouth's opinion on the stolen medicine.

"You have heard the Voice talking on the River That Calls?" I asked.

"Everyone hears it who goes there."

"Have you heard that it has left the river?"

"It has left the river," he assured.

"Where is it?" I bluntly demanded.

"A strange spirit flies through the sky along the Pembina River above the fort. It makes a loud noise."

"A strange spirit? What foolish talk is this? How can you say that unless you have seen it?" I reproached.

"I have seen it," he astounded me by replying. "It floated on the water through the darkness and sang its medicine song."

"What did it look like?"

"Like a big white swan."

His hesitation before answering satisfied me this was a bit of imagination.

"The Pillager chief heard a loon cry and said it was a spirit," I scoffed.

"The loon has the voice of an evil spirit. Ugly, like the snarling of two foxes fighting."

By implication I was to understand that the strange spirit on the Pembina had a very sweet voice. This in itself was no clue for a white man to follow, for the senseless thudding of a war-drum is soothing and beautiful to the Indian ear. I was glad old Tabashaw and his people were back in the hills. Once they heard they held this mighty medicine Voice a captive, they would stop hunting and depend upon their prisoner to charm rum out of my strong room.

That night, after I had turned in, there came a pounding on the stockade gate. I ran out. It was White Buffalo who answered my angry challenge.

"Listen up the river, the Pembina," he requested in a trembling voice.

I turned my ear to the west. At first I heard nothing; then it came down the river to me. It was faint and far off, containing a wailing sweetness much like the soft passing of a bow over a violin. It was like nothing so much as a human voice without suggestion of spoken words. Rather a humming, moaning sound.

CHAPTER IV

SUPERSTITION VERSUS RUM

FLAT MOUTH would not utter a word when I attempted to question him about the strange sound. I thought to betray him into some expression by making light of the incident and attributing it to some animal call. He smiled grimly and turned away from me. He knew that I knew no animal was ever heard in the Red River country to give voice to that peculiar cry.

The effect on the Crees was tremendous. Their expressed determination to fight the Chippewas and compel a return to the Voice was not repeated after White Buffalo called me to the gate to hear the wailing up the Pembina. They became meek and humble in bearing, and their leader pathetically explained:

"The new milk made us talk bad. We cannot fight against the Chippewa medicine. We only want to stay where we can hear the Voice."

For several nights I remained awake, hoping the phenomenon would be repeated. As nothing happened, the edge of my interest wore off and I became busy with the ordinary humdrum which occupies the attention of the *bourgeois* of a post, as the French called a manager. We turned the horses out to graze on the plains and fired the dead grass along the east bank of the river. Two skin canoes, loaded with beaten meat and a few skins, came down the Pembina from the hills hut. I sent back several kegs of mixed wine and orders for our man to keep the Indians there, to tell them they would get nothing to drink if they came to the post.

77

That the X. Y. was pursuing its silly policy of attempting to carry on trade without rum was again evidenced by the arrival of several small bands of Indians, Chippewas who were bringing their hunt to me although they had taken debts from the opposition. They denounced the X. Y. for refusing them liquor, and again I marvelled that Angus did not come to me and borrow a few kegs.

Then came the Rat with two prime packs of beaver. As he was still in the employ of the X. Y. I hesitated to trade, fearing he had stolen the skins, but they bore none of the MacKenzie marks, and finally I believed him when he insisted he was trading them in behalf of two tents of Crees who were afraid to visit me from fear of the Chippewas. And the Rat wanted rum.

I accommodated him and questioned him concerning affairs at the post. He was curiously silent; not a bit like his usual loquacious self. When he spoke it was to return evasive replies. To my pointblank query, "Isn't Angus planning to come here for liquor?" he replied—

"No, I don't think."

I next took up the Crees' fear of the Chippewas and demanded to know on what it was based. He shook his head. I decided they believed our Indians had stolen the Voice from Rivière Qu'Appelle, but as he did not touch on the subject, and as I was not anxious to have it revived, I held my tongue. I did say, however:

"Tell the Crees they are welcome here. No Chippewa will bother them when they bring in their hunt."

Presenting him with two quarts of liquor for bringing the trade, and a keg for the Crees, I saw the rascal to his canoe and was glad to be rid of him.

About the first of May old Tabashaw and seven other chiefs, including a Cree and two Assiniboins, descended upon me for their annual spring presents. I gave each a keg of liquor, a new coat, some red feathers and tobacco. The usual drinking match followed, keeping me busy for two days preventing murder. It was the Chippewas who seemed hungry for trouble, the others, especially the Crees, appearing to be cowed. Tabashaw, in particular, was in a mood to tickle the devil. Twice I took a knife away from him while a Cree sat with a bowed head, singing that he was not afraid to die.

This meek submission to a ranting scallywag like Tabashaw was not a bit like the Crees' ordinary behaviour, and I could only attribute it to the theft of the Voice. However, although I kept with them and listened sharply to their words, I heard nothing said which would indicate the Chippewas felt they held any advantage in medicine. If the news of the Voice had penetrated the hills, none of my visitors revealed that fact. After the second day I drove the whole party back to the hills to finish their kegs and turned to stringing eighty fathoms of sturgeon net across the river. Flat Mouth, who was my helper on the opposite bank, ceased his labours and stared downstream. I turned my head and beheld two canoes, the clerk Angus occupying the first. The second held a figure heavily cloaked and with a *capote* drawn over the head.

I smiled grimly at Angus as he slowly paddled to the shore. He had been forced to come for the rum. If he had held off another month I would have cleaned up all the spring beaver in the department.

Angus jumped out, pulled up his canoe, turned and did a similar service for the second, and briefly announced—

"Miss Dearness, of the X. Y., come to talk with you."

With this astounding statement he walked rapidly towards the post, leaving me alone with the hooded figure.

More than one Northman had taken an Indian wife, and whenever Dearness's "woman" was mentioned I had taken it for granted that an Indian spouse was meant. Instead of his wife it was his daughter, the woman who had talked to me in three languages from behind the rawhide curtain at the X. Y. post. This discovery was so overwhelming that for a moment I forgot to be surprised at Dearness's departure without her.

"I am honoured," I began, bowing to her.

She threw back the *capote,* and I was stricken dumb at the revelation. Expecting to find a mixed blood, I could only stare foolishly at the clear skin, an English skin, and the glory of her red hair. There was no mistaking her being her father's daughter. For nearly a year I had seen only the coarse, greasy black hair of the Indians and the dishevelled locks of the few white men. Here was a head with a fiery nimbus. Not auburn or yellow, but red—a red that would fire the heart of a warrior about to take the war-path. I have a vague recollection of a skirt of blue cloth, such as the Spanish far-south trade with the Missouri Indians, and a coat of dressed leather that fitted her superb figure snugly. But it was the hair that held my eyes, much as fire draws a moth.

"I didn't know you had been left behind," I heard myself observing. "Or did you and your father go only as far as the Forks?"

"I stayed behind to look after the post, to see it wasn't burned down, while the clerk was away," she answered, her blue eyes levelled on me with the utmost composure.

"Then Angus is only a clerk and you're the *bourgeoise?*"

"Quite correct! And your name is Franklin, according to the agreement you signed at the post. You represent Mr. Chabot here this summer."

"You and I are of equal rank. I represent the N. W.," I corrected.

"That makes it all the better." She smiled graciously and nodded her head. Then reproachfully, "You have been trading rum for skins which should have been traded at our post."

"I've traded rum for skins," I qualified. "Whether they should have gone to you is another question. It's customary to trade rum, you know."

"Rum would have kept the skins at the X. Y.," she quietly informed.

"Of course—I had no idea you were down there.

Really, I had no idea you were you. The hunters spoke of the 'woman.' I supposed you were his wife."

"His Indian wife," she gravely amended.

I nodded and continued:

"I took it for granted Angus was there alone with the interpreter. I've been prepared to let him have a few kegs any time he asked for it. It wasn't my place to force it upon him, but you are more than welcome. How much do you want?"

"I don't want any. Some of the X. Y. stock is stored at the post."

I sank down on the nose of a canoe, almost doubting my ears. And her blue eyes were gathering storm signs, which was also bewildering.

"Well," I helplessly replied, "if you have rum and don't want any from the N. W., I don't see how I can help you. You've refused to trade rum for skins. Surely you're not going to make the startling suggestion that I do the same?"

"It would be a very sensible suggestion. I had thought of making it. Now I see it would be wasting my breath—that you would never consider it."

"Not for a second! Why, Miss Dearness, nothing but rum will bring in the skins. You know that. I can't imagine your father getting a hunt without using high wine. It's the one thing the Indian cannot resist."

"He has always used it and always will," she calmly admitted. "But I will not."

"Then you'll do no summer trading on the Red," I assured her.

"That doesn't follow," she murmured, half closing her eyes and watching me sleepily. "I'm only staying till my father returns."

"Does he know you're killing his trade in this way?"

"Not unless he has very strong medicine." Her teeth flashed in a smile.

"I see," I mumbled, my brains quite addled by the red of her hair and the deep blue of her eyes. "Of course."

"When I came here I was prompted by an impulse," she ran on. "Before I jumped ashore I knew my errand was foolish."

"Don't say that," I begged. "You've given me the greatest surprise in my life. Surprises up here are good for one."

"I've nothing to say to your trading rum," she imperturbably continued. "It's customary. But there are some skins owed the X. Y. on debts taken before my father left for the Forks. You had no right to trade for those. Even the rum was passed over for them."

"It's not nice, this taking skins owed on debts. But your father has had few scruples, if you'll forgive me for saying it."

"Black Chabot had none. I should never have come to see him."

This was either a compliment or a reflection on my youth.

"I know the fur trade quite well," I said. "It isn't for the N. W. to safeguard the X. Y. interests. I can't imagine Sir Alexander MacKenzie going out of his way to prevent Simon McTavish losing a profit. This is a trading-post."

"Quite so—and you approve of Black Chabot's way of fighting women for their furs," she sneered.

"You know better. I have never fought with women. There is a vast difference between holding up a woman and taking her furs by force, whether she owes them on a debt or is free to trade where she will, and trading for skins voluntarily brought here."

"Then you refuse to stop trading with Indians who have not settled their debts with us?"

"I must. The proposition is absurd. Your father would never make such a request. When the X. Y. and the N. W. make a bargain to that effect, all well and good. But the liquor you have stored and won't use would bring in every debt owed you."

"I'm disappointed in you," she said.

It was on my tongue to say I was in no way disappointed in her, but there was something in her clear gaze, a strength in her simple dignity, that held me constrained and awkward. She made me feel as if I were very young and callow, a capacity some women have, I've discovered. I resented it.

"You can't prove your experiment a success if I stop trading rum," I argued. "If your medicine is strong, the only way you can prove it is by overcoming opposition."

"I believe I understand that much quite thoroughly," she gravely said, yet making me feel she was laughing at me all the time.

"Are you afraid of the Indians? Angus wouldn't be much help in time of danger. The Rat is—well—a rat."

"I'm not afraid. They never bother me. I come and go. I'm something of a mystery to them. They seem glad to keep clear of me when they see me outside the fort."

"Do you go any distance from the fort?"

"Oh, I go as I wish. I've been as far as Grandes Fourches in my canoe—alone. Several times I've gone on my horse to the Pembina and followed it to the hills. Now I'll be returning to the Scratching. But please remember, I think you're making a mistake in taking furs belonging to the X. Y."

"I shall have to risk it. You go up the Pembina. Do you sometimes sing when you're travelling alone?"

She gave me a quick little glance and admitted—

"I sing if I wish to."

"Then you're the medicine that has stolen the Voice from Rivière Qu'Appelle," I exclaimed, very proud I had solved the mystery.

"I have been on the River That Calls. I know the Indian story about the Voice. But I don't catch your meaning," she said, turning back and waiting for me to explain.

"Why, the Crees and Assiniboins say the Voice has left the river—probably high water and a change in air currents, perhaps just their imagination. The fact remains they believe the Voice has been stolen. They say the Chippewas' medicine took it away. They've heard you singing at night. That's a positive proof to them the Chippewas have the Voice a captive down here on the Red and its branches."

As I eagerly said all this she turned her head aside and half-closed her eyes. If her clear-cut profile had not remained immobile I would have sworn she was laughing at me.

"Very interesting! Very real to the Indians, too. From what I've learned in going about with my father there are no unfair practices among rival posts," she murmured. "That is your code?"

"We have spoiled the Indians. We stop at nothing which does not involve premeditated murder. Your father, you know, advised Little Crane to kill me for preventing his trading our skins to you."

"Very likely, although I did not hear him," she coolly commented. "I'm glad to get your point of view. I've said I thought you were making a mistake in trading for our skins. I meant a mistake that would hurt you morally. Now I'll make a little prophecy. You've made a mistake in a business sense. I see fur coming back to the X. Y. post on the Scratching. And I thank you."

"For what?"

"For helping me bring the trade to our post."

Again she stared at me sleepily through her half-closed lids.

"So you've changed your mind. You will use the rum your father left behind."

"No, I'll trade superstitions."

I didn't catch her meaning.

"Superstition has brought many troubles to the Indians," I reminded.

"So it has to the whites. Superstition was here before

the whites came, but we brought rum into the country. We're responsible for that."

Her quaint and prim notions concerning rum and Indians amuse me. But as she amused, she also thrilled me. She was a white woman, wonderful to look at. I did not even know that I approved of her, but still she fascinated me.

"You'll trade superstition," I repeated, groping for her meaning. "And I have helped you?"

"Superstition was here before rum. It's stronger. You may think you are holding them—you will hold them at times, when the rum is under their noses—but you'll learn that superstition has the first call on them. Yes, you have helped me immensely with your story of the Voice stolen from Rivière Qu'Appelle. I know the river and the strange song it makes at times. You tell me they heard me singing and thought it the lost Voice. I confess it. I took the Voice." And she paused to smile at me triumphantly.

"But what of it?" I asked, tingling beneath the electricity of her smile.

"If they would have it back, they must come to me—bring trade to me."

"Impossible!" I jeered, wondering how she could be so credulous. "You forget that I only have to tell them what you say to make them see they're mistaken."

"Tell them. I shall be obliged to you if you will. You have refused a very reasonable request In declining to stop trading for skins taken on X. Y. debts. Without intending to do so, you have given me the advantage. I'll strip your spring hunters of their furs. The N. W. will have some unpaid debts as well as the X. Y."

Tender, gentle women arouse one's pity when they attempt defiance. She struck sparks with every word.

"Rum against superstition," I challenged, hungering to trade with her and to best her.

Like the average man, my instinct toward the sex was to protect, but I was keen to humiliate this woman.

"So let it be. I'll wager all the furs I've taken on rum."

Without heeding me further she walked to her canoe and whistled a long quavering note. Angus came on the run around the corner of the potato-field stockade. He had been trained to leave her to look after herself, for he made no move to push off her canoe, although his bearing was as skulking as that of a whipped dog. Staring at me without seeing me, she sent her craft out into the current. Then, resting her paddle, she lifted her head and sounded a bell-like call that rose and fell and trilled far up the river with a strange sweetness. With never a glance at me she adjusted her *capote* and started down the river. And, as she went, she sounded the call again, distance giving it an eerie note.

I was aroused from my meditations by the splash of a paddle above me. It was Flat Mouth, and now he was running toward me. I greeted him with a laugh and pointed after the woman, saying—

"There goes the white woman whose voice the foolish Crees and Assiniboins took to be the Voice of the Calling River."

The fellow's behaviour both irritated and amused me. His strong face showed a curious touch of timidity. His gaze followed the dancing canoe until a bend in the river snatched it from view.

"The white woman is very big medicine," he grunted, speaking to himself rather than to me.

"But she is the trader's daughter. She sings when she is out on the river. Foolish Indians heard her singing at night and thought it was a spirit's voice," I impatiently reminded.

"There was a spirit on the River That Calls. It is gone. This woman with the medicine hair——"

I was greatly disappointed in the Pillager chief. I had been with him on so many trips and always had found him so brave and loyal and sensible.

With a wealth of new thoughts I resumed my daily tasks. Old Tabashaw unexpectedly arrived from the hills with Black Robe and the latter's family. The Robe hadn't a single skin and would give no answers when I inquired for his hunt.

Tabashaw asked for liquor and, despite my vow to give none except when skins had been killed, I measured him out a dram—just enough to make him mad for more. Then I asked him why the Robe came empty handed, and why the hillmen were not sending in anything. He was dying for another drink, but surprised me by simulating ignorance, talking vaguely about certain difficulties which I knew did not exist. The Robe got never a drop and, after hanging about the fort for several days, disappeared.

Shortly after his going I discovered that a nine-gallon keg was missing from my stock. It would never do to let an Indian get clear with stolen property, especially if it were rum. From Flat Mouth I learned the Robe had gone down the river. Believing he had made for the Reed camp, where he would go on a drunk with Probos's hunters, I put after him.

I followed the west bank down to the Scratching, searching it carefully for signs of the thief. If I did not find him at the Scratching I intended searching the east bank going back. I landed a short distance above our abandoned post and cast about for a trace of him. Then, fearing lest he might get inside the fort and set it afire, I left the woods and ran to the post.

Entering the stockade, I found him asleep near the gate, but there was no sign of the keg. I kicked him awake and demanded to know where he had hidden the rum. He scrambled to his feet, intending, as I supposed, to lead me to the liquor. With the ferocity of a cornered Canada lynx he was on me, his knife slashing at my breast. My stout leather coat protected me long enough to bring up the end of my paddle under his chin.

Down he went, but was up again, insane from rum and rage. I feared I would have to kill the brute when Miss Dearness's voice, trilling and wailing, penetrated his black mood. He ceased fighting and the knife dropped from his limp hand.

I wheeled just as she reached the gate. One sweep of her blue eyes took in the situation. Puffing and panting from my exertions and anger, I do not suppose I presented a very pretty picture. Anyway, there was disdain in her glance, and before I could speak she was saying:

"It isn't for the X. Y. to return goods stolen from the N. W., but I suppose you want the liquor this Indian took. I saw him carrying a keg into the woods."

Then to the Robe, speaking his own tongue even better than I could, she commanded—

"Go!"

He ran to the timber and I ironically observed—

"I thank you for your good intentions, but you've allowed him to escape."

"If there is any liquor left he will bring it," she coldly retorted.

Something thudded behind me and I whirled and raised my paddle, only to find Black Robe sullenly standing beside the keg. I tipped it with my foot and knew that less than a quart had been taken. The expression of disgust on her face as she watched me make an inventory of the liquor was maddening. One might think she regarded me as an animal instead of a Northman in the making.

Her own father was famous—she would say "infamous" if he were not her father—for the big trades he made by means of alcohol and water. He was accused of one trick I never had been guilty of—using a mug half filled with tallow on an Indian too drunk to realise he wasn't getting a full drink. But then, Chabot did it, too. The annoying fact remained that by some influence she had compelled Black Robe to bring back the stolen liquor. I would have given twenty kegs if the rascal, on striking the woods, had kept on going. I wouldn't tickle her vanity by asking how she did it; I did say, however—

"I'll send down to you the next furs offered me by an Indian owing you a debt."

"Owing the X. Y.," she carelessly corrected. "Why not one of the packs received by you yesterday?"

"None came in yesterday," I informed.

"Then the day before," she went on, smiling.

"It's fully a week since any of my Indians have brought in a hunt," I explained. "No X. Y. Indians have offered me furs since your visit."

She opened wide her mouth and laughed with such a mocking lilt as to send the blood sizzling into my scrawny face. Sobering abruptly and with no trace of merriment in her lips or eyes, she coldly reminded—

"Superstition against rum."

Raising her fingers to her lips, she whistled an ear-splitting signal, and in twenty seconds Angus came running through the gate.

"How many skins have we traded this week, Angus?" she shot at him.

"Between sixty and seventy."

Had he told me that and she had not been present, I should have informed him he was a little liar. As it was, however, I clenched my teeth, knowing only too well he spoke by the book.

"And how many of them were brought by hunters owing N. W. debts?" she sweetly continued.

This made Angus uneasy. He did not want to answer. She snapped her eyes, and he replied—

"All but four of them, Miss Dearness."

"Now I understand why my Indians haven't come in," I confessed. "Yet it's only half a test. This thief has brought his hunt to you." I pointed at the Robe. "If he hadn't stolen the rum he would have returned here and stolen the skins back to trade to me for high wine. You've started a dangerous game. I shall stick to what I've told them—no rum without skins. Rum they will have, and they can't steal skins at our post. You're responsible for anything that happens down here."

"Mr. Franklin, you understand that you and I think alike on lots of things concerning the fur trade," timidly spoke up Angus.

"You go back to the post. We've left it alone in the Rat's care," she gently commanded, and Angus left us forthwith, accepting the rebuke without a word.

Her eyes were laughing as she faced about and confessed:

"The Crees and Assiniboins bring me trade as a bribe to me to send the Voice back to Rivière Qu'Appelle. The Chippewas bring their hunt to keep the Voice on the Red. So far as being in any danger, you should know I am a medicine woman to them. My hair is very great medicine. Old Tabashaw says I am a spirit-medicine. I have no sex for them."

"My, but you're a tearing beauty!" bawled Black Chabot's bull of a voice behind us. "No sex, eh? And I never guessed it. I blundered right by and never knew it."

I was amazed to behold him there on the Scratching when he should be on the Lake of the Woods or Rainy River. He had been drinking, of course, and never had I seen his eyes look more evil. He glared at the pliant figure of Miss Dearness until his gaze became defilement. She, cold as ice, did not flinch before his lecherous staring. I could not see that his brutal presence quickened her heart by a single beat.

"You did not go through with your brigade?" she remarked. "Did you overtake the X. Y. and my father?"

"I overhauled the X. Y., all right," he hoarsely responded, edging a step closer to her. "That's how I learned you, his daughter, was here. All white—and a red head."

"Then you did overtake my father?" she demanded.

"I'd have to travel considerable to overtake him," he informed. "He's dead."

Her face went blank and with a little sigh she leaned

limply against the stockade. With the grunt of a wild animal Chabot snarled—

"I come way back here to overtake you, my pretty."

It was beastly. He lunged forward to seize her. I shoved the paddle between his feet and brought him crashing down on his face, and as he fell I gave him a thump on the head. He lay very still, his face buried among the broad chips left from hewing the stockade timbers. Across the clean chips the blood trickled until I believed his fall, or my blow, had ruptured a blood-vessel.

"He's a black-hearted liar," I told her. "I haven't a doubt but what he's made it up out of whole cloth. Don't you be afraid. I shall kill him if he bothers you again. The N. W. would expect me to do it."

"Black-hearted, yet he told the truth," she whispered. "My father was suffering with incurable heart trouble. He knew it was only a question of time. He was very loyal to Sir Alexander and his partners, and he hoped to last until he could send someone out here to take over the post. He didn't dare send me while he stayed, for fear he would die before his successor could come. He had a horror of the post being without a master, so I stayed and he went."

She talked like one dazed, and yet she had not given way to her grief in the usual womanly way.

"Pack up," I directed. "I will have a canoeman here just as soon as I can make our post and start him off. He will be Flat Mouth. You can trust him absolutely. Take Angus with you; he'd be helpless up here alone. Flat Mouth will see you to the Forks. The rest of the trail is easy."

She pointed to Chabot, who was now showing signs of life, and directed:

"Take that away. Don't send your Indian."

"Your clerk is not *voyageur* enough to take you through alone," I protested. "Once the Indians learned you were leaving the country, taking the Voice with you, they might do anything."

She walked through the gate, and I followed her. She halted and wearily informed me:

"My father left me to look after the post until some one came. I shall stay. Good-bye! You'll get more skins now—just for what you did to that." She nodded towards the fence, behind which Black Chabot was trying to collect his drunken senses.

She was gone by the time he had managed to stagger through the gate. His long black beard was full of blood, a ghastly sight even in the fur country.

"Where is she?" he whispered, glaring about.

"Miss Dearness? She went back to the post to get her father's double-barrelled gun. Said something about shooting you on sight."

"I'll tame her," he vowed. "A regular red head! But I'll tame her. Come back a purpose to."

"Scarcely worth the game," I carelessly remarked. "A risk is a risk, and danger is a danger, but when she's got all the Chippewas, Crees and Assiniboins believing she's a great tribal medicine, when the whole outfit is willing to murder every white in the North-west if she gives the word—— But what's the use of talking all this to you? You know your own business. You're old enough to take care of yourself."

He combed some of the blood from his beard and stared at his fingers curiously. Slanting his eyes at me, he muttered:

"How did I come to fall? Felt like something was mixed up with my feet—like something hit my head."

His low voice was the danger signal. I was carrying the keg on my left shoulder, the paddle in my right hand. I dropped the keg as if to rest me and shifted the paddle, leaving a hand free to snatch for my knife.

"Looked to me as if your last drink was what got mixed with your legs," I boldly replied.

He combed more blood from his beard and stole murderous glances at me. He knew I had mauled him over the head and he proposed to get even.

"Indians think she is big medicine, you say?"

"Ask any of them," I advised.

He picked up the keg and drank wolfishly; then he made for his canoe and, by some miracle, embarked. In spite of his drams he handled the paddle smartly. I placed the keg in my canoe and followed him. Instead of keeping inshore he swung out into midstream, where he had to contend against the full force of the current.

He had a reason in this, as I soon knew; it was to get a view of the X. Y. post. I trailed him, and we both beheld Miss Dearness standing on the shore, her face turned toward the north, looking down the path her father had taken for the last time. Her hair looked like a torch.

The sight of her seemed to drive him mad. He stood erect and shook his fist at her and raved:

"I'm coming back to get you! It'll even up what I owe Red Dearness."

I reached over with my paddle and gave his canoe a shove, and he shot into the water.

Without a word he turned and began paddling up-stream. He had gained a lead of a rod or so when an arrow whipped from the bushes and hissed close to his wet beard. With a yelp and a howl he toppled backward and all but went overboard again. By the time he had scrambled back to his knees a second shaft stuck in the bow of the canoe.

Then came the girl's voice, clear as a bell, warning:

"Tell him he dies unless he goes downstream at once, Mr. Franklin. Tell him he dies if he comes back here before I have left the country."

I had no need of telling him, for he heard her. Snarling with rage, yet weak with fear, he hesitated, and a third arrow all but got him. The Black Robe, for I knew it must be he, was shooting marvellously straight for one so recently drunk. Howling like some wild animal caught in a trap, he frantically spun his craft about and, hugging the east bank, paddled for his life downstream, making for the Forks. I watched him till he was out of sight, but did not see any other arrows pursue him.

I half expected the Robe to take a shot at me, but he did not, although he had many opportunities had he so wished. Perhaps it would be better to say had she not forbid his doing so.

Thus closed Black Chabot's career in the Red River Country—expelled by a girl with fiery red hair. I had much to ponder over as I fought my way upstream.

CHAPTER V

THE RIVER SETS A TRAP

FLAT MOUTH was cleaning a string of catfish when I went to the river bank next morning.

The Pillager wiped his knife on a tuft of grass and rose, saying—

"He will not come back here."

He referred to Black Chabot. There was no need of names between us.

"How do you know that?" I asked.

"A very strong medicine will keep him away," he replied, smiling grimly.

"A red medicine," I suggested.

"White man call it 'afraid.' "

"You have heard how he came and went away?"

"My *wabeno* medicine tells me much."

"What else has it told you?"

"The father of the medicine woman is dead," he said.

In some such way did news travel up and down the river, often outspeeding a messenger. You might start post-haste for the hills with news and find it ahead of you when you arrived. The natural inference was that Black Robe had brought word of Chabot's attempted assault on the girl, but the Robe had not put in appearance and, unless he travelled during the night, he could scarcely have arrived before I woke up. That he would paddle day and night was hardly probable.

Of course there would be a flare-back, once Chabot reached Grand Portage, but I was not worried over the outcome. Miss Dearness's testimony would offset any charges Chabot could prefer against me. What I had

done was for the honour of the N. W. company. The
rivalry between my company and the X. Y. was at its
height, nearing the point where one must give way, or
both go down with a smash; neither of us split hairs
in overreaching the opposition.

Still, there were things which could not be permitted.
The gentlemen of the North did not bother with the
morals of their representatives so long as the returns
were good. The leisurely procedure of the H. B. company had changed to a frantic endeavour to suppress
us, its most powerful rival. Sir Alexander MacKenzie,
once a partner in the N. W. but now head of the X. Y.,
was very bitter against Simon McTavish.

With all this bad blood almost anything would be
overlooked that gave a trade advantage—but a ruffian
attacking a white woman—no! Tell headquarters that
so-and-so is taking too many Indian women as wives,
and the gentlemen would overhaul the factor's last statement, note how many black, silver, red and cross foxes
his sheet showed, or how many beaver and dressed
moose, then gravely reply it was for the good of the
company's trade relations with the tribes.

We determined a Northman's reputation in terms of
beaver, marten, mink, and wolverines, bolstered up by
his trade in black, brown and grizzly bears. But all
this only when Indians were concerned. To trouble a
white woman, especially when she held the unique position of representing the X. Y. company, was a vicious
slap at Sir Alexander and his powerful associates. The
N. W.—all question of decency aside—had enough
trouble without seeking trade in that way.

So I wasn't worried over the final outcome, although
I looked for Chabot to spread wild reports about an
Indian uprising, with me turning renegade. This would
result in the company's rushing a brigade up the Red
and relieving me of command, and, doubtless, in sending me under arrest to Grand Portage or Montreal, where
I would ultimately be vindicated.

While at the bank watching the Pillager, two canoes

came up stream, containing Bad Axe and White Partridge with their families. White Partridge had kept clear of us since Chabot nearly kicked him to death for stealing a horse. Now Chabot was gone, he was back, anxious to become one of our family. As he had a number of skins I let the past sleep and gave him and the Axe a dram. The Axe had started to hunt moose and red deer on the east side of the Red, but had turned back, he said, as the country was overflowed from the spring freshets. I knew this to be a lie, as the river had dropped rapidly, and because of the trip the Pillager and I had taken to the Red River district.

It does no good to tell an Indian he lies, so I told the two I would give them tobacco and ammunition if they would take their families and paddle up to the Goose and get beaver. As an additional incentive I promised a big keg if they should return with enough skins to wipe out their debts. They were much disgruntled over two points; they wanted the keg at once, and they did not propose to hunt beaver on the Goose at any time, as it was above the Red Lake country, where they were sure of being gobbled up by the Sioux.

I spoke to Flat Mouth, who disappeared. When he proudly returned he was flourishing the four scalps, now nicely stretched on small hoops. With great relish he inflicted his new song upon them, relating our adventures and picturing himself always in the lead and at death grips while I lounged in the rear. The scalps impressed them mightily, and they eagerly offered to trade anything they possessed, even their daughters or wives, in return for some of his war-medicine.

At the risk of spoiling a trade I interrupted the babel to declare there was no need of war-medicine up the river now that the Sioux had gone home, for they would not dare return to the Red until the following spring.

"And before then, tobacco will be passed among all the Chippewas, Crees and Assiniboins. A great war party will go after the Sioux and dig them out when the

leaves begin to turn yellow and drop off the trees," I
added for good measure.

Flat Mouth boasted:

"The Sioux are still running like frightened calves.
If one is left behind because he is lame, shout the name
of Eshkebugecoshe, war-chief of the Pillager Chippewas,
and the lame man will run like a fox to get away."

They wavered, and I tipped the scales in favour of
the trip by giving them another dram and consenting
to furnish a gallon of mixed wine for them to take along,
the big keg to await their return with a good hunt. I
was anxious for them to go, as the beaver signs were
unusually good along the Goose, because none of our
Indians had dared tarry there and neither the X. Y.
nor the H. B. had cared to risk establishing a post above
us.

Aside from such unvisited streams, beaver was not
plentiful in the lower Red River department. The
scarcity was not because the animals had been trapped
out, but resulted from some disease that had killed off
the valuable creatures by thousands. They seemed
immune so long as they remained in swift flowing waters,
but the colonies in ponds and stagnant waters were
wiped out in numbers sufficient to make a Northman's
heart ache. They died while at work cutting down
trees, in the entrances to their homes and while constructing their little canals.

My Indian hunters had told me this wholesale exter-
mination was to be found all the way to Hudson Bay.
Now that Chabot would surely endeavour to prejudice
headquarters against me, I was anxious to build the
best of defences—a heavy trade and the exploiting of
regions heretofore left practically untouched.

Flat Mouth's medicine and my promises of rum won
them to the venture and I had the satisfaction of seeing
them on the way with their families, kettles, ammunition and traps.

Taking the Pillager, I crossed over to the east side
of the river and shot three black bears, one on the shore,

drinking, and two out of an oak, where they had climbed to escape me. Their fur was prime and the skins very acceptable. I mention the incident to show how easily some of the idlers at the post and the hills could pay off their debts and buy plenty of mixed wine if they would take the trouble.

Black Robe, very penitent and very thirsty, came in the next day and left a moose as a peace offering. He had shot the animal in the river while coming up from the Scratching. I read him a lecture on the awful crime of stealing rum from a white man and showed him the three bears, telling him to take his family and go and do likewise. Of course he wanted rum at the start. I advanced some cloth for his woman, gave him a few inches of tobacco, some powder and balls, and informed him that bear pelts were the only medicine that could get rum from me.

In a final effort to touch my heart or arouse my fears, he told me of meeting Tabashaw in the woods back of our Scratching River post and learning some important news from him. Tabashaw, he wished me to understand, need no longer lean on the white man. I encouraged him to proceed, and, hoping for a drink, he explained:

"Tabashaw came down from the hills to the strong timber. He was three days without eating. While singing his new song a man, dressed like a white man, came to him and told him of many things. This man-spirit told Tabashaw he must not ask the sun to help him when he made feasts or new medicines, as he, the man-spirit, the great Kitchimanito, was the father of all life and the only power to help the Chippewas. This great spirit told Tabashaw that the traders did not treat him well, and that he, the great spirit, would give him rum and tobacco and ammunition if he gave his medals back to the traders and have nothing more to do with them. Tabashaw told me all this."

"He is a liar," I scoffed, yet glad to know the old rascal's latest plans for regaining control of the tribe and thereby forcing the traders to grant all his whims

"Kitchimanito goes everywhere to turn the Indians away from the whites. Tabashaw saw his moccasins worn to pieces by his long travels," persisted Black Robe.

"If you believe him, go to him. Tell him you will not hunt for the traders. If he is not a liar he will give you rum which the man-spirit gave to him," I advised.

The Robe drew a long face and grunted in despair.

"I will take my woman and my children and go and hunt bear," he surrendered.

There were now two long tents of women and children at the post, their active men being away on the hunt. I used these in finishing the planting and in doing odd chores. The day after the Robe crossed the river old Tabashaw arrived. His manner was subdued and he was very humble when he came to me for some new milk.

"Where is the milk the man-spirit was to give you?" I jeered. "And where are the medals you were to give back to us?"

"I had a bad dream," he muttered, turning away.

His manner was strange. He forgot to threaten me. He wandered apart and placed his *wabeno* drum before him and stared at it gloomily. To draw him out I called him inside the fort and gave him a drink. Even after that his downcast demeanour continued. This was not play-acting. I tried to get him to talk, but he would only say that he had had a bad dream.

The arrival of several hunters, all Chippewas, called me from him. I quickly observed these were sullen and uneasy about something. I traded their skins and gave them rum and sought to set their tongues to wagging, but, like their chief, they remained moody and taciturn. The situation began to get on my nerves. The Indians were children. Ordinarily it was very simple to learn their intentions, despite their expressionless features, but to get behind their thoughts it was necessary to make them talk. So long as the chief and the hunters sat in gloomy silence I could learn nothing, while my imagination pictured all sorts of disagreeable events about to happen.

Anxious to get at the truth, I went after Flat Mouth. I despaired when I observed that even this intelligent and—with me—very frank fellow was sobered almost to the point of dejection. At first he would make no reply to my questions.

"My friend, the great war-chief of the Pillagers, looks sad when four Sioux scalps hang in his tent. And he refuses to tell his white brother, who would drive the shadows away," I complained.

"My brother can not drive the shadows away," he grunted.

"Medicine is strong."

"Was it strong enough to bring the Voice here from the River That Calls?"

I knew I had it. By indirection I had learned what a month of cross-examination would not have told me.

"Flat Mouth is sad because the voice has gone back to its home on the Qu'Appelle," I boldly stated.

Assuming I knew all about it, he said—

"It has gone back. The woman with the medicine hair sent it back."

Old Tabashaw's gloomy bearing and the depression of the hunters was now easily understood.

"That is why your people are so sad even when they have new milk," I said.

"It was great *wabeno* medicine while it was with us," he regretted.

"How do the Chippewas feel toward the woman?"

"They are very angry, but they are very afraid of her."

"They would like to have her scalp nailed to a tent pole," I suggested.

"They are afraid to go near her. No one dares harm her."

"No one can harm her," I cried. "She is mighty medicine. She called the Voice here. She has sent it back. She can call it again when she will."

This possibility caused his eyes to glisten.

"I will tell my people, so their hearts will not be hard against her," he said, rising and making for the stockade.

The result of Flat Mouth's interview with his friends was soon apparent. Tabashaw began beating his drum and the hunters found much vivacity in their wine. Scarcely had this improvement taken place when two tents of Crees and two of Assiniboins brought in their hunt. Their arrival was marked with poorly veiled hostility toward the Chippewas, and yet they seemed striving to hide elation. They eyed the Chippewas askance and kept their bows and arrows in their hands and camped by themselves.

This was unusual, as the three tribes ordinarily fraternised when meeting at the posts. The weaker party during a drinking-match usually desires to keep its weapons close at hand, but this precaution is taken to protect them against the effects of the rum, rather than because of any tribal antipathy. To be on their guard when not in liquor had an ugly look.

"What's the matter with you?" I demanded of a Cree. "You act as if you had passed war-tobacco with the Assiniboins against my Chippewas. What do you mean?"

"We are afraid of the Chippewas. Our hearts are warm toward Tabashaw and his people, but their hearts are black against us," he replied.

"Why should you fear the Chippewas?"

"The Voice is back on the River That Calls. The Chippewas are sad and angry at losing their medicine. They will trade no more skins at the X. Y."

"What about your trade?"

"We bring our hunt here. The Medicine Hair told us we could have no new milk. We can get milk here."

"You took your hunt there when you could not get milk," I reminded.

"That was when she had the Voice. Now it is back on the river we come here."

"See that you are very careful what you do, or the Medicine Hair will take the Voice away from you," I warned. "If any of you have not paid your debts to the X. Y., take your furs and do it, or she will be angry."

It seemed that one hunter did owe the X. Y. a debt, and as a result of my talk with the Cree he was made to do up his skins and hold them out of the trade with the N. W. This was scarcely good policy when the rival companies were bending every energy to get the best of each other, but I had passed my word to her. She had meant it when she said I should receive more furs—that she would let the trade come to me because of what I did to Chabot. Royal pay for a slight service, but somehow there was scant consolation in it. It was like having an opponent clearly demonstrate he can defeat you at your own game and then quit playing from weariness or some whim.

Could I have secured the trade with rum, leaving her hands empty despite her taking advantage of the Indians' superstitions, I should have felt much better. However, the trade continued coming in, with very little going to the X. Y., and the bulk of that returning down-river because I refused to buy from a hunter in debt to my rival.

The monotony of refusing, then judiciously dealing out drams; of threatening, then cajoling the hunters, wore on me. My thoughts were too much given to wandering down the river. I gave too much time to picturing the woman. I resented her attitude of aloofness. After all, we were both young and of the same race. Even though we were trade rivals, there was no reason why, as human beings, we should not see each other and enjoy each other's company.

There was no escaping the fact that the girl was in my mind and was bothering me. Then, suddenly, came the chilling fear that she might be gone. I had refrained from going down the river. Her attitude had not been friendly. She wanted to be alone. Very well, I had

haughtily told myself, it should be as she wished—
then the dread lest she had been relieved.

Once the X. Y. people learned of her father's death,
they would lose no time in shifting a man from the
Assiniboin to the Scratching to permit her leaving the
river before cold weather set in. The idea became fixed
in my mind and tormented me. She was buying no
skins; there was no excuse for her remaining. If a
summer man was not sent out, then Angus could look
after the post, and I was booked for the summer and
winter—a whole year—without another opportunity of
looking on a white woman.

It wasn't love for her that called me, I stoutly told
myself; for I knew we could not exchange a half dozen
sentences without quarrelling. But she was a white
woman, the only one in the department. She aroused
my resentment, and yet I was miserable for wanting to
see her.

At last I ceased trying to fool myself and made for
the river. I would canoe down to the Scratching, make
an errand of looking over our post and at least get a
glimpse of her, if she had not already departed from the
country. I found the Rat talking earnestly with Flat
Mouth, and his presence aggravated my fears. Addressing him in Chippewa to provoke a more voluble flow
of language, I asked—

"What is the Red Hair doing?"

"She makes ready to go away," he replied.

My heart gave a jump.

"When does she go down the river?" I carelessly
inquired.

"Up, not down," he corrected.

I scowled at him, thinking he was lying to me. He
eagerly explained:

"She goes to make discoveries in the Red Lake River
country. She thinks to send hunters there."

"She can get no hunters," I sneered.

"She thinks she can get some Crees, some Assiniboins," he retorted.

I began to believe that she could. All she need do would be to threaten a second theft of the Voice from the Qu'Appelle. I began to feel normal, to look on her as a rival whom I must best in trade.

"Is she going herself?"

"She takes a guide—maybe a family of Crees."

"When does she go?"

"She did not tell me. She talks with no one."

"But you should know if you go with her. Would a deep dram of strong milk make you remember?"

He groaned at his misfortune and replied:

"I do not go with her, so I do not know. She asked me, but it is too near the summer war-path of the Sioux."

"Flat Mouth, chief of the Pillager Chippewas, has scared the Sioux back to their holes," scornfully cried my Indian. Then to my amazement, "I go with the Medicine Hair."

"Did the Rat come to hire you?" I sharply demanded. The Rat drew away, looking very uncomfortable. Flat Mouth readily admitted—

"She knows I am a great warrior."

"She doesn't make any bones of hiring my men, it seems!" And my resentment grew very strong.

"Her hair is great medicine. She calls the Voice. It comes. She tells it to go to sleep. It is gone. I go with her," calmly answered the chief.

Her cool impudence in securing a guide at the post without even asking my leave somehow hinted at the eternal feminine, a quality I had steadfastly refused to detect in her. It was good to think I might see her again, even if only to reproach her for her insolence; I could not get over the conviction that it was decidedly raw for her to send the Rat to hire my best Indian. I could not forgive her going over my head in that fashion. Did a man wish to borrow the Pillager, he would offer me some skins as a bonus. Being a woman, she quietly appropriated what she desired. It wounded my self-esteem, and yet prolonged meditation brought me to the point where I could appreciate the irony of it and grin a bit.

I had wild thoughts of trying to talk Flat Mouth out of the trip, but retained sense enough to know that such an effort would be about as successful as to attempt conversation with a wounded buffalo bull.

He was the best of his complexion I ever met. At times you would forget he was an Indian. But superstition could drive him every which way. He liked me. He enjoyed many privileges because I both liked and trusted him. We had been friends. Yet, without a word of warning, he was to leave me and guide a rival to one of the few remaining beaver localities, and all because of some red hair.

I grinned more broadly, although sardonically. Her lack of logic grimly amused me now; perhaps because it revealed the woman in her. How fiercely she had upbraided me for following the time-honoured custom of trading rum for pelts—a custom that was followed from Hudson Bay to the Willamett. Then she deliberately stole a man without even a "thank you," or "by your leave."

I sternly told myself she needed taming. I found the Rat and asked him—

"When do you go back to the Scratching?"

"At once, unless I am asked to stop for a dram. It is very dry at the post and I am very thirsty. My throat is like the prairie after the fires have scorched it."

"Come inside! You shall have a dram, and a keg to take back with you," I promised.

"New milk is good," he murmured, his mouth watering. "I will take a dram. Let the keg wait for me here, till after the woman goes up the river."

I assured him the liquor would be held in trust for him. He confessed that she was making life miserable for him and Angus by refusing them liquor.

"After she is gone, the clerk and I will have a big drunk," he gloated.

"Then why do you stay with her? I will make it a

big keg for you two. Why not come up here? I will hire both you and Angus. If a man behaves he can have plenty of rum here.''

He sadly shook his head and drifted into French as he answered:

"It is to be wished, to be prayed for—the beautiful rum! But I would be cursed. A bad sign would be on me.''

"Bah! She has made you believe such foolishness?''

"She says nothing. If I went and told her I was leaving the post, she would say nothing. She does not seem to know I am at the post. Since her father died, her eyes look very far away. I do not want to stay, yet I know it would bring me bad luck to leave her. After she goes up the river I will call for the keg—the big keg.''

"You will start down the river at once,'' I directed. "You will stop at the mouth of the Reed and find Probos. Tell him I say for him to come up here at once. He is not to bring the Indians. He will stay here for a few days.''

The Rat readily promised to carry my message, downed his dram and returned to the canoe and set off. I waited till he was out of sight and then attempted to pump Flat Mouth. The chief did not seem to know just when his services would be required. I got the notion he was evading me. I knew it would be useless to press him.

That night I had a stroke of luck. One of the Red Sucker band dropped down the river and brought me five wonderful white buffalo skins, four of them young bulls slain in January below Grandes Fourches, and one, a calf, killed recently. The hair on the bulls was like that of sheep—fleecy and soft and all white. The calf-skin was white except for a black spot encircling the right eye. The Chippewas prize these white robes and skins only for what they will bring in trade, but there are other tribes, especially those on the Missouri, which will barter any of their possessions to secure one.

So I called it a stroke of luck, my getting them; for I planned to use them to the great advantage of the N. W. company before I quit the country. The Indian said he had seen no sign of Sioux, that he had talked with my two hunters on the Goose, and that they were taking beaver.

The story of our victory over the Sioux—rather Flat Mouth's victory, for he was being given all the credit—had spread throughout the country with that celerity with which news ever travels in the wilds. It was taken for granted that, after such a rebuff, the Sioux would not travel north on another path until spring. They would be sure to expect the Chippewas, emboldened by the great coup, to venture south and seek a second victory.

Probos came in due season and I manufactured excuses to keep him, but it was two days after my arrival that I got up one morning to find Flat Mouth had gone. No one seemed to know when he departed. Old Tabashaw, I suspected, had an inkling of the Pillager's engagement, for he performed on his drum with sullen zeal, as if sending his medicine after some one he feared. He sang, without giving any names, and called on the Great Mystery to revenge the Chippewas.

I knew I held a thread to the puzzle in the ten-gallon keg of high wine I intended to present to the Rat and Angus. Depositing the liquor on the bank and seating myself beside it, I waited. An hour of impatience and then the nose of a canoe scraped the willows on the west bank, announcing the arrival of the Rat. From the slack water under the willows he spied on the landing-place before the fort, then scanned the upper reaches of the river and propelled his light craft forward.

"When did she pass the post?" I asked, kicking the keg toward him.

"About the middle of the night," he replied, tenderly setting the wine in his canoe. "The clerk stands on the bank before the fort, his tongue hanging out like a blown bull's, waiting for me to come back."

"You followed her?"

"Not too close. I timed myself to arrive here after sunrise. Ran the canoe into a sunken tree in the night and dared not try to shove off till light came. At the speed she was paddling, I know she must have passed here in the night."

"Flat Mouth has gone. Did he know when she was coming?"

"Yes, she was to sound her call, if she came in the night. He was to be waiting for her."

"Did she bring any Indians with her?"

"She came alone."

I swore and wished I had made it a smaller keg. The rascal had said nothing about Miss Dearness's plans to make a signal to the Pillager.

"I thought he would tell you," he artlessly remarked, sending his canoe into midstream with a deft sweep of the paddle.

"Do you know where they go first?" I called after him.

"To the mouth of Rivière du Lac Rouge where the war road of the Sioux ends. Where the Sioux wait many days when watching the Chippewa hunters to come down the Thief, the Clearwater and the Wild Rice Rivers."

Thanks to the fear my double-barrelled gun had instilled in the Sioux, the woman and her guide would be free from any danger even if they passed the mouth of the Red Lake River and proceeded so far south, even, as the mouth of the Cheyenne.

Now that I knew they were only twelve hours ahead I was undecided as to what I should do. I had called Probos from the Reed, intending to follow them. Now, face to face with the business, I weakened. I had no warrant to follow her. She did not wish my company. She had planned to pass the post in the night so that I might not know of her presence. This was not because of any trade delicacy on her part, as she had not scrupled to hire my best man to guide her. If she wished to avoid me, what an awkward situation I would be in should I follow and find her.

I set Probos to work to arrange a place for the season's hay, some three thousand bundles if we had luck; then I developed great energy in having defective stockade posts of poplar replaced by some of oak. In truth, for nearly an hour I was desperately busy trying to make myself believe I had washed her and her red head out of mind. Could Simon McTavish have dropped in and witnessed my industry, he surely would have appointed me to head an important department.

This attempt to fool myself soon gave way before a satisfactory purpose. I would deceive her. I would go up the river and encounter her, but I would have a legitimate errand and our meeting should appear to be the work of chance.

Once I cast aside all pretences and squarely admitted I would make an errand to take me after her, the way became easy. There were the white robes. I would pack them in my canoe and stalk her until I knew she and her guide had entered the mouth of Red Lake River; then I would turn in after them, pretending I had come down the river, where I had traded for the skins.

Flat Mouth would understand this was some subterfuge of mine but he would never tell her. The scheme tickled my fancy. I would display surprise on overtaking her. I would pretend I thought I was following two of my hunters. Naturally I would exhibit displeasure at her hiring the Pillager. Whether we got along or quarrelled, I would simulate fear of the Sioux and stay by her down the river.

Procuring the skins and baling them neatly, I put them with my gun in the canoe, together with tobacco and a hook and line—the men were now taking many fish on the line. With a final word to Probos to look after things until I returned, and a stern command that he should give out no liquor, I started on my eccentric journey.

I was much ashamed of myself, for I feared I was weak; somehow, though, I was brazenly contented with the thought that I should soon see her. I passed the mouth of the Park at sunset. A short distance beyond, I came to a dead fire and the bones of several catfish, showing where they had paused to eat. There were two canoes and she was doing her own paddling. I kindled a fire, caught some fish and made my camp there.

Nothing broke the monotony of the river until I reached the Big Salt and began paddling by the long slough which extends from that stream to the Turtle River.

Paddling cautiously, I glided along close to the bank, my gaze sweeping the shore at the mouth of the Turtle. The tall reeds a short distance ahead became alive with motion, and, with a twist of the paddle, I was backing into cover.

A canoe darted out, filled with women and children, the former bowing low and paddling frantically. They were closely followed by a second canoe, likewise holding women and children. A few rods behind the second came a third canoe, and in this I recognised Bad Axe and White Partridge.

As they bore downstream, those who were not paddling kept a constant watch to the rear. It was plain that my hunters were afraid of something and, with their families, were fleeing down the river.

The warriors, as was proper, brought up the rear, to stave off death and permit their women and little ones to escape. I have never known this trait to fail of expression in the Indian. He may kill his wife when drunk, or brutally disfigure her, but in event of an enemy attack there is none so cowardly as not to take the fighting position in the rear. I waited until the two canoes of women passed, then drove my craft across the course of the warriors and held up my hand and called out my name.

With a powerful sweep of their paddles they swerved wide to run by me and yelped something I could not understand. Turning my canoe downstream, I laid to the paddle and drove alongside of them until the canoes locked. White Partridge was in the stern. I grabbed his shoulder and forced him to desist paddling until he had explained his flight.

He turned a face on me that was distorted with terror and gasped out "Sioux!" and tried to cast off my hand.

"You saw red deer," I cried. "There are no Sioux on the war road since we killed them at the mouth of the Thief."

"Bad Axe saw them creeping through the woods on the east bank of the Red just below our camp on the Goose," he cried, his teeth chattering.

"He lied to you! He wanted to get back to the post and get rum," I said. "He is a lazy dog."

"We saw their horses," protested Bad Axe over his shoulder. "We counted them. There were so many." And he opened and closed his left hand until he had indicated thirty. "I had crossed to the east bank after a bear. I came upon them in the woods. They did not see me. I was very near. Some were making new moccasins. Some were sticking willow sticks in the ground and painting their faces. Some were creeping to the river—right toward me!"

The recollection caused him to give a little yelp and redouble his efforts at the paddle. White Partridge took up the tale and said:

"There were ten warriors left with the horses. They left all their horses on the west bank. They will kill every one on the river."

He now succeeded in jerking himself free of my grip and, with the two paddles working as one, they sped after their families, leaving me to chew over the problem.

I had not had time to ask the hunters if they had seen anything of Flat Mouth and the woman. I believed they had not seen them, or else they would have mentioned the fact; or, rather, the Pillager and Miss Dearness would be returning with them.

Then I angrily declared there could be no Sioux.

Still, I would have felt easier in my mind if Bad Axe's tally of the warriors on the east bank and the Partridge's count of the horses on the west bank, guarded by ten warriors, had not squared up so nicely. Neither of the men was in a mood which would permit calculation. The number of horses agreed with the number of warriors.

Quitting my shelter, I resumed my journey south with rapid strokes, eager to make the mouth of the Red Lake River. Should there be any truth in the Chippewas' alarm, and had the enemy unaccountably returned to spread along both banks of the river, then the girl was in danger.

Once more I caught an agitation among the reeds and grass on my side of the river. Knowing that all the Goose River Indians had passed me, I drove my canoe into cover for the second time. Once in the swamp growth, I could see but little. A rod in front, flowed the river; as for the rest, I had to depend upon my ears.

Five minutes passed, I estimated, before I heard a *flap-flap* at the edge of the river where it merges with the rank growth of the slough. With the gun ready to be cocked and discharged, I pulled my knife and waited.

The commotion drew nearer until it was nearly abreast of me. Whatever it was, it was in the clear water but close to the reeds. It turned into the marsh grass in the path left by my canoe and I laughed aloud in relief as I glimpsed the long, grey neck, twisting like a serpent, and the flapping wing.

It was a swan, disabled by mink or some other wild thing, and it was floundering along most awkwardly. I sat very quietly while the bird worked its way nearer the canoe. The grass permitted of only occasional glimpses, and I saw it was likely to blunder full against the canoe. With much splashing it came through the last thin barrier, its head moving from side to side in a curious way.

Like the jab of a red-hot knife-blade I remembered

my loud laughter which should have frightened the bird away. Its neck—it was never still. I fastened my gaze on the head and followed it back and forth until I discovered the eyes were dead. It grazed against the boat and at the same moment I drove the butt of my gun down on the feathery mass.

Instantly a brown hand shot up and gripped the side of the canoe with the lithe quickness of a water-snake. Before the canoe could be capsized I had seized the hand and was hanging over the opposite side, my free right hand holding my hunting-knife.

The body of the swan toppled to one side, revealing the head of a Sioux hideous with war-paint. As our eyes met, his left hand came up with an axe and he opened his lips to sound his yell of discovery. But, as the body of the swan fell and uncovered him, I pulled on his hand, propelling myself toward him before he could use the axe, and drove my knife through his neck.

For a moment he stood there, his lips parted for the yell and only bloody froth coming through them. He sought to strike with the axe and hit the gunwale a feeble blow. I released him with a shove and with both hands thrown above his head he settled back into the muddy water and sank from sight.

I crouched low in the canoe, expecting that the sound of our struggle would bring more of the enemy. The slough seemed calm enough; the water-fowl were returning to feed; the river just ahead of me flowed on serenely. My nerves grew quiet and I sensed the stench of a dead buffalo stranded somewhere near by. The stench grew intolerable and I edged my canoe forward through the last fringe of grass and glanced up and down the river. Above my position, a moose was climbing the eastern bank, having swum across. Dipping softly, I crept upstream.

Before coming to the mouth of the Turtle I turned toward the east bank and crossed at my best speed, darting like an arrow under the low-hanging willow boughs.

I reconnoitred from this position and found the river's banks quiet enough.

Not satisfied, I left the canoe and crawled up the bank and advanced some distance south, seeking signs of the Sioux. At almost every rod I aroused red deer from among the willows. At last I realised that the Sioux, if in that neighbourhood, would do the same and thus give me warning of their approach.

Returning to my canoe, confident no menace was stalking me on the east bank, I paddled up the river, giving almost all my attention to the west bank. I camped that night a few miles below the mouth of Red Lake River and was nearly devoured by mosquitoes. I dared not make a smudge and could only pull my white robes over my head and endure it.

Two hours before sunrise I was afloat again, gliding up the silent river and giving my attention to the beaches, which were beginning to appear as the water lowered. There were no signs in the muck, that I could find, that would indicate the passage of a war party from bank to bank. On arriving at the mouth of the Red Lake River, as wide as the Red at that point, I swerved inshore and remained quiet for an hour before daring to proceed.

Once above the mouth, I beached my canoe on the east bank and had not stolen along three rods before I came to signs which substantiated Bad Axe's story. Fully a score of savages had crossed the river at this point, with no return trail showing.

Moving inland, I managed to follow the trail through a grove of strong timber and much prickly ash until it led me back to the Red Lake River only a short distance above its junction with the Red.

This was a favourite hiding-place for Sioux war parties. It was famous for sturgeon, many being found during the winter. Red deer, bear, moose, and buffalo abounded, while the wild-fowl could never be counted. From this spot the Sioux could watch for hunters coming down from the Red Lake country, or from the Goose and other upper tributaries of the Red.

Within a quarter of a mile from where I struck the river I came upon some huts of elm bark, such as the Sioux build when on the war-path. These huts were a season old and must have accommodated fully a hundred men. I looked them over carefully and failed to find any fresh signs. I noted many poles used in stretching beaver, showing they had combined business with pleasure.

Except for the Indian I had killed at the edge of the slough and the tracks in the mud, I had found nothing to indicate there was a Sioux in the country. If I had not met Bad Axe and White Partridge by accident, I should have walked or paddled right into their arms. Even now they might be watching me from any point.

Skirting the huts and warily keeping to cover, I followed up the Red Lake River and observed that I no longer scared up red deer. A few miles behind me, and on the same bank, the woods were full of them. The coming of the enemy had driven them away.

A short distance above the huts I came upon some little sticks, painted with vermilion. These were fresh signs and such as Sioux war parties left wherever they paused to renew their war paint. I counted the sticks and they tallied with the tracks in the mud. A score of the devils were on my side of the river, and it was a miracle that Bad Axe could have discovered them and retreated without being seen and slain.

A more disturbing thought was that Miss Dearness and Flat Mouth were in that immediate vicinity. It looked mighty bad for the girl. If already caught, a quick death was the kindest fate I could wish for her. The thought of her glorious hair flapping at a Sioux bridle made a madman of me for the time being. I forgot to be cautious and prowled through the woods with red lights always flashing before my eyes.

The undergrowth directly ahead of me gave way before incautious steps; my head cleared suddenly. I drew aside from the deer path and stood close by the river, intending to discharge one barrel of my gun and drop under the bank to seek a hole among the roots of one of the giant elms, where I could reload. The slight noises were repeated, and I now caught the sound of laboured breathing. I was puzzled that a Sioux should display exhaustion. The berry bushes swayed and parted. I raised my gun, and caught a glimpse of dishevelled red hair. I lowered my gun and Miss Dearness staggered toward me, one hand pressed to her side, her blue eyes contracted with pain.

She did not see me until almost upon me. Her gaze widened in surprise, questioned, and then lighted with hope. She could not speak. I sprang to her side, passed my left arm around her waist and felt her splendid arm thrown about my neck. Her hot breath was in my face as I bowed my head and whispered—

"They're on your trail."

She nodded and swallowed convulsively, not from fear but from exhaustion.

"Have they got Flat Mouth?" I murmured.

She lifted her head to listen; I did likewise. Off to one side rang out the scalp cry of the Pillager Chippewa. She smiled wearily and choked—

"Leading them off my trail."

"Don't try to talk," I whispered. "I have a canoe back on the river. We must reach it. If we can get out into the open we may stand them off."

"——after me?" was all I caught of her low query.

"But they haven't got you yet," I comforted.

She frowned and laboriously corrected—

"No; you came—after me?"

"Of course," I answered, inclined to be impatient at time wasted on what was perfectly obvious.

She caught at her throat with her free hand and I saw she was nearly choked with thirst. At the risk of being overtaken, I relinquished my hold about her waist and slipped down the bank, bringing back my hat filled with water. Her eyes lighted with thankfulness. She swallowed some and poured the rest over her face. I made to go for more, but she took my arm and warned—

"No time."

Encouraging her to lean on me, I began the retreat. The path was narrow and encroached upon by the bushes. Two could not walk it abreast without betraying themselves. I gave her my gun and, picking her up, ran for it. Concealment was impossible, as our feet had left tracks any Sioux would read at a glance, and more than once we had advertised ourselves by rustling the bushes. Either the enemy was not within hearing or else he was already pressing after us. She murmured a protest at my reckless pace and, as I set her on her feet to get my second wind, I briefly explained that it made no difference.

"Then let me walk," she said.

"Faster my way," I said, taking her up in my arms.

This time I did not stop until back within sound of the Red River's voice. Then I let her walk behind me while I advanced to the bank and hunted for my canoe. We had come out almost upon it.

I jumped down the bank and, turning, caught her as she came after me.

"The Indian? He was very brave—led them away— but not all of them," she gasped.

The bank reached above my head. Stepping on a rock, I secured a view of our back trail for a short distance.

A lithe figure, bounding along with the elasticity and silence of a *loup-cervier*, suddenly popped into the foreground. He was the first of her trailers. The upper half of his face was painted red and looked like a mask of blood through which the small black eyes glittered ferociously. Shoving my gun through the dead grass, I gave him the right barrel and he went down with no time to sound his death howl.

Shoving off the canoe, I lifted her into it and gave her the paddle, directing—

"Downstream while I reload!"

"The Indian?"

"He must take care of himself—downstream!"

"No, across!"

She pointed to several Sioux now breaking cover on the bank below us. As I beheld them, they gained the river's edge and stood ready to swim out should we attempt to descend.

"Across it must be!" I agreed, kneeling in the stern and reloading.

The Indians below us began shooting arrows, which flew wild, as the wind was strong from the south.

I held my fire until one of the Sioux waded waist-deep into the river and prepared to aim a gun. The weapon was a London Fusil, a number of which had trickled into the Sioux country through the hands of traders, and I have seen a savage do very efficient work with one. I gave him a barrel and he went under, taking his gun with him. The others scrambled for cover.

The girl now sounded the bell-like call which the Chippewas believed she had stolen from the Qu'Appelle and had given back. As the last note died away, the Chippewa scalp-yell rang out from the bank above us and a slim figure burst from the timber, taking to the river in a head-dive.

"The Pillager!" I yelled.

A volley of arrows hissed from the woods behind us, and one ripped a hole in the stern, through which the river began to gurgle most menacingly. More warriors had arrived and several were holding knives between their teeth, intending to swim after us. The group below also reappeared. The pursuit was to be pressed in force.

I could easily have bagged two of them, but I must keep one shot in reserve. I contented myself with catching the first man to slide down the bank. At the same moment a dark hand came out of the water and gripped the canoe. I raised the gun to smash the fingers, but the girl poked me with the paddle, crying—

"The Chippewa!"

Sure enough, it was Flat Mouth. He grinned up into my face sardonically and endeavoured to give his yell of triumph, but a mouthful of water stopped him.

"We're sinking!" I told him.

He struck off for the opposite bank, swimming abreast of us and watching our progress with much concern.

I crowded my knee against the hole and reloaded. My last shot had driven the Sioux to cover, but now they were popping up all along the bank. Below and above us several had taken to the water, thinking to head us off while our attention was held by the fire of those directly behind us.

Flat Mouth threw himself half out of the water and raised his fiendish howl of triumph. There was no mistaking the fact that he had made his kill, for a ghastly bunch of fresh hair was caught through the rawhide lacing of his skin shirt.

Arrows and an occasional ball followed us. Above and below bobbed the heads of the swimmers. Our approach to the west bank was very slow and the canoe grew sluggish. I tried to bail with my hat but nearly lost my gun overboard. The craft settled slowly but steadily. I glanced forward and decided we could ground her nose before she filled.

Flat Mouth gave a bark of warning and dived. The situation above, below and behind us remained about the same. I turned toward the west bank and the girl gave a little muffled cry, yet held steadily on. Ten or a dozen of the enemy were crouching in the grass at the top of the bank ready to receive us. These were the Indians left to guard the horses.

"I want to thank you for what you've done for me," the girl called over her shoulder.

"Don't thank me until I've pulled you out of this," I growled, raising my gun.

"You said back there you came after me. Did you, or was it just chance?"

"I came after you, to help you," I replied, staring at the top of the bank.

"Your sense of duty—I'm sorry," she sighed.

"I didn't know you were in any danger when I started. I came because I couldn't help it. It looks bad for us. I'll be honest with you—with myself."

There's never any understanding a woman; which is not surprising, as she does not understand herself. Logically she should have been twice as sorry on learning I had followed her without suspecting I was running into danger. Instead she quietly called over her shoulder—

"Now I'm glad. Don't let them take me alive."

"Of course not." That was why I had taken pains to reserve one barrel of my gun.

The canoe now was very low in the water. She paddled gently and we crept closer to the bank. Then, with a muscular swing, she sent us into the mud with the water up to our waists. The Indians on the bank jumped from cover. I blew a hole through the leader. Flat Mouth came out of the water as if shot by a gun, was half-way up the bank, had cut a fellow's throat and was yanking off the squirming skunk's hair quicker than you could skin a partridge.

CHAPTER VI

BESIEGED

THE sudden appearance of Flat Mouth from the river and his fierce charge up the bank, perhaps, had as much to do with the Indians' failure to press the attack as did my gun. Their hesitation gave us an inch of room and, while I reloaded, the Pillager snatched up a dead warrior's bow and two quivers of arrows and, sheltered by the bank, began firing rapidly. The Indians scattered and ran to escape his shafts. While this was happening Miss Dearness secured the pack of white robes from the submerged canoe and threw me two and two to the chief and draped the fifth over her arm to serve as a shield.

The Sioux ahead of us had lost two of their number, and while they could have smothered us in a rush, had they remained instead of fleeing, they knew the victory would cost them dear. Ducking and dodging, they picked up their discarded shields of bull-hide. This retreat on the part of the enemy was to be commended from their point of view, as the Indians crossing the river would soon be landing above and below us. Then we would be hemmed in and they could kill us at their leisure.

With the canoe out of commission and the water road closed, there remained but one course—to attack at the weakest point. In other words, go ahead. The fewest warriors opposed us and with them were the horses of the entire war party.

"We must have horses;" I cried to Flat Mouth in Chippewa.

"Good cover here," grunted the Pillager, motioning for me to climb up the bank and survey the plain.

I joined him and saw that the growth on the river several hundred yards below us extended some distance into the plain.

I called to the girl to follow. Four savages were cautiously approaching the bank, depending on their shields, while their mates ran to procure some of the horses. Flat Mouth snatched up the white hides and held them before him with his left hand and ran toward the enemy. They began to fall back, shooting their arrows wildly. I gave Miss Dearness a hand, took my robes and fell in behind her to guard the rear. I had nothing but admiration for her coolness as we made for the woods, for she bothered to pick up the arrows the Sioux were wasting.

Once she turned to me and held up a knife she had picked up beside the two dead devils down the bank, and cried out—

"Use both barrels if you have to." Meaning that if the worst came she would kill herself to escape capture.

The four Sioux refused to dispute Flat Mouth's advance and began falling back. Either the white robes worried them, being big medicine, or else they believed they had the game in their own hands and could afford to wait. Suddenly they turned and ran zigzag toward the horses. This behaviour puzzled me. I glanced behind me, but as yet none of the Indians had mounted the bank. We were advancing obliquely toward the woods.

Now Flat Mouth called on us to hurry and turned to make cover along the shortest line. Miss Dearness ceased hunting arrows and ran like a deer. I pounded along at her heels, with no immediate danger visible and yet realising that a crisis must be at hand, else the Pillager would not flee so precipitately.

He slowed up so that the girl and I caught up with him.

"Big medicine!" he exulted.

"The robes?" I panted.

"They sent the Sioux running away like old women!"
And although we needed to conserve our breath he halted
and indulged in a long-drawn-out howl of triumph.

There was no doubt now in my mind as to the effect
of the robes. While an albino buffalo counted only as
a hide among the Indians in the Red River department,
the skins were objects of reverence among the tribes on
the Missouri. The possessor of one was most fortunate.
He was destined to be successful in the hunt, on the
war-path, and in his accumulation of wives. He would
part with his dearest belongings to secure such a robe.

Their value was so high that often the price was
beyond any individual. When one was infrequently
put on sale the village would undertake to purchase it.
The robe was then cut into strips, and each contributor
to the fund received a portion. Even a narrow width
of the hide would guarantee good luck to a lodge.

Believing all this, it was natural they should view
our five hides as a stupendous display of mighty medicine, worth any price to possess, yet to be sought for
very cautiously. There was nothing partisan about a
hide's medicine. It would benefit and protect us so long
as we could hold it, but its benevolence would instantly
be transferred to a new owner.

"They come from the river!" bawled Flat Mouth as
we struck into the edge of the timber and turned to look
back.

The warriors from the eastern shore were popping
their heads above the bank. None had crossed directly
behind us, out of respect for my gun. By going up or
down stream they had lost time. The Sioux on the plain
were now mounted and busy rounding up the rest of the
animals. But the horses were reluctant to cease feeding
and viciously rebelled. Two managed to break their
hobbles and run clear of the herd. Flat Mouth watched
the runaways through half-closed eyes. I gave my
attention to the Indians.

Our situation was desperate. The strong timber we had entered followed a rivulet only for a short distance. It was only a thin grove on each side of the tiny stream, and to the north of it was the open plain again. It was surrounded on all sides by the plain except in the east, where the river flowed. Could we have had a brief respite we might have raised the canoe, patched it up and trusted to luck. While I was regretting our inability to do this, two of the Sioux scrambled over the bank, dancing and hooting and waving pieces torn from the damaged craft.

"That closes the river to us," Miss Dearness calmly observed.

I cut a slit in one of the robes and dropped it over her head so it formed a long apron in front and behind. She thanked me with a smile. She knew she would not be taken alive and this knowledge gave her strength.

I put on a robe, only I allowed it to hang on both sides. While this left my back and breast exposed, it gave me free play with the gun, and in case of arrow-fire I could turn sideways. Against a ball the robe would offer but small protection. Flat Mouth grunted in approval as he watched me prepare myself. Taking two of the robes, he slit them in the middle and put them on as I had done, making his armour doubly thick. The calfskin he hung down his back.

"Dig holes," he said, walking to the edge of the timber.

"What is it now, Eshkebugecoshe?" I called after him, fearing he planned a fanatical display of bravery by charging the Sioux single-handed.

"We must have horses. It is the only way," he answered without looking back. Standing in the open, he paused to study the enemy. Again he cried out:

"Dig! Dig! I will watch."

I found a hole where an uprooted oak had torn the soil. Jumping into this, I began excavating with my knife. The girl joined me with her borrowed blade. We worked side by side, her red hair falling over her face and at times brushing against mine. I threw out the dirt with my hands and placed it as a breastwork, the butt of the tree with its long roots forming a good half of the defence.

Digging was slow work, however, and we soon shifted to dragging fallen timbers and building a barricade. Leaving her to finish the little fort with a mask of willow branches, I searched until I found a spot near-by where several mouldering trunks lay crisscrossed. This I fashioned into a refuge for the Pillager. Having accomplished this while the chief stood guard, I crept forward and announced—

"We have dug the holes."

He did not appear to have heard me but continued staring at the Sioux. Those from the river were warily advancing. Only one of them that I could see carried a gun. I took careful aim and fired. It was a long shot and I missed, but the ball must have passed close to his painted head, for he ducked wildly and threw himself down, the whole line following his example. I let them have the second barrel on top of the first, believing I had ample time to reload. This double discharge from one gun was acknowledged with yelps of alarm.

They remained in the grass, their brown bodies scarcely to be distinguished from the brown earth. The effect of the two shots on the other group was equally pronounced. Abandoning the herd, they galloped to the river and took up a position behind those afoot. I reloaded and, aiming high, fired twice at the horsemen and wounded one of their animals.

Flat Mouth considered this to be a suitable time for his endeavour. Loudly singing his song of triumph, he stalked from the timber. He was rather imposing in his white robes. Nor was the effect lost on the Sioux, for I heard low cries of envy. They shot their arrows but the distance was too great, and he remained untouched. To rush him they would have to enter the zone of my gun-fire, crossing from east to west in front of me. The mounted Sioux now realised their mistake, and galloped back, making a deep detour.

I began to believe he might succeed in securing at least one of the animals, one that had broken its hobbles and had halted to graze on the short grass. Dropping his voice to a monotone, the Pillager began to advance toward this brute. The Sioux afoot and on horseback set up a loud howling, to frighten the animal, and discharged arrows in high arcs in the hope one might descend on the horse and send him galloping off. But the runaway continued feeding, quite used to his master's hullabaloo. When Flat Mouth was within ten or a dozen feet and moving slowly, the brute raised its head and glared viciously. The Pillager made to pass him, still chanting.

"He'll get that one!" Miss Dearness exclaimed.

For the moment I had forgotten her, so intent was I on watching the chief. One horse might mean freedom for her.

A warrior leaped up from the ground and yelled to the horsemen. They began a turning movement and started a shrill "*Hi-yi-yi!*" to alarm the animal, at the same time recklessly charging the Pillager. I could have easily brought down one if not two of their ponies, but held my fire for fear of startling Flat Mouth's prize. The chief needed to exercise much patience. The enemy were coming toward him at a smashing gallop. The grazing pony was suspicious and kept turning so as to watch him. If not encumbered by the robes, he could have covered the distance in one spring and caught the beast by the nose. As it was, he manoeuvred as coolly and deliberately as if he were alone on the plain.

"To the left!" softly cried the girl, tugging my arm.

I pivoted and beheld the warriors leaving the grass to run forward. The menace of the double-barrel was sufficient to send them to earth again.

"Good!" cried the girl. "I'll watch them."

Back went my gaze to the Pillager. The Sioux horse-

E

men were perilously near, and I prepared to shoot. He was close to the pony, which snorted and jumped back a few feet, then ducked its head to snatch a mouthful of the poor feed. In the next second the Pillager had him by the muzzle, was on his back and darting like a white streak for the herd, the flapping of the robes giving him the appearance of some gigantic bird.

The advancing horsemen, as if afraid of the sacred robes, swerved deeper into the plain, then conquered their reluctance and bore down on him. I took two quick shots, one a clear miss, the other wounding a warrior. His fellows instantly reined in.

"On the left!" cried the girl.

I wheeled and bumped into her, because she was standing so close and she had interposed her body between me and the men in the grass. I threw my arm about her and swung her behind me as a volley of arrows struck the ground around us, several rattling harmlessly against my robe. I raised my empty gun and the line of kneeling men flattened out, none daring to learn if I could fire more than two shots without reloading. They must have approached in a most subtle manner, or the girl would have warned me. At the least they had managed to get within long arrow range.

"Now you can stand between them and me," I told her.

Behind cover of her white robe I hastily reloaded without them seeing me; then I again placed her behind me. One of the scoundrels was lying on his back and sending arrows in a high curve.

Leaving her to watch them, I turned my attention to Flat Mouth. He was guiding his animal with his knees and sending arrow after arrow at the horsemen as he rode. Now he was up at the edge of the herd and the horsemen were manœuvring on the opposite side of the wide circle and wheeling into position to charge.

I fired one barrel and hit a nag, sending the rider flying to the ground. This halted their advance long enough for the Pillager to gather up two halters, lean low and cut the hobbles. When he turned to retreat the brutes balked and dragged back. The horsemen started to interfere, yelping fiendishly. I fired my second barrel and, although I could not see that I scored, my shot stopped them. Now the Pillager was coming at a hard gallop and I swept the Indians in the grass with my empty gun. To my great relief they did not rise, although they continued shooting their arrows until the chief had smashed into the undergrowth.

"For the Medicine Hair," he proudly announced as he leaped to the ground and made two of the ponies fast to an oak branch.

"I'll let you ride one of them, Mr. Franklin," she encouraged with a sad little play at cheerfulness.

"I will go back and get all of them," cried Flat Mouth, fighting his vicious beast to a standstill against a tree before he could mount him.

"No!" I cried, pointing to the line of Sioux, who had quit the grass during our minute of forgetfulness and were now racing toward the herd.

They were bent half double and grotesquely leaped from side to side as they ran to escape my lead.

"They will try to ride us down in force," muttered Miss Dearness.

I believed this to be their plan and urged her to fall back to our fort. She insisted on remaining with me until the attack was under way. The path to the river was open, but we had no canoe. We could pass through the timber and race north, and, at night, I would have asked for no better chance. Flat Mouth secured his pony and began gathering arrows from the grass. I could account for two with my gun and the Pillager was sure to score as good a tally, yet we must go under if they pressed the charge home.

I called for the Pillager to return to the timber and asked him which it should be—a break through the woods and a gallop north, or a last fight where we were.

"Stay till night," he promptly decided. "They can not dig us out. In the dark we will ride home."

"Can't they ride in here and get us?" she asked him.

"They could if they would pay enough," he admitted. "But they want scalps without losing any men. They have lost heavily on this war-path and they lost heavily when they brought the pipe the time before. If they ride at us they will not come too near. At night they will creep in. We shall not be here."

CHAPTER VII

THE SIOUX RECEIVE REINFORCEMENTS

THIS encouraged us tremendously. Miss Dearness stuck more willow branches around our two forts, while I remained with the chief, who was curiously watching the Indians on the plains. All of the Sioux were now mounted, the horses the Pillager had captured being replaced by those whose owners had fallen. For some minutes the band milled about; then one man rode aside and began haranguing in a loud voice. The Pillager, who had travelled and lived on the Missouri, readily interpreted the speech, which consisted of exhortations for the Sioux to remember they were brave men, that our scalps must go back to their village to wipe out their disgrace in having lost warriors. The white woman was to be taken alive. I was glad Miss Dearness was busy with her willow wands, for the Pillager interpreted word for word, and she understood the Chippewa tongue almost as well as she did English.

When the speechmaker desisted the Sioux swung into a long line, a manœuvre beautifully executed. In this formation they came towards us at a walk, tossing up their lances, waving their axes and singing lustily. I made ready with my gun, picking the leader and a man on the left end as my two victims, but Flat Mouth folded his arms and did not even see to it that his bow was taut.

"Make ready!" I nervously advised.

He grunted in disgust. All but half a dozen of the horsemen began to pivot on the left end of their line and, almost before I could understand what they were up to, this huge segment was galloping madly along, parallel to the woods and away from us.

"When night comes we shall ride very swift or very soft," mumbled Flat Mouth, resuming the task of gathering arrows.

In short, the Sioux were perfectly willing we should break from cover and ride south, and left the six men to keep watch on us. But if we attempted to ride north we must pass through the bulk of their band.

Miss Dearness came up to us, and I told her how the Sioux had thrown most of their men to the other side of the grove. She promptly said:

"It doesn't make sense. If they didn't dare attack when all together what good will it do them to divide their forces?"

"They will wait until dusk and creep in from both sides——"

"And be shooting into each other," she shot in.

"Or stay out on the plain and wait for us to try and break through," I concluded.

"But if they don't dare attack in force they must know we can stay here as long as they can stay out there. We can creep to the river and fish. We can make some kind of a raft and cross, or float downstream. We can stay right here and eat our horses. The rivulet furnishes water. And there is a chance that some of our Chippewas may come up the river and give them battle. There's more to it than a waiting campaign. They're anxious to cage us up here until what? Whatever it is the time will be short."

She spoke in English and I translated it to the Pillager. His small eyes sparkled appreciatively and he declared:

"Medicine Hair sees beyond the woods and hill. She can call and send away a voice. She can send her eyes far up the river and over the plain. Look! Tell me what that means!"

He was pointing to the south and at first I could make out nothing. Then I spied it, a thin stream of blue smoke. The girl promptly said in Chippewa:

"The Sioux know help is coming. They will not attack until their friends come. That will be some time before morning. Soon the others will send up a smoke."

The meaning of the smoke was very obvious. Not a half-breed hunter, not a man at any post in our department who could not have read it. Even Probos would have understood. Yet the Pillager, a master at such things, heard her as if she had been an oracle.

"Can the Medicine Hair's eyes, when she calls them back, tell how many Sioux there are at the bottom of that smoke?" he humbly asked.

"As many as were here before you killed any," she calmly replied. Then in English to me: "It's reasonable to believe they belong to the same party and split up in two equal bands. So long as he believes in my *manito*, so much the braver will he be."

The chief began talking to himself in a guttural and almost audible voice and fell to fingering his bow nervously. His emotion was occasioned by the sight of the six warriors out in front. They were beyond arrow range, and only by luck could a ball score any damage.

They began running back and forth, and we saw they were heaping up dry grass. They paid no attention to us, being intent solely on answering the signal.

With a leap the Pillager was on his horse and riding towards them, his bow held with arrow notched. He was not singing now, and as if in a trance the girl and I watched his progress. As the drama of the situation got into our heads we instinctively clasped hands. Back and forth scuttled the Sioux. Forward rode the Pillager. Then one of them chanced to discover him and, with a shout of fear, turned and made for his pony. I saw him go down with a Sioux arrow buried to the feathers in his back.

With screams of rage the others snatched up their weapons, opened fire and then mounted their horses. With a whoop the Pillager charged at them, and they separated in haste to let him pass through, but, when a bit beyond the fallen warrior, he brought his pony round on two hoofs and was making for the timber, swinging very low from the saddle as he rode. For a moment the speed of his mount was checked, then picked up a rattling pace, and the chief was sitting erect, waved something round his head and sounded his terrible scalp-cry.

"By heavens! But that was a coup worth counting!" I fiercely exclaimed.

With a little shudder the girl reminded:

"They could have come through the woods while we stood here. We've been very careless and——"

She ceased abruptly and stared down at our clasped hands.

I was as much surprised as she. Certainly I was no more conscious than she of having taken her hand. It was three years since I had taken a white woman's hand. In no way was the experience displeasing.

"He may need help," she said, releasing her hand and looking toward the Pillager.

I leaped out in front with my gun, and the warriors behind the Chippewa vanished over the sides of their ponies and swung off to the west. On rushed Flat Mouth, still singing and shouting. But the climax of his arrival was weakened by a puff of smoke from a mound of grass. The signal fire was burning, and the Indians were heaping wet grass and green branches upon it.

Leaving the two to watch the smoke, I hastened to the north side of the grove. Had the enemy but known it he could have massacred the girl and me easily, as we watched the Pillager's sensational exploit. When I came to the end of the growth I noted the Sioux had heard the Chippewa's scalp-yell and were very uneasy. They were riding back and forth, their eyes fixed on the timber, while one of their number was galloping madly toward the tip of the grove to learn what had happened. After watching them for a minute and failing to detect any sign of an advance on our position, I returned to my companions and related what I had observed.

"The name of Eshkebugecoshe fills the Sioux hearts with fear. It makes them old women," loudly boasted the chief.

"It was a big coup," I declared. "You may paint the marks of death and the feet of horses on your body and on your tent to show you killed a man while riding hard."

The chief toned down his vanity on meeting the girl's clear gaze and confessed:

"Eshkebugecoshe is a mighty warrior, but the white woman's medicine helped him. It made the Sioux blind till I could creep very close."

"Couldn't we get across the river? I can swim," eagerly spoke up Miss Dearness.

Flat Mouth said it would be foolish to cross before dark, but he suggested that I reconnoitre the river while he watched the Indians. He did not seem to think much of the suggestion, but as it came from the girl he was bound to consider it, probably believing her medicine suggested the plan. I thought very favourably of the idea. The Indians' belief that we planned to use the ponies in attempting to escape would tend to blunt their watch of the river. I followed the rivulet until I came to its mouth, a bit of a beach grown round with reeds and tall grass. The river rolled brown and silent except for the murmuring of air currents. Midstream a huge tree floated with roots upraised, like arms held up in surrender—desolation and solitude. As I watched the water I decided a man could well risk the danger. A long swim under water, timed to take advantage of some of the driftwood ever passing, and the trick could be turned. But the water was icy cold and the danger was not for a woman to run unless absolutely necessary.

Yet at night, with the aid of a log, Miss Dearness could be ferried across. I began to look about for some fallen timber which would serve as a raft. It was while occupied in this task that I received ample proof that the Sioux had not forgotten the river. The proof was an arrow which whizzed by my head and disappeared in the reeds. I drew back among the trees and, cocking my gun, searched the top of the bank. I could see nothing suspicious, yet a savage could remain below the bank with the top of his head masked by the fringe of dead grass. Thus concealed, he could follow my every movement and loose another arrow when I presented a fair target.

The thought made me uncomfortable, and I retreated deeper into the grove. A mocking yell told me that my flight had been witnessed, and, incensed, I turned back, determined to get a shot at him. The rascal was too cunning in his hiding, so, returning to my companions, I reported the incident.

Flat Mouth slipped out of his white robes and without a word stole to the river to match his woodcraft against the sentinel's. As he had reported that the Sioux on the north side of the timber were quiet, and as no danger could take the girl unaware from the south side, I surrendered to my desire and followed him.

Armed only with his bow and arrow he slipped through the growth with the softness of a lynx, following my trail along the rivulet. Keeping well back, I watched him. He was studying my tracks rather than looking about for the enemy. He halted a short distance from where I had stood in the open when the arrow missed me, then glided to the edge of the reeds and, bending low, pulled an arrow from the muck. As he straightened I saw his arm twitch and a red blotch appear on the biceps. Leaping to one side, he fitted the arrow to his bow, gave a keen, sweeping glance overhead and discharged the arrow. Almost with the twang of the bow there came the shrill death-cry from the sentinel and I saw a dark body bump along the trunk of an oak and lodge against one of its branches.

Gliding back to me, the Pillager announced:

"Sometime I will climb up and get his hair. The arrow in the mud showed that it came from overhead and not from the bank."

With this explanation he registered the kill with his terrible war-cry.

We hastened back through the grove, the Pillager swinging to the north to reconnoitre, while I made direct for Miss Dearness. She had heard the two cries, one of death and one of victory, and stood facing the river, her hands twisted together, her face white and drawn. On beholding me she hastily turned toward the plain and her hands fell listlessly to her side.

The column of smoke had replied to the message from the south and was now dying out. She informed me that while I had been gone the Indians had used their robes to confine the smoke and then released it in puffs. Had the Pillager witnessed it he could have read the code. However it was not difficult to guess the message; it told those in the south to hasten if they would be in at a triple kill.

Until now I had had no chance to exchange more than a few words with Miss Dearness. She gestured for me to sit beside her on the robes, and I took the opportunity to say:

"You should have started back east the minute you heard your father was dead."

"I told him I would stay till some one came to take his place."

"But it's no place for a white woman," I protested. "It's bad enough for a man to be cast away among these savages."

She smiled faintly and reminded—

"The only danger I've faced—until to-day—was from a white man, Black Chabot."

"I wish the Robe had hit him with his arrows."

"I told the Robe to be very careful and not hit him, the drunken beast!"

"If we could only get word to my Chippewas," I sighed.

"It would do no good so long as I am with you," she discouraged. Then with a grim little laugh: "I'm bad luck. If you were alone they would come; but not while

I'm with you. They believe I stole the voice from the Qu'Appelle or that my medicine wasn't strong enough to keep. If I hadn't sent the Voice back they would dare anything to help me.''

''Then the Crees and Assiniboins?''

''They've heard the Chippewas tell that my medicine is weak. Now they believe I would have kept the Voice if I could. They feel no gratitude. It would be as dangerous for me to meet Cree or Assiniboin away from the post as it has been to meet the Sioux.''

''Nonsense!'' I scoffed. ''They're afraid of you, even if they don't like your medicine.''

''They hate me and they don't fear me. When I went on the river alone at night and sang to forget my loneliness I little knew what I was stirring up. I went to get away from the drinking and fighting. I sang, as I was always singing back in the east.''

''But the Assiniboins would listen to me,'' I proudly insisted.

''Mr. Franklin, you don't know them. You've met those that come to your post. Their territory extends far to the west. They're a mighty people. You've met men from one band only. Meet them away from your fort and your rum and you will find they're very much savages.''

A horseman suddenly darted toward us, his bow drawn, seeking to learn if we were keeping watch. I covered his bobbing figure as best I could and held my fire until he should come within decent range. Just as I began to hope, he pulled his pony about and scuttled back to his mates.

''Who are you? Where were you born?'' I asked, lowering my gun.

''English—England,'' she murmured, her gaze wandering far beyond the wild horizon.

''And I'm an American. Flat Mouth thinks your hair is medicine.''

With a little frown she gathered up the dishevelled mass, and, before my eyes, performed the miracle of restoring her hair to glossy smoothness by the simple process of patting, twisting, and poking. Stay out in the Northwest for three seasons and you will appreciate how keenly this simple task appeals to a white man.

She faced me suddenly, her blue eyes prying deep into mine, and abruptly asked—

"Why do you look at me like that?"

"Like what?" I defended.

"As if you had never seen a woman before."

"I haven't seen a white woman for three seasons," I sighed.

"I understand." And she turned to resume her watch of the Indians.

"A white woman even if she be as ignorant and unattractive as a scullery maid would seem a goddess to you now."

"Scarcely that," I demurred. "Three years out here is a long time, but not an eternity. I never dream of scullery maids. I——"

Her grave reproachful gaze caused me to shift and ask—

"You'll be willing to start back east after you get out of this?"

"When my successor comes. The X. Y. people allow nothing to interfere with the interests of the company."

"Except rum," I reminded.

"That was my whim. The company will disapprove. My defence will be that the drinking made it dangerous for me. They will let it go at that. The companies know liquor is bad for the trade. If it weren't for competition they wouldn't use it. It isn't sound business. You must depend entirely upon the Indians to get furs into the posts. The richest fur country in the world would be worthless unless you had Indians to work it. Then where is the sense in killing off your workmen with rum? Every drinking match means so many wounded and usually one or more dead. It's bad enough when the quarrels are kept within one tribe, but let a Chippewa stab a Cree, or a Cree an Assiniboin, and you have a season of war between the two tribes, and no trade. Except when fighting an opposition the Hudson Bay Company is very careful about giving out liquor. So would the X. Y. and the N. W. be if either could have all the trade.''

"If the N. W. and the opposition posts should shut down on rum to-morrow you'd find these Indians hunting for some free trader to give rum for their goods. They will travel any distance to get new 'milk.' They will have rum and we must have the furs. There is no other way.''

"Oh yes, there is," she murmured. "Give one company a monopoly of the trade, and the furs will come in and no rum will go out.''

"But which company? The N. W.? Then I agree with all my heart.''

"The companies should combine into one. No company would refuse if it knew a monopoly was to be granted.''

She became silent and I was satisfied to study her profile. During the stress of fighting and retreating I had defended her from a sense of duty. The puzzling and disturbing emotions which had driven me up the river to find her had abated. From the moment we met in the woods, and I learned my work was cut out for me, she became quite impersonal, something to be saved. The Pillager placed her on a pedestal and looked on her as mighty medicine because of her hair.

Now that I took time to study her she became a personality again, to be protected differently than one protects a pack of beaver. This knowledge was borne in upon me after I had decided she was very tired. Weariness suggests weakness. The strain had told on her and this fact humanised her. I began to pity her. I was guilty of feeling glad she was weary, for it proved that she was no superwoman.

I was horribly afraid. The Sioux would make all haste

on reading the smoke which told of three victims—one a woman—awaiting capture. I believed they would arrive before night. Did they do this we must stand an attack in force and go down fighting. I prayed for a storm to spoil their bow-strings and leave my gun master of the situation, but the wind continued strong from the south, and there was no hint of rain in the sky.

Had it been a case of the Pillager and myself we would have taken to the river, trusting to reach the opposite bank and find a hiding place in the thickly timbered country. By separating, one of us would stand some chance of escaping. Together with the girl it would be a miracle if we could conceal ourselves even if we reached the other bank of the river. Only a black night would reduce the advantage of mere numbers.

The Indians were dismounted and stretched across the plain to prevent our making a break. There were no shadows now, and the light had perceptibly dimmed. I knew how quickly the light fled in these vast areas of loneliness, once the sun gave up the fight. Only a few minutes more and we would hope for the best. A warrior sprang to his feet and stared toward the river. I believed he had glimpsed the Pillager. He said something, and other warriors stood up, one even standing on his horse.

Then came a high-pitched call from the river. With an extravagant display of joy they answered the call, sprang to their ponies and began riding back and forth. From the other side of the timber came a yelping chorus.

"Mr. Franklin! Mr. Franklin!" called the bell-like voice of Miss Dearness.

I ran back, much alarmed, and found she had come as far as the rivulet in search of me.

"They're coming!" she said.

I raced to the edge of the woods and beheld them, riding far apart, waving their weapons and shouting their war-songs as they slowly cantered towards us. Dropping on one knee, I covered the man riding in advance of the line whose elaborate head-dress marked

him as the bearer of the pipe on this expedition. I
sent a ball through his chest most neatly, and as his
spirit fled to the land of many lodges his followers came
to a confused halt. I fired again, this time knocking
a man half round in his saddle but not dismounting him.
Instantly the survivors scurried back. As I was reloading Flat Mouth came through the bushes and motioned
for me to follow him. I hesitated to leave the girl, but
she urged:

"Go! They've learned their lesson. They'll keep
back."

Flat Mouth hurried diagonally across the timber and
emerged on the lower edge near the river. Drawing me
down beside him, he pointed to the east bank and
grunted—

"Sioux!"

"I heard their signal," I informed him.

"They came down the river on the other side. When
it gets very dark they will bring their horses over. They
heard your gun and they don't want to try it just now."

"When they cross we cannot break through," I said.

"We will all be killed if we stay in the woods. You
must stop them from crossing their horses for a little
while. The Sioux on this side feel sure of a coup. They
will not fight till their friends join them. Stay here till
it gets too dark to shoot. I will take Medicine Hair and
the horses to the end of the timber. When they attack
on both sides we must ride after the sun."

"West?"

"It leads from home but it is the nearest way there
We can strike the Cheyenne near the Lac du Diable
country. There are many good hiding places there."

The bushes across the river swayed and a painted face
showed through the dusk as one of the newcomers stood
up to signal the horsemen on our side. Knowing I could
not begin too soon to teach them their place, I rested
the gun on Flat Mouth's shoulder, aimed a bit high and
had the satisfaction of seeing the brave go sprawling

down the bank, his head and shoulders remaining under water. This kill wrung a chorus of devilish yells from the hidden warriors. Flat Mouth hurled his war-cry at them and danced in great glee.

I reloaded and urged the Pillager to return to the girl and prepare her for making the tip of the grove. Reluctantly he left me, swinging to the north to take a final look at the horsemen there, and I settled down to waiting.

Objects began to fade out of my vision. Trees near-by became blurred and unreal. I knew our supreme effort could not be long delayed. The surface of the water became a black waste, and I thought I heard a faint splash opposite my position. Now voices began calling loudly farther down the river. The newcomers had gone to find a crossing. I could see no reason why I should not put after the chief and the girl; then the soft splashing was repeated, this time nearer.

Quitting the bushes, I crawled through the mud to the edge of the bank and heard a rippling sound that was not made by the *lap-lap* of the water on the narrow beach. Suddenly a vague shape stood before me, within twenty feet, and I fired. He did not have time to utter his death cry before slumping back into the current. Trailing my gun, I ducked into the woods and followed up the rivulet.

The Pillager and Miss Dearness were about half-way to the end of the timber when I overtook them. It seems she had refused to go further until I joined them.

"Take her and go on," viciously directed Flat Mouth, thrusting the bridles of the three horses into my hands.

"No time for you to count a coup," I warned as he turned back.

"Very soon I shall be at your heels," he promised.

I gave the girl the bridles to hold while I recharged my gun. We had nearly reached the end of our cover, and the underbrush was thinning out, when the girl caught my hand and whispered—

"They're trying to burn us out!"

I sniffed and detected smoke, a thin reek of burning grass. I wet my finger and tested the faint breeze. It still held from the south. Creeping to the edge of the plain I could make out moving shapes as the Indians rode up and down the front of the timber. But there were no fires burning on this side, and a blaze lighted on the north would sweep away from us.

Returning to Miss Dearness, I reassured her.

"Then there is only one other explanation," she said. "Flat Mouth has set the grass afire on the north side of us."

"It will burn to the Turtle, perhaps to the Park."

"Some one is coming!" she warned, and again her hand instinctively closed over mine.

I cocked the gun and rested it over a saddle, not bothering to release my hand.

"It is Eshkebugecoshe," softly called a voice.

The girl dropped my hand hurriedly.

Without pausing, Flat Mouth took charge of the horses and pressed ahead while I guarded the rear. Now the smoke was very noticeable and our animals showed a tendency to bolt.

"You fired the grass?" I whispered.

"In many places," he grunted. "The Sioux are spreading out and watching for us to ride through under cover of the smoke. The warriors on the other side will think we're escaping and will ride into the woods."

We were at the end of the timber, and the girl mounted her pony and adjusted her white robe.

Dead ahead sounded the pounding of hoofs and an Indian screamed something. Flat Mouth interpreted:

"He says for the men to ride through the woods, some to go to the river, some to come up here, some to follow the fire and see if we are there, some to keep in front of it. Wait for me here and do not fire the gun unless you have to."

Before we could restrain him he was galloping toward the messenger, his white robe making him resemble a

Sioux warrior whose skins were white with clay. I heard him salute the Sioux in that tongue. The other asked something in a sharp, insistent voice. The next moment there was the blurr of a struggle, then the clump of a falling body. A horseman was riding toward me. I cocked my piece, but Flat Mouth softly commanded:

"Hurry! Hurry!"

Then he took the girl's pony by the halter and led the way out into the plain.

CHAPTER VIII

WE MEET BLACK CAT'S PEOPLE

OUR escape must have been quickly discovered, as we had not travelled more than two miles before we heard shouting to the north and abreast of us. We slowed our animals to a walk, our course tending a bit south of west and which, if persisted, would bring us to the Cheyenne River. The Sioux knew we were somewhere south of them and were concentrating all their efforts in throwing a barrier across the plains to prevent our turning north towards the Pembina.

I rode up beside the girl. She reached out, patted my arm and said—

"I've made you a lot of bother."

"Life out here is made up of bothers. I'm glad to find one that's worth while."

"You say it very nicely," she approved. "But I won't be a bother to any one again if I can get out of this. So long as I could manage without being helped it was my place to stay. Now that I find I have to shift my responsibilities I am anxious to go back east. I never had believed it, but I do now; a woman is sure to need help some time."

"She wouldn't be a woman if she didn't," I declared. "Even men expect to help each other in this country."

"He doesn't have to ask another to see to it he isn't taken prisoner," she gravely replied. "I had no right to ask you. Another example of dodging responsibilities."

"God forbid it should ever have to be!"

"But you wouldn't let them take me alive?" she fiercely demanded.

"No man would," I answered.

Again she patted my arm and murmured—

"If we had met back east we might have been such friends."

The wind whipped a strand of her hair across my face, and in that moment she was all feminine—dependent, and her presence became a tonic. I was saved from replying to her last speech—a foolish speech, as there was nothing to prevent our being "such friends" out here—by a warning hiss from the Pillager.

He leaped to the ground and ordered us to do likewise. I helped the girl to dismount, and the chief caught her pony by the nose to keep him from giving an alarm, while I muzzled my own beast and waited. A thudding of hoofs, not more than four men, as the Pillager whispered, drew nearer. They were bearing directly down on us, and I was anxious to release my animal and make ready to fire. Flat Mouth warned:

"Be still! See that the horse doesn't call out. They can't see us."

I knew this must be true, as we could see nothing of them. On they came and raced by in front of us and very close—a suggestion of motion as if something had disturbed the darkness and left a swirl of darkness behind it. These were spies sent out to learn our true position. Above us on the right the enemy kept calling back and forth as they patrolled from east to west. Still on foot, we resumed our flight, the chief picking his course without any hesitation. I suggested the necessity of a turning movement before daylight, but he discouraged it, saying:

"We must keep this way till light. Then we must hide. This is a big war-party. It will be ashamed to go back and face the women without scalps to pay for the braves we have killed. These are the Sioux of the plains, very cruel and fierce. Once they held the country along the lower Red River. They are always at war with the Chippewas."

"For just where are we striking?"

"The bend of the Cheyenne. It is very rough and heavily wooded along the river. The Sioux claim the country. We can hide there a few days and then go home."

From what he said I judged the distance to be covered was about forty miles. I knew that we rode and walked all night long with the Sioux hovering to the north of us during much of the journey. When the east began lighting its fires, and we were permitted to see the plain around us, I was delighted by two discoveries; the plain was empty of Indians, and a short distance ahead a thick growth marked the course of the Cheyenne where it made its northern loop.

The girl swayed in her saddle, and I rode closer to her.

"I was asleep," she drowsily murmured, leaning against my arm. "Dreamed the Indians had captured me, that you came."

Again her head dropped, and it was a long time before I learned of the heroics I played in that particular dream.

Searching the edge of the growth, I collected an armful of dry sticks which I knew would not smoke, and by the time I had done this Flat Mouth appeared with several wild geese. He attended to the cooking, making a fire so small as to seem ridiculous to a white man. As he broiled the fowl he told me the trees were ripped and seamed by bears' claws and that both banks of the river must be teeming with the animals. I had nothing but contempt for the black and brown varieties, knowing them to be harmless, but the grizzly was a different proposition. Flat Mouth insisted, however, that these seldom attacked unless cornered or wounded.

The girl woke up, and, after she had eaten, the chief and I stuffed ourselves. Then he insisted that we try to get some sleep. The sun was half-way through its day's work when I opened my eyes. The girl was seated with her back to a tree, her hair a marvel of neatness. She had thrown a robe over me, and this little act, so meaningless to those never initiated into the wilds, affected me strangely. It was the first time in many years that any one had taken thought for my comfort; certainly the first wherein a woman had given me any attention since I was a child in the States and under my mother's care. My first sensation was that of being "mothered." I liked it. All men do, let them disclaim to the contrary as they will.

I half closed my eyes and for several minutes pretended to be asleep, that I might watch her. Her blue eyes were serene; her fine features were softened by repose. Here, in a position of great danger, she impressed me as revealing her true self, her genuine womanliness. At the X. Y. post, where no physical harm could intrude, she had been cold, hard and unapproachable.

At last she caught me spying and coloured furiously, instinctively feeling of her hair.

"Where is the chief?" I innocently asked.

She pointed, and I arose and beheld him sleeping, lying on his face. When I stepped toward him he came to his senses and sprang to his feet like a wildcat. Our voices had not disturbed him but my step had. Subconsciously, perhaps, he had catalogued our voices, but a stealthy step was not so easily classified. He always insisted a person woke up more easily and more completely—woke up all over as he expressed it—if he slept on his face. The girl insisted that he finish out his nap, but he replied he was "filled" with sleep and would need no more till another day.

The girl said that during our slumbers there had been no signs of life on the plain except the buffalo and their lurking escort of grey wolves. She had heard sounds back in the woods, and once a red deer had poked his head through the bushes to look us over.

I went with Flat Mouth to the river, where he fashioned several drinking-dishes out of bark, and while there we saw seven grizzlies descend the opposite shore to drink. They were huge brutes and more to be feared than the Sioux, should they take a notion to attack.

The Pillager observed them unconcernedly, however, assuring me that they would not bother us if we did not trouble them.

The river, he reminded us, was seldom visited by Assiniboin, Cree, or Chippewa because the Sioux claimed it. From fear of attacks from the northern Indians, the Sioux, in turn, seldom came there except in war strength. So all animal life had been left to develop undisturbed by man. The bears had not been hunted and did not know man as a destroyer. This was all very comforting as long as I could believe it, but the thought of the girl back in the little glade alone, with these monsters wandering about in batches of seven, made me anxious to return.

We took water to her and on the way started up red deer which were nowhere near as shy as those on the Red River. Leaving her again, we visited the horses and found them contentedly grazing inside the fringe of bushes and willows. Leaving the chief with them, I rejoined the girl.

"Must we wait until night before starting home?" she eagerly asked.

"I believe that is the chief's idea. He knows the country and the Indians far better than we do. We must take no foolish risks."

"If you were alone would you start now?" she asked.

In truth I should have, but I said nothing.

"Then pretend I'm a man. Let's go at once," she cried with a show of impatience, and she stood and began gathering up the robes.

My imagination was incapable of detecting anything masculine in her splendid womanhood. I could not suppress a small smile at her suggestion. Instantly she was the woman of the X. Y. post and was commanding:

"Call the Indian! Tell him we start at once."

Flat Mouth appeared on the scene before I could remonstrate with her. In Chippewa she repeated to him her intention of starting for the Red River. He shook his head, saying—

"We must stay here a little longer."

"You two can stay. I will go alone. The country is perfectly safe. The Sioux have lost the trail entirely."

I have no doubt she would have taken a pony and set forth if I had not stopped her, saying:

"You can't go alone. We'll take orders from the Pillager."

"I'll take orders from no one," she haughtily informed. "I suppose I may have one of the horses, seeing that they belonged to the Sioux?"

"No."

"Very well, I can make it afoot," she calmly said.

"What's the matter with you?" I angrily inquired. "Can't you reason? Or is it your temper?"

I thought she was trying to annihilate me with her furious gaze. By an effort she mastered herself and quietly retorted:

"My temper is nothing to you. We're thrown together by a series of mishaps. I appreciate your coming to find me, but if your coming makes you feel any responsibility for my acts I'm sorry you came."

"The Lord forbid I should ever have to be responsible for such a bundle of spite as you seem to be," I peevishly protested.

She smiled with her lips, turned and walked towards the plain. I caught up with her and demanded—

"What do you plan?"

"I'm on my way to the X. Y. post," she lazily informed.

"Unless you return to cover at once the Pillager and I will tie you."

"You would never dare!" she gritted, turning on me like a cat.

All my silly resentment dropped from me, and I gently explained:

"Miss Dearness, I should never dare to look a man, red or white, in the face if I allowed you to start alone for the Red. I won't threaten again to tie you, but if you start for the Red I'll go with you. It's hardly fair to let the Pillager go with us as he is of a different race.''

She fought the battle with herself, her red hair being a true gauge of her temper. Suddenly she surrendered, murmuring: ''I was wrong. We'll go back to the chief.''

''You're tired. Your nerves are out of tune. In a few hours it will be night; then we can go.''

''It isn't my nerves,'' she contritely corrected. ''It's just temper.''

''My temper is off the key. Of course I spoke foolishly when I said I would tie you.''

''I'll obey orders.''

Flat Mouth had watched us without a lineament of his strong face betraying that he could either see or hear. When we joined him he gave her a quick look and walked towards the horses. She remained silent, not inclined to talk. I waited some minutes to see if she desired companionship, then went after the Pillager.

The chief was crouching behind some cherry trees and had, I observed, shifted the horses deeper into the growth. He was staring intently out on the plain. He motioned for me to drop beside him. My heart gave a thump, for I had been so positive we had shaken the Sioux off our trail that this hint of their presence weakened me for a moment.

''Assiniboins,'' he said.

''Where?'' I demanded. He pointed to the northern rim and by much staring through half-closed lids I managed to make out some dots.

''Buffaloes,'' I decided.

''Assiniboins,'' he repeated.

''Then they're friendly. They won't do anything worse than try to steal our horses.''

''They've killed traders when catching them alone. These are not of the same band that comes to the Pembina.''

''All the Assiniboins are good robe-makers. They're all friendly with the whites,'' I persisted.

"These are not any Red River band. If they see us they will do their best to kill us and take our horses. I am an Indian. I tell you I know this."

"Say what is to be done and we will do it," I agreed.

"We will wait until they go. If they came down here we will follow up the river," he replied. Then very significantly—"They must not see the white woman."

"She was big medicine to them once," I reminded.

"To those who came to the Pembina. But the Voice is back on the River That Calls, and this band would kill her to prevent it being stolen again."

I remembered what the girl had told me, much to the same effect, and if Flat Mouth was not afraid, I was.

"What's the matter, Mr. Franklin? Are the Sioux near?" cried Miss Dearness.

"Not a Sioux in sight. The Pillager and I disagree about some dots out on the plain. He says they're Assiniboins. I say they are buffaloes."

"And he fears they saw smoke," she cried, wringing her hands. "Now I've brought new danger on you two by my thoughtlessness. It was so dreary waiting. I forgot myself. I threw some green bark on the hot ashes to see it curl up—it burst into flame—then I fed on some green sticks—I bring bad luck."

"Nonsense," I sharply replied. "Is it surprising that a band of thieving Indians should stumble upon us here? They will stand clear of my gun. It's stood off their betters."

I turned to Flat Mouth and boasted the same to him.

He shook his head energetically:

"It's no medicine to the Assiniboins, the Crees, or the Chippewas. They have seen it and its two barrels, and the truth has gone through the three tribes. They are two shots afraid; that is all. Soon the Sioux of the plains will know about it. Then it won't be medicine to them."

He ran back to watch the dots, and Miss Dearness and I followed him. Now they were no longer dots but mounted men. They had drawn near enough for us to be sure of this, and yet they strangely resembled buffaloes. It was not until a line of them raced parallel to our hiding place that I discovered the cause for my fancy. Each warrior wore on his head a covering of buffalo hide to which were fixed two horns. In some cases this strange head-gear comprised the whole head of the creature, the skull bones having been carefully removed, and the skin worn as a hood.

They seemed to be racing about aimlessly, and I rejoiced to the Pillager—

"They didn't see the smoke."

"It was such a tiny smoke they couldn't," added Miss Dearness.

The Pillager's answer was a silent drama. Without a word he reached over his shoulder and pulled arrows from his quiver. Without removing his gaze from the swiftly manœuvring horsemen he placed the arrows before him in a row, then caught up his bow and drew the cord taut. Miss Dearness glanced at me with a little frown worrying her forehead.

"They think we're here?" I asked Flat Mouth.

"They know it," he tersely responded.

To my way of thinking the horsemen were not acting suspiciously. One of them, the leader, whirled a disk of rawhide from the point of his lance and the riders raced to where it fell, jabbing and spearing until one managed to pick it up. He, in turn, carried it triumphantly aloft until hard pressed, when he sent it sailing from him, and again the mad scramble to obtain it.

I doubted the Pillager's bald assertion until I noted that the rawhide was always being sent in our direction. Each rush brought the band closer. Now the chief had the piece of hide and his men were strung out behind him in undulating loops like the letter S greatly prolonged. My eyes were distracted by the constantly shifting loops. Yet the leader, with each manœuvre, brought them nearer to the woods.

"They're coming!" I softly warned as the first loop

suddenly swung far forward so as to line up fully thirty warriors riding abreast with their chief on their left.

"Fire the gun and get back to the horses!" ordered Flat Mouth, snatching up an arrow.

With a terrific shout the whole band came toward us. I fired both barrels into the front rank, and a miss was impossible. Flat Mouth's bow began to twang, and his arrows streamed into the centre of the assault.

"Get to the horses!" he cried and then raised a war-cry.

It was not the Pillager's yell, but the cry of the Sioux, and faster and faster flew the arrows. I seized the girl's wrist and urged her to the camp. I had barely slipped the hobbles and gathered up the halter ropes when Flat Mouth came gliding to us, his face exalted with the lust of battle against great odds. Without a word he took his horse and began leading the way along a deer-path that led up-stream. The girl rode behind him, and I, on foot, brought up the rear.

I managed to reload one barrel and, as nothing happened, I halted and charged the other. The way was rough and at every rod we read the signs of much game. Little piles of hair at the foot of trees whose bark was worn smooth showed that the buffaloes penetrated the thickets in considerable numbers. Signs of bears were the most plentiful, however. It was a pelt-hunter's paradise if he could gather the toll without losing his scalp.

After an hour of continuous travel the Pillager halted and briefly explained:

"They didn't dare to enter the woods at first, thinking the Sioux were there. My Sioux war-cry and the Sioux arrows fooled them. They'll soon find out their mistake. Their men are creeping in now; soon they'll see where only two men and a woman camped. Soon they will come fast."

"What shall we do now?" asked Miss Dearness.

"Cross the river and strike for the Mandan villages on the Missouri," was the astounding answer.

I gasped aloud in dismay. Leave the post with only foolish Probos on duty, with old Tabashaw having free rein to intimidate, to bully, and to consume the company's rum! Run to the Missouri to escape while home was so near?"

"It must be so," growled the chief, guessing my reluctance. "Only in that way can we save the white woman."

"To the Mandan villages it is, then," I agreed.

"I'm willing to risk turning back," spoke up Miss Dearness.

"Eshkebugecoshe is not willing," grimly retorted the chief. "I killed some of them, and the gun killed some. When they see how they were tricked only one torture will satisfy them. Wait while I look at the river."

The crossing was not difficult and we made it easily and surmounted the opposite bank, but left a trail a bull buffalo could read. Flat Mouth held up his hand for silence and cocked his ear. I heard nothing beyond the usual noise of wood life.

"They're following our trail," he warned. "If we stick to the woods they will overtake us. Our only chance is to take to the open now and ride for it. Our horses are fresh, theirs are tired. Once on the plain, we can leave them."

"But they'll chase us?" asked the girl.

He nodded and, to cheer her up, added:

"We shall find some Mandans, or some of the Big Bellies (Minnetarees) hunting buffalo. They will help us."

We broke through the timber and started for the south-west at a gallop. We had gone not more than a fourth of a mile when a ringing cry sounded behind us. Glancing back, I beheld a warrior dancing and waving his arms at the edge of the timber. We had not advanced more than half a mile before nearly a hundred horsemen emerged from the woods.

Flat Mouth was worried, for well he knew that it would take more than an ordinary hunting party to stand off such a force. At the start the chances favoured us, as our animals were well rested, whereas the enemy's had been ridden far and fast. There was no question as to our maintaining a safe lead, providing none of our animals met with an accident. Realising this my eyes became focused on the flying feet of Miss Dearness's mount. At every stride I expected to see a hoof stick into a hole and hurl her to the ground, leaving one of our mounts to carry a double. I glanced back once more and beheld even more warriors quitting the woods.

Flat Mouth grimly explained:

"Big war-party going to fight the Mandans. We shall have them all the way."

He insisted it was the medicine of the girl's hair that permitted us to drop them before the night came. I felt a great uplift when, with the last light, I failed to make out their figures against the northern skyline. The chief quietly assured me they would be on our trail in the morning.

We camped that night in the bed of a dry coulée. The chief managed to kill a buffalo calf with his bow and arrow, and we ventured to build a small fire, fencing it about with our white robes. Over this we broiled some excellent steaks and cooked enough to carry with us on the morrow. At daybreak we were up, and beheld figures creeping over the horizon.

The country grew rougher with each hour, and we lost the Assiniboins only when we dropped into the hollows. On surmounting ridge or hillock we raised them to view again, tenaciously sticking to our track. Flat Mouth had eyes only for what was ahead, seeking for some opportunity of shaking the enemy off. I was always staring behind me, fascinated by the implacable purpose that held the savages to the chase. The girl rode with head bowed, seldom bothering to lift her gaze from the ground. Her fear was an accident to her pony.

We began to encounter coulées filled with water, each a sign-post for the Couteau du Missouri, the rough and

hilly country we must cross before descending to the
Missouri River. The Pillager believed the Assiniboins
would not venture beyond this height of land. Yet they
were in such strong force they might recklessly risk
an encounter with Mandan or Minnetaree.

.   .   .   .

Ahead were the steep red banks of the Missouri. At
our feet were two cows freshly slain. Flat Mouth in-
spected them, and for the first time since our flight from
the Cheyenne his immobile features showed animation.
"The brains have been taken to dress hides. Hunters
did it, not a war-party after meat. Only Mandans hunt
here."

The Pillager dismounted to demonstrate what an
Indian pony could do and with the beast scrambling
like a cat he led the way up the slope. Miss Dearness
made light of it, although she was forced to climb it
afoot. On reaching the top we had a more intimate
view of the river. The valley was some two miles in
width and caged in by steep banks. The current was
sluggish and swollen, dotted with much driftwood and
many black dots which I knew to be drowned buffalo.
Immediately below us was a growth of big cottonwoods,
and from our position to these woods ran a well-beaten
path.

For the first time since our race began, I presumed
to take the lead, but before I could do more than press
ahead to the brow of the ridge, Flat Mouth was halting
me and explaining that the way was full of dangers and
that he must go first. I placed my gun across my
saddle, but the danger was not animate and consisted
of certain deep holes, or pits the Indians had dug for
trapping fox and wolves. These pits were ten or more
feet deep, with the openings masked by the dead grass.

We descended slowly and cautiously, skirting several
of these menaces, and I know I should have plunged
into the first one, had I had my way. At the foot of the
ridge the Pillager reined in and warned:

"We must say we have come from Fort Assiniboin,

that the Medicine Hair is the daughter of the big white chief there and that we work for him. The big white chief wishes to open a post here and sends his daughter because her medicine lets her see things we men cannot see. He has told us to stay but a few days and to ask for warriors to go back with us as far as the Mouse. The Mandans must not know we were driven here by the Assiniboins. They would think the white woman's medicine was weak and that her father was a little chief if they knew the Assiniboins had made us run."

"Why can't we start back as soon as we get fresh horses?" I anxiously asked, my mind reverting to the incompetent Probos in charge of the post and to old Tabashaw bullying him for rum.

"And why must we travel by the way of the Mouse?" demanded Miss Dearness, referring to the long route to the confluence of the Mouse and the Qu'Appelle, thence down the Assiniboin to the Forks, where we would turn south up the Red.

"We must stay and look about, as if looking for a good place for a post," Flat Mouth patiently explained. Then to the girl—"We must come from Fort Assiniboin to show why we are here. We must go back the same way to make our talk sound straight. Even if we could pick our trail we must return by way of the Mouse and the Assiniboin. It is the regular path and safer."

I told Miss Dearness the chief was right and that a few days wouldn't make much difference, that we ought to be thankful at having escaped the Sioux and the Assiniboins—this to cheer her up.

"Oh, we will go through with it," she wearily replied. "I was thinking of you and your affairs more than of mine. I have no trade to lose. Angus can watch the post till I get back, or my successor arrives."

"Remember our talk!" warned the Pillager, kicking his horse into a gallop and riding ahead.

Off at one side and at a distance was an Indian with a gun. Around him were women and children working. These were the gardeners and they were planting and hoeing under an armed guard. This was impressive proof of their daily danger. Even at the very outskirts of their villages they did not dare to move about without a sentinel. Just as the Red River of the North always contained the menace of the Sioux, so did the stretch of woods hold for Mandan and Minnetaree a hidden danger.

At the Pillager's gesture the girl and I halted while he rode to the man with the gun. I saw the fellow nervously cock his piece, then stand keenly at attention while Flat Mouth, with both hands above his head, talked to him. Suddenly the gun was lowered, and the guard was shaking hands warmly with our companion.

"He recognises him," murmured the girl.

The two conversed for several minutes, then came to us. Flat Mouth announced it was all right, that we were to proceed and find quarters at the village a short distance ahead. The guard smiled broadly and shook hands with me, but seemed to stand in awe of Miss Dearness. Later I learned the Pillager had filled him with tales concerning the wonderful medicine she possessed and her powers as a magician. Then the guard looked at my pony and at the chief's and said something we could not understand.

"He asks where our presents are," translated the Pillager.

He might well be puzzled, for beyond the white robes snugly wrapped in my blanket we had no possessions. No voluntary visitor to the villages would fail to bring a pack-animal or two loaded with gifts.

Before I could scare up an answer the girl was haughtily saying in Chippewa:

"Tell him the big white chief does not send gifts by his friends. He has slaves to bring them. They will come later. He will decide how much to send after he hears how we have been treated."

Flat Mouth's eyes twinkled as he listened, but his bearing was stern and haughty as he translated her words to the guard.

The guard next informed us that an H. B. man was living in the village across the river, but was now on the headwaters of the Missouri looking for trade in spring beaver.

The man returned to his charge, and we rode on.

As we entered the village we were discovered and quickly surrounded. They greeted us cordially, shaking hands and seemingly much pleased at our coming. Some recognised Flat Mouth and hailed him as a friend. Then they commenced asking where we had left our packs. As he had explained to the armed guard, so now did the Pillager explain to the tribe that while we represented the greatest traders of the North we had brought no goods with us either for trade or for gifts. Their faces fell.

The chief continued to explain how our errand was to investigate the chances of trade. Of course he described Miss Dearness as being a medicine-woman and the daughter of the big white chief at the head of the fort on the Assiniboin. It was grimly amusing that I should pose as an *engagé* instead of *bourgeois*, that she, of the opposition, should masquerade as my superior.

The interest Miss Dearness aroused was accumulative, and it was plain she created a tremendous impression. One young buck standing close to her pony reached up a hand to feel the texture of her fiery hair. As quick as *loup corvior* her hand rose, and the handle of her leather whip landed on his wrist, causing him to spring back in dismay. I think it was the blazing fire of her blue eyes, rather than any physical hurt from the blow, that startled the fellow.

Flat Mouth took occasion to warn that the hair was medicine and that the white woman had saved the young man's life by preventing his touching it. After that incident the circle widened. In turn the Indians informed us that the Sioux had been very troublesome ever since the snow melted, and that since Le Borgne (The Blind), the great war chief of the Minnetarees on the Knife a few miles above, had gone out with a hunting party, the Mandans had kept their huts barricaded every night. On his return an alliance was to be formed with the Cheyennes and aggressive measures taken to teach the enemy a lasting lesson.

Flat Mouth, further to increase our prestige and make them forget we came without gifts, now stated that the goodwill of the white woman was worth a war-party and that her anger was equal to a blast of lightning.

Firmly believing as he did that the girl possessed powers of magic, he did not hesitate to draw a long bow, and I was fearing that she might be requested to bolster up her reputation by some little display, when a newcomer distracted the attention. This was none less than Poscopsahe, or Black Cat, the chief of the village. We were presented to him and he was duly impressed by the girl and assured her that the big white chief would do well to send traders there and to the Minnetaree villages above, but especially to his village of the Mandans. This jealousy, when it came to acquiring the white man's goods in trade, was very keen among the villages, although they would unite readily and solidly enough in opposing their ancient enemies.

Through the Pillager, the girl calmly replied that she had heard the Mandans had a good trade in robes and buffalo tongues and a fair trade in beaver; that she would look the villages over for a day or so and then report back to Fort Assiniboin.

With these ceremonies out of the way, we were shown to a hut reserved for visitors. I took my pack of white robes inside and turned the horses over to a young man. One of the chief's wives followed us to the hut with a huge dish of boiled corn and beans, a tasteless mess, and another of dried meat. The latter was impossible because of the Mandans' preference for tainted to fresh meat, so on the whole we made a sorry meal of it.

Despite our explanation that we had no goods to trade, nor gifts to bestow, the men, women, and children crowded about our hut, eager for us to open our packs. The fact that they had seen all our possessions, namely my bundle of robes, did not spoil their imagination. White people always had gifts, always wanted to trade. They believed that in some mysterious manner we would produce articles of the white man's making which they were so eager to secure. It was with the greatest difficulty that Flat Mouth persuaded them to believe we had nothing to trade, and their attitude was sullen when they finally withdrew.

After they left us in peace the Pillager advised that we take up different quarters, urging that by doing so we would create a better impression. So we decided that Miss Dearness should remain in the guest hut with the chief's wife as attendant, while the Pillager and I found shelter elsewhere. Leaving her with the Indian women, we went out to look the village over. The Mandans, being a settled people, had no need for dogs, so this nuisance was not in evidence. The children, too, were quite decently mannered, although they would have stolen the clothes off my back had I given them a chance. The population of this and the village across the river was about two thousand, Flat Mouth said. I suggested we cross over and visit the second village. Flat Mouth called out to some young men, and, on my giving them a few inches of tobacco, they readily agreed to set us across.

One man did the paddling, and his paddle was a five-foot pole with a strip of board lashed across the end. With his first stroke the boat turned nearly around, but he quickly reversed us with a stroke on the other side. First one was looking upstream at the mass of floating trees and dead buffalo, then downstream. It made me dizzy, yet our man was an expert, for we drifted less than a quarter of a mile, whereas the average boatman would have drifted a full mile.

The news of our arrival in the first Mandan village had spread across the river, and on landing we were met by a crowd of natives, headed by Big Man, a

Cheyenne prisoner and now adopted into the tribe—a man of prominence. He shook us warmly by the hand and anxiously asked why we had left all our packs in Black Cat's village. The tedious explanation was given by Flat Mouth and the interest of the assemblage flattened out, and many turned away to resume the work of towing trees and dead buffalo ashore.

Through the Pillager I learned from Big Man that the Minnetaree village was much excited over the arrival of six Cheyennes seeking a peace treaty. Messengers had been sent for Le Borgne to bring him back from the hunt. Black days were waiting for the Sioux, once the treaty was perfected. We paraded the village, finding it a duplicate of the one across the river. We were invited into several huts to eat, but always found the meat abominable. On the outskirts of the village women with hoes made from buffalo shoulder-blades were working in their gardens, with armed men stationed at intervals. Their danger was imminent, much like that which surrounds some of the smaller wood-folk who live under stumps, sporting and raising their little families while death stalks them day and night.

The Pillager mumbled to me—

"We must go back now."

I had known him long enough to realise that he was disturbed at something. Thanking Big Man and telling him he should have presents when our traders arrived, we returned to the river and were ferried across.

"Something makes my brother sad," I remarked in Chippewa after we had stepped ashore.

"I was glad when I heard that The Blind was away on a buffalo hunt. My heart is heavy now, for they send to bring him home to meet the Cheyennes."

"You believed we should find him here before we arrived," I reminded.

"I knew and hoped for the best. When we came and found him gone my heart sang. I believed we should get away before he returned. Now to find he will come back, makes me sorry."

"The Blind does not like white men."

"He likes white men," was the laconic response.

"Then why feel sad to know he is coming back?"

"He likes women. He has never seen such a woman as Medicine Hair. He is a mighty war chief. His word is law in both Minnetaree and Mandan villages. When we fought the Sioux and the Assiniboins I thought only of escaping to a place where we would not be killed. I knew we would not be harmed in these villages. Now I have had time to think. What The Blind wants he takes."

The danger must be pressing when an Indian would be troubled over the fate of a white woman. His words reduced my complacency to ashes. I could only say—

"We must start before he comes back."

"They will think our coming is a trick if we go away too quickly," he warned. "I will talk with the Mandans and ask if they have seen any signs of Assiniboins or Sioux to the north. We must visit the villages, but in one or two sleeps we might start for the Mouse. Once we reach Fort Assiniboin the Medicine Hair will be safe."

"But Le Borgne would be very blind to make the whites angry by taking one of their women," I protested.

Flat Mouth smiled in grim pity at my ignorance.

"You do not know The Blind," he murmured. "He takes what he wants. No chief is as powerful as he. When I was here before, he took a woman from a Mandan chief who went with his war-club to bring her back. They buried his war-club with him. He likes white men. He will treat you better than his warriors, but he doesn't let anything stand between him and the thing he wants."

From the end of the village rose the girl's wonderful voice, singing her quaint song, in which one heard the rush of the river and the sighing of the wind, a voice of sadness and pathos, yet coloured with a rare beauty.

For the first time I realised there were no Indians hanging about us begging for tobacco and gifts. We walked to the guest-hut and found the entire village grouped about it. Black Cat was seated on a robe, before the entrance, smoking his Missouri tobacco—villainous stuff—and wondering at the medicine of her voice.

"When she sings her medicine song I see the leaves turn yellow and drop, and I feel the first of the snow. I hear the ice breaking up and smell the first grass," said Black Cat as we stood beside him.

"She calls the voices from rivers and sends them back when she is tired of them," Flat Mouth boasted. "She is very strong medicine. It is her hair. The Chippewas are afraid of her."

"The Chippewas are old women," snorted Black Cat.

Flat Mouth's visage grew very wicked. From inside the robe he was wearing Mandan-fashion he pulled forth a grisly string of Sioux scalps, shook them in Black Cat's face and hoarsely taunted:

"I am a Chippewa. I do not hide in a village when the Sioux of the Plains come near. I go out and kill them. Have the Mandans any old women who take scalps like these?"

It was the master-stroke for putting the beggars in their proper place. The Cat was unable to speak for a full minute. His eyes glowed and gloated over the trophies. He sprang to his feet and loudly proclaimed:

"My Chippewa brother is a very brave man. I will adopt him as a son. He shall have a new war name. He shall have many wives. He shall carry the pipe for us against our enemies."

I feared Flat Mouth would indulge in more boasting and scornfully flout the chief's offer, but his finesse was sharpened because of the girl's peril. He replied—

"After I have taken Medicine Hair back to her father."

This gave the Cat great pleasure. He pictured himself basking in the glory of his new son, the recipient of homage, the possessor of many scalps. He loudly announced he would give a feast for the mighty Chippewa and forthwith directed his wives to prepare an abundance of stinking meat, corn, and beans. The Indians scattered in all directions to make ready for the festival. Black Cat hurried off to see his commands were obeyed, and, with a glance at me, the Pillager walked beside him.

I remained before the hut. The door swung open a crack, then wide open, and Miss Dearness confronted me, her eyes searching mine anxiously.

"When can we start from this place?" she whispered.

"Very soon—in a few days."

"A few days!" she faintly exclaimed. "Something tells me we must start at once."

"The Pillager would say it is your medicine," I bantered.

"It is instinct. It has never failed me since I came to the Indian country. Let us start to-night!"

"But that would invite danger. We must make a pretence of looking the villages over for trade purposes," I protested. "If there is any vital, any immediate danger, of course we will start at once and fight for it. Now tell me just what has happened."

"Nothing has happened," she slowly replied, her eyes staring into mine and yet not beholding me. "But I'm afraid—I am horribly afraid—different from anything I ever felt in my life—I'm never afraid of death." With this she closed the door, leaving me standing there gaping.

CHAPTER IX

AT THE MINNETAREE VILLAGE

EARLY next morning Flat Mouth and I went to Miss
Dearness's hut and, on her joining us at the porch,
asked her to make ready for a trip to the Minnetaree
villages a few miles above, situated on the Knife River.
To attempt leaving the country without visiting these
"Big Bellies," as the trade had named them, would be
to incur the wrath of Le Borgne and throw discredit on
our story of representing the N. W. company and its
plan to set up an opposition to the already established
H. B. trader.

The girl was afraid. Her bearing was calm and
collected enough, but there were transient flashes in her
big blue eyes, a curious trick of glancing sidewise
through half-closed lids, that bespoke a furtive fear.
However, she readily agreed we must visit the upper
villages to sustain our rôle. She only insisted that we
make all haste to have it over with.

Flat Mouth improvised a legend which he sung as we
slowly made our way through the crowd. It was to the
effect that beams of sunlight became imprisoned in the
girl's hair when she was born, and that their struggles
to escape created the powerful medicine she possessed.

Big Man walked by my side and informed me a hunting party of a hundred braves was due to arrive home
after a three days' trip and that, if we would postpone
our visit to the Minnetarees, we could procure some
fresh meat. I immediately feared lest the Minnetaree
chief, Le Borgne, would be with this party, but Flat
Mouth explained that the Minnetarees hunted to the

south-west of the Knife and the Mandans to the south-east, the river being the boundary. We needed fresh meat badly, but the hunting party would greatly delay our journey up the river, so we pressed on more determinedly than ever.

I assured Miss Dearness that we could make the villages, ride through them and start back for Black Cat's village before dark. On returning and recrossing the river we could decide whether to start north immediately, unaccompanied, or wait till morning and endeavour to obtain an escort from the Mandans. The girl was for an immediate departure.

I had planned to take my white robes with me, thinking I might have a chance to trade them for horses, they being about the only thing the Minnetarees would exchange horses for. Flat Mouth, however, insisted such a trade would consume all the day, that the horses we had were fresh enough, and that the hides had better be left behind in the hut, where they would be perfectly safe.

So we rode forth.

The first pause in our journey was at the Minnetaree village at the mouth of the Knife, consisting of half a hundred huts and called the "little village." We very quickly learned there was a great difference between this and either of the Mandan villages in regard to manners.

The moment we were sighted a mob of young demons surrounded us, hooting and deriding. Their elders sat smoking their miserable tobacco on top of the huge circular huts and enjoying the spectacle. More troublesome even than the children were the dogs which swarmed from all directions. They were as vicious as wolves and much more daring.

Miss Dearness, who had drawn her *capote* over her head when we neared the village, gave a cry of alarm, and I spurred forward and brained a brute with the butt of my gun as he leaped high to pull her from the saddle. This act caused much scowling and mumbling from

the spectators, which I interpreted to be threats. Flat
Mouth leaned low from his saddle and did for another
beast with his axe. The mumbling broke into a sullen
roar, and the men on the huts began rising and preparing to descend.

Flat Mouth pulled out his string of Sioux scalps and,
waving them above his head, shouted his name and the
fact that he had once lived among the Mandans and
the Minnetarees. Then in their own tongue he chanted
his record of coups, touching a scalp as he narrated the
details of each encounter. The men on the huts gathered
to the edge and allowed their feet to hang down while
they listened.

Finishing the story of his exploits, the Pillager
explained how he was serving the woman with the
medicine hair, the most wonderful woman ever on the
Missouri, whose father was the mightiest of all traders
and who had intended to build a post among the villages
so the Indians could always obtain whatever they
wanted in arms and ammunition. He significantly concluded with saying:

"The big white chief will send no traders where his
daughter is met by mad dogs and screaming children."

Then, turning to Miss Dearness, he directed her to
reveal her hair.

She obeyed, and as the Indians stared at her fiery
hair, those on the ground drew back and forgot their
scowls, while those on the huts stood erect and forgot
their smoking. As the Pillager rapidly translated his
speech to me I understood their concern; each village
was anxious to obtain all the white man's goods possible and was extremely jealous of every visit made by
a trader to a neighbouring village.

Their lack of hospitality was an excellent excuse for
us to save time by pushing on. Although they beseeched
us to enter their huts and partake of food and tobacco,
we held on steadily through the village and into the
road leading up the Knife. They followed us outside the
village but we gave them no heed. We followed the

road for about a mile when the Pillager halted and announced that we were opposite the big Minnetaree village.

This time we met less of the rudeness which had greeted us below, and yet there was no suggestion of hospitality. They were rude in another way. We were ignored. They were most arrogant in their bearing. After ordering a woman to show us to a big hut, set apart for visitors, they paid no attention to us. A physical characteristic of all Minnetarees was the large aquiline nose. The Pillager assured us we were safe among them, but added that this was the case purely because they must have arms from traders to protect themselves from the Sioux, and they believed that we were paving the way for permanent traders. The village originally contained a thousand huts, but the deadly smallpox had whittled it down to its present proportions.

The hut we were shown to was a duplicate of the one in Black Cat's village except that it was dug down three feet below the surface. As in the Mandan huts we found earthen pots and a copper kettle. The kettle, it seems, was used entirely for boiling meat. Why they couldn't cook meat in the earthenware, as they did their corn and beans, I do not know. Some foolish superstition was behind it, of course. I asked the woman about it, and she said the meat would make the earthen pots crack.

I quickly learned it was unsafe to move outside the hut unless armed with a club. The first time I stepped to the door to survey the scene, I was set upon by a huge dog. I kicked myself clear of the brute, and after that I never ventured abroad without a club in my hand. So long as we remained in the hut we were left by ourselves. The moment we passed through the door we were surrounded by impish brats who would go through our clothes and filch anything they could. Miss Dearness went out with us once, but the repulsive sights and the constant attendance of the vicious-mannered mob which accompanied us every step was experience enough for her.

"You and the Pillager carry out your plans," she urged after we returned to the hut. "But let us start back to the Mandan village before dark."

"It's a beastly place," I admitted, pitying her deeply. "I almost wish, for your sake, we had tried to win back north without coming here. I think we could have made it."

"No, we stood no chance. The Sioux were too close, the Assiniboins too many. Our lives are safe here, but we ought to be starting for the Red River within a day or two." After a pause she asked, "When do you think Le Borgne will come?"

"Not till after we have gone. You have heard of him?"

"My father spoke of him when we were on the Assiniboin. The Indians had much to tell of him. But go and finish your business so we can be getting away."

The undercurrent of her thoughts was Le Borgne, that sinister master of the Minnetarees, who ruled as an autocrat, an unusual condition of affairs among the Indians. I did not care to ask her what she had heard about the chief; it was sure to be something disquieting. I picked up my club and, followed by Flat Mouth, passed from the hut.

We had a brisk battle with the dogs but finally put them to rout. Young bucks swaggered close, glaring murderously at our success over their pets. One was so bold as to step before the Pillager to block his path, or to make him step aside. Flat Mouth slapped him in the face with his string of Sioux scalps, called him a "child," and asked how long before he could grow up and kill a Sioux.

The buck, maddened beyond self-control and knowing the warriors were watching his shame, grabbed for his axe. Flat Mouth smiled evilly and dangled the string before his face. The hand on the axe relaxed.

I was using the medicine bag taken from the war-chief killed in the Red Lake River country as a tobacco pouch. Now I produced it, filled my pipe and through the Pillager advised the young man and his friend not to bother mighty warriors who never bothered to slay any but chiefs carrying the pipe.

The display of scalps and the sight of the medicine pouch brought the elders to sharp attention. Several approached, their bearing very decorous, and questioned the Pillager. He proudly proclaimed himself a hero and gave his new name of Sioux Killer. He declared I came next to him and said the white woman with the medicine hair was more powerful than both of us.

The lowering glances continued, yet our exhibit of trophies had made a deep impression and forced their respect. Their great chief, Le Borgne, would have been proud to recite the coups the Pillager had recounted. Harsh commands were given, and the band of children drew back, the young men ceased their insolence, and women clubbed the dogs to the outskirts of the village.

Then Le Borgne's brother, Caltahcota, or Choke-cherry, as the traders knew him, deigned to make himself known and inquired minutely into the purpose of our visit. He was pleased with the story I told through the Pillager, and said his brother would be very glad to welcome us, but that we had done wrong in not bringing guns, powder and ball with us, as the Sioux were very thick and troublesome around the village.

The Pillager sneered and loudly declared he would drive the Sioux away and double the length of his string. Choke-cherry seemed to accept him at his own estimation, and his respect took on a touch of awe. He insisted we go into his hut and eat.

We followed him and were presented with bowls of meat that only one word can describe—putrid. Even for politeness' sake I could not endure the stench of it, let alone tasting it. Choke-cherry gobbled at it voraciously and gave us some dried beans and corn, bruised

in a mortar, cooked without salt, and very tasteless.
Still it could be swallowed. Flat Mouth was not particular as to what he ate, yet there were limits to even
his Indian appetite and stomach. He partook only of
the corn and beans. While we were bolting our portions
he assured me that the Minnetarees would kill a buffalo
in winter, leave it in the snow and wait until decom-
position had set in before using it for food. I could
well believe it.

Escaping to the free air, I asked Choke-cherry when
his mighty brother would be back. He believed in a few
days. He was very vague, indicating he knew no more
about it than we did. The six Cheyenne envoys had
withdrawn a mile north of the village to await the
coming of more of their people. Upon their arrival the
treaty between them and the Minnetarees would be duly
cemented. The Minnetarees would adopt a Cheyenne
youth and many presents would be "placed under the
stem." While Le Borgne was too big a man to abandon
a hunting trip for any purpose except to follow his own
will, it was probable he would return very soon.

With the Pillager interpreting I said:

"We must go back to the lower villages to-night.
When your brother comes send a man to us so we may
come to him."

He urged that we remain with the Minnetarees indefinitely, but I explained we had certain trade preparations to make, and he finally agreed to inform us when
the chief arrived.

Utterly disgusted with the villages, determined to get
away where I could feel clean once more, and sensing
that it must be hell for Miss Dearness, I made up my
mind on the spot to make a break north from the
Mandan village early the next morning. Fear of the
Sioux would keep the village Indians from pursuing us,
while the presence of the Cheyennes on the Knife,
anxious to make peace, would tend to make both Sioux
and Assiniboin chary about remaining in that neighbourhood.

The Mandans, while peacefully disposed and much less arrogant than the Minnetarees, were known as dogged fighters. Allied with the Cheyennes, they could carry a good fight to the Sioux, and the latter knew it. By striking directly north and travelling much by night I believed we could make the big loop of the Mouse. After following the Mouse a short distance we would be within the sphere of influence of the N. W. company, represented by Fort Assiniboin, and our dangers from hostile red men would be over. Nor did I expect any difficulty in leaving the Mandan village. We had come and gone as we pleased, our story was believed, and we had visited the Minnetaree village to consult with Le Borgne's brother.

Leaving Choke-cherry—Cherry-on-a-Bush was his full name, I believe—we returned to the hut and found Miss Dearness seated on a robe before the empty fire-hole and looking very sad. I briefly explained my purpose, and it was worth great risks to behold the wonderful lighting up of the blue eyes as she turned them on me.

"It will succeed!" she cried in English. "It must! Oh, you've removed a big load from my heart. To be out in the open—to breathe clean air again—anything but this!"

"You've seen so much of Indian life in travelling with your father that you must be prepared to withstand what would shock an inexperienced white woman," I remarked.

"True," she murmured. "I can force myself to indifference to much that's repulsive—a make-believe indifference, anyway. I've said the Indians talked of Le Borgne on the Assiniboin. I've also heard the H. B. men describe him in talking with my father. He likes to meet white men. He treats them better than his warriors do. He's shrewd enough to know he must have arms, and he can get them only through the white traders. From the Indian standpoint he is a very great man. Yes, he's that even by our standards. He controls these villages absolutely, and you know how dearly an Indian prizes his personal liberty. Le Borgne overrides many hard-and-fast rules of ordinary Indian usage. What he wants he takes."

Her face went red as she finished; then the colour receded, leaving her cheeks a ghastly white, and her hand fumbled at something inside her leather coat, probably her knife.

"You understand him as well as the Pillager does," I gravely commented. "Perhaps it's best you should."

"The truth is always best," she simply replied. "The fact is there. It would be foolish to hide from it as a calf hides his head in the grass to escape a hunter."

Flat Mouth, who had listened and picked up a word here and there, now broke in:

"When I was here last, Le Borgne would go into a hut and take a warrior's wife away from him. The warrior never made any fight. Le Borgne is a great chief."

His lack of finesse in making the brutal speech would have angered me more if I did not believe the girl knew all that he knew. She glanced with a curious little smile and quietly said—

"Well, he will never take me."

"What nonsense! Of course not!" I cried hotly. "To hear us one would think this raw savage was all-powerful. Then again, let's give him credit for having some sense. He wants traders to come here so he can stand off the Sioux. Is he fool enough to spoil all the chances for saving his people from the Sioux by turning every trader against him? Of course not. Miss Dearness, you haven't any cause to worry."

She reached out and patted my hand and murmured—

"Comforter!" Then she reminded—"Yet there is some danger, so great that you plan to return to the Mouse without an escort."

She had me. In all honesty I insisted our proposed flight was impelled by idle fears, so far as we knew.

Beyond the general character of Le Borgne we had no reason for deducing he would bring down the wrath of the American Government upon him by stealing a white woman.

"Tell that to these Indians and they will laugh at you," she jeered. "You can't make them believe but what they are the most superior and the most brave people on earth. There may come a time when your Government can control them. Now they have no more respect for or fear of your Government than that of China, which they never heard of. Why, they even believe they outnumber the whites. Tell them of big white villages beyond the Mississippi, and they will tell you that you lie. I've travelled enough with my father and have heard enough trade-talk to know at least that much."

I had to admit the truth of her statements and shifted to the contention that the chief's imperative need of guns would come first in his heart. He might laugh at the United States Government as a shadowy thing, but he would never laugh at the Sioux and a powerful trading company. Believing we all three represented the N. W. company, he would be anxious for us to carry back pleasant reports and thereby hasten the establishment of a permanent post.

"And yet you plan to escape at the earliest opportunity—to-morrow morning if we can manage it," she monotonously reminded.

"We can wait and see the chief and have him send an escort with us," I boldly declared.

With a little shudder she protested.

"No! No! We must start to-morrow. Instinct tells me we must do so. I only wish we could start now. I tell you I am afraid, and I'm not bothered with any silly imagination. I feel as if something were about to happen."

"For heaven's sake don't let your friend here know that, or he'll sit down and sing his death song, waiting for some one to club him to death. You're big medicine to him. So long as he can believe that, he can do much.''

"Medicine Hair big medicine," murmured Flat Mouth, catching at the familiar words, although puzzled by the rest of our talk.

She raised her head and stared at us both haughtily. The effect at once registered on the Pillager. Smoothing out her wonderful hair, she softly sounded the ululating call that carried the whispering of the wind and the prattling of shallow rivers. The chief stood very straight, his head tipped back, his nostrils distended.

There was a warrior's ambition in his small eyes. If he had been disturbed by her downcast mien he was now restored to all his old-time strutting complacency. He was the chief of the Pillager Chippewas. The Minnetarees were low dogs who lived cooped up in a village and ate stinking meat. The hand that struck against his robe where hung his scalps was itching for more bloody work. Then the door of the hut swung open, and Choke-cherry stood before us, blinking at the girl.

He was wearing a gorgeous headgear made from a turkey-cock's tail, and he seemed much puffed up with his own importance. For a few moments he forgot his errand and stared at Miss Dearness and her lustrous hair. With an effort he recalled his business and, in a loud voice, began reciting. As he talked he pounded his chest and glanced from me to the girl and then to the impassive Pillager. When he had finished the Pillager explained that the messenger sent to inform Le Borgne of the Cheyennes' presence at the village had found the great chief a short distance up the Knife. But, being a great chief, it did not please his fancy to quit the hunt, even for making the peace treaty. Accordingly he had sent the messenger back with directions for his brother, the renowned and redoubtable Choke-cherry, to treat with the Cheyennes and to adopt the Cheyenne youth.

These delegated powers had swollen Choke-cherry's

conceit almost to the exploding point. Out of five brothers to Le Borgne he had been picked. He had sent word to the Cheyenne camp that he was coming to act for his illustrious brother and, to give more tone to the ceremony, he desired his new friends to be present.

Miss Dearness's face remained cold and proud, but her soul was on her lips when she whispered to me:

"Thank God, he isn't coming. You two go, and I will wait here."

On being informed of her decision, Choke-cherry violently objected. He needed the medicine of her hair, he said. Never had the Cheyennes seen such hair. Her attendance was absolutely necessary, he insisted.

"You'd better come," I urged after Flat Mouth had interpreted. "It will give us better standing with them. We can ride directly from the ceremony to the lower village."

"If you think best," she surrendered, rising and gathering up her capote.

Choke-cherry had had small chance to wear the purple, I took it, and his dignity and conceit were terrific. As Choke-cherry, the warriors would have laughed at him; as the mouthpiece of his illustrious brother, his orders were obeyed with great celerity. Our horses were brought to the hut, and the buck who acted as hostler did not even pause to beg for the usual piece of trade tobacco. We found the village humming with unusual activity, and Choke-cherry, every few rods, halted his pony and hoarsely harangued the people. These speeches had no point, I deduced from Flat Mouth's grim smile of contempt, but they killed the time which I believed to be precious.

Finally we were ready and rode beside Choke-cherry at the head of two hundred or more mounted warriors. They had decorated their ponies with white and red earth, some showing white or red hand-prints to advertise that their riders had grappled bare-handed with an enemy. Others were marked with stripes.

As we galloped along behind Choke-cherry, Flat Mouth festooned his scalps down the front of his robe, while I hung the Sioux medicine pouch on my breast. Several groups of young men now swung in ahead of us, riding ten abreast and chanting their war-songs and sounding their rattles. Choke-cherry produced the ceremonial pipe from a case carried across his saddle, and held it high in one hand so that it could not touch his horse.

Now, while we went in superior numbers to sign a peace pact, yet we moved in a compact body as if fearing an attack. Nor was this because of any ceremony. We were afraid of an attack. Word was given for the young men to cease racing their ponies and stay close with the main body, and more than one of the gun-bearers saw that his piece was properly primed and slipped an extra ball into his mouth.

When, within about a quarter of a mile of the Cheyenne camp, a score of warriors came racing out to meet us, on horse-flesh that was far superior to anything the Minnetarees owned, their animals' heads were cunningly concealed in masks representing buffalo and red deer heads. The riders were all young men and they rode up to us, shook hands and cried out greetings in their own language.

On beholding Miss Dearness they seemed strangely affected and lost much of their noisy manner. Flat Mouth and his decorations also impressed them, although he wore none of the finery the Minnetarees were displaying. But he had the proof of having been at hand-grips with the Sioux.

As they galloped back to their camp they repeatedly turned to gaze at us. Choke-cherry took all this to his own credit, but I knew it was the girl and her vivid hair that attracted these backward glances. She, too, was moved by the stirring spectacle, and her blue eyes flashed and sparkled and roamed back and forth to take in all the details of the lively panorama. For the moment she was forgetting the filth and the annoyance and was beholding only the barbaric grace of the riders, and the pictorial rioting of colours.

Choke-cherry, the old wind-bag, now halted the long line and rode from front to rear, pausing every rod to spout and roar his orders, determined to live his brief authority to the limit. He lectured them on the virtue of keeping their finery unsoiled, so as to do honour to their tribe. He exhorted them to carry themselves carefully, so as to give no offence and spoil the peace. He severely scolded a band of Mandans, who rode at one side and out of line. Flat Mouth said the Mandans had to stand much overbearing conduct from their allies, but added that, aside from Le Borgne, no Minnetaree ventured beyond certain limits.

Because of Choke-cherry's love for speech-making I feared we would never make the camp and have the ceremony of adoption done with, but fortunately a great war-chief of the Cheyennes now dashed out to meet us on a white stallion and put an end to our leader's mouthing. This man was a magnificent specimen. He wore a blue coat, procured in trade with the Spaniards through some of the southern tribes, and a gaily-striped blanket. He all but rode us down and had his horse's hoofs pawing the air over my head in a most disconcerting manner.

He shook hands with me and Miss Dearness, at whom he stared overlong, and with the Pillager. Choke-cherry, who was a few hundred foot behind us, now galloped up and fussily took over the management of the situation. The chief shook hands with him cordially, but his gaze alternated between the girl's hair and the stern cold face of the Pillager with his wealth of Sioux hair. The business of handshaking done with, he fell back, and a large number of his men rode forward and mingled with the Minnetarees and Mandans, shaking hands and shouting a welcome.

At a signal from their chief the Cheyennes fell into long lines with a military precision and galloped to their camp. We followed at a sedate pace. When we arrived, the chief and several of the older men rode back and forth through the camp, reminding their people that the Minnetarees were their friends, that they were to be fed and protected from thieves. There were a hundred leather tents in the camp, white as snow and set in a horseshoe with the opening toward the north. The speech of the Cheyennes is much more pleasing to the ear than that of the Mandans or Minnetarees and reminded me much of our northern Crees.

Thus far all had gone smoothly. Then, like a bolt, a band of Cheyennes darted from their camp and rode like mad along our back trail. At first I supposed this to be one of their graceful manœuvres, but quickly perceived by Choke-cherry's excitement that something unusual was up. He yelped to his warriors and two-score wheeled their horses and started on a course parallel to that of the Cheyennes.

I rode up a low hill to discover the trouble and beheld two horsemen desperately riding to meet the Minnetarees before the Cheyennes could get to them. Behind me both the Cheyenne camp and the body of Minnetarees were in a boiling commotion. The women accompanying our party were hurriedly getting the horses to the rear. Choke-cherry was bleating badly. Flat Mouth and Miss Dearness galloped to join me.

"Be ready! We may have to ride fast from here. If we do we will strike for the Mouse without going back to the Mandan village," said the Pillager.

I asked for an explanation. He pointed to the two horsemen, now inside the double line of Minnetarees. I looked and recognised the head-dress of buffalo horns.

"Assiniboins!" I cried. "Why don't the Minnetarees kill them?"

"They came into the village. They can not be harmed. The Cheyennes are their deadly enemies. Knowing the Minnetarees are stronger to-day than the Cheyennes, they foolishly followed them out here. The Cheyennes want to kill them. The Minnetarees say they shall not be hurt. Instead of peace we may have a battle. If that happens we will ride for it."

Now the Minnetarees were returning, the two Assiniboins in their midst. The Cheyennes shouted furiously and gesticulated with their weapons as they demanded the surrender of the newcomers. Choke-cherry rode up to the Cheyenne chief and asked him to call his young men back. The chief offered ten of his best horses for the Assiniboins, and there was no logical reason—the dictates of humanity aside, of which the Minnetarees knew nothing—why the intruders should not have been given up. But according to the Indian reasoning the two were safe once they entered the village and so long as they remained in the village. As almost all the village had gone to visit the Cheyennes the Assiniboins followed our road and were held to be, theoretically, still in the village and entitled to protection.

It was a curious example of the power of custom. The Minnetarees were determined to protect the two hostile Indians even if it cost them the friendship of the Cheyennes. The men were finally brought well within our lines, thrust into a small tent and told to keep out of sight. Next followed an hour of vehement speech-making. At last the Cheyennes said they would get their chance later. Choke-cherry was nervous and uneasy and at once began preparing for the ceremony.

Miss Dearness became so deeply interested in the Assiniboins that I made some comment upon it. She replied:

"They were with those who drove us down here. They are spies. They came to learn if we were here, and when we are likely to go. Their main body is in hiding somewhere near."

"They must not go back to tell what they've learned," I said.

"Oh, not murder," she protested.

"Self-defence," I grimly qualified.

I turned to the Pillager and found him perfectly composed. He said he had known the moment he beheld the two, that their errand on the Knife concerned us.

I said to the girl:

"It's very simple. I'll get word to the Cheyennes to watch the two and bag them if they leave the village. Flat Mouth shall tell them, as he talks the sign language."

"But the war-party outside waiting to catch us?" she murmured.

"Flat Mouth shall tell of that, too. The Cheyennes shall go and drive them away."

I began to feel rather obliged to the two fellows for coming in and revealing the unsuspected danger.

So far as I could observe, the wrangling over the Assiniboins terminated without any obvious gain made by either side except that the Minnetarees kept the two Indians alive. With the dissension smoothed away, next came the ceremony of completing the treaty. The terms were simple and accepted by both tribes. The alliance was to wage war on the Sioux and their allies. Choke-cherry, by formally adopting a Cheyenne youth as his son, would be creating binding ties between the tribes. The Cheyennes, however, were reluctant to proceed with the business.

Flat Mouth got hold of a Mandan and learned the Cheyennes were angry that Le Borgne did not consider the treaty of enough importance to be present. It had only needed the incident of the Assiniboins to bring this resentment to the surface. The medicine tent was not up, nor had they formed a smaller ceremonial horseshoe of the white leather tents. After much arguing and oratory the medicine tent was finally erected.

Choke-cherry made a long-winded speech and called to him Two Crows, a Minnetaree chief, and gave to him the long pipe-stem he had so carefully guarded from being profaned by touching his horse. This stem was adorned with feathers, and Two Crows, in accepting it, danced grotesquely back and forth, while two young

Minnetarees beat on a drum and rattled antelope hoofs together.

After a certain amount of prancing came the ceremonial visit to the tent of the Cheyenne who was to be adopted. Choke-cherry tried to reason with him, but he would not come out of his sulks.

The situation was growing serious. Flat Mouth gained the side of the Cheyenne war-chief, who was sardonically watching Choke-cherry's embarrassment, and talked rapidly with one hand masked by his robe. Only the chief could read his talk, and, as he comprehended, his eyes darted fire. Striding to the young man he spoke in his ear, whereat the stem was accepted. Choke-cherry and Two Crows now took him by the arms and led him to the medicine-tent and seated him beside some new red strouds—coarse blankets. Choke-cherry sat on his right and Two Crows on his left. The musicians continued their efforts, and a figure danced in with the head of a buffalo on his shoulders, the nostrils and mouth of which were stuffed with dried grass. He placed the skull of a bull on the ground opposite the Cheyenne.

Now came the gift-making, and again the Cheyennes held back. Some of the Minnetarees brought ammunition and placed it on the strouds, and the Cheyenne held the stem over it. Two Crows rose and addressed the Cheyennes, urging them to bring something to put under the stem. After much waiting three warriors brought in a few robes and some dressed leather and piled them on the ammunition. This encouraged the Minnetarees, and they gave three guns. The Cheyennes came back with three poor ponies. Choke-cherry growled and grunted in great wrath, and his followers brought two more guns and some corn and beans. This resulted in another sore-backed nag from the visitors.

Then did Choke-cherry explode and demand what the Cheyennes meant by putting worthless creatures under the stem when the Minnetarees were giving good guns and powder and ball. The Cheyennes replied they would bring good horses when more guns were put under the stem.

Choke-cherry forgot diplomacy and roundly accused the Cheyennes of plotting to induce the Minnetarees to give up their weapons so that they might be helpless before an attack. This accusation of treachery was immediately followed by the Cheyennes hurrying back to the tents. We waited, thinking they were gone to bring more ponies. Then the warriors outside the medicine tent began calling out loudly, and we ran after Choke-cherry and Two Crows and beheld the Cheyennes striking their tents and preparing to ride off.

The young man who was to have been adopted galloped by us, riding one of the gift nags, leading the others and carrying the guns and ammunition. More than one bow was drawn taut as he flew by, but Choke-cherry, although convulsed with rage, knew better than to let war come while his brother was absent, and his stern commands, liberally mixed with mention of his brother's name, saved the young man's life.

The Cheyennes rode off in a body. The peace treaty had fallen through because of the Assiniboins. Yet the Minnetarees did not seem to attribute any blame to them and treated them kindly as we rode back to the village. Before arriving at the huts Choke-cherry turned toward the river, a mile away. On reaching it he directed Two Crows to bring a white buffalo hide. Flat Mouth explained to me and the girl that Choke-cherry feared he had handled the peace treaty badly and anticipated his brother's anger. To guard against this he now proposed to sacrifice a precious white robe. Such a hide, as I have remarked before, is the most highly valued by the Minnetarees of all their possessions. I could understand how the chief's brother was considerably worked up.

Two Crows came galloping back, not with a whole hide, for that was a liberality that even the gods had no right to expect, but a long strip. This seemed to answer perfectly, however, and was soon placed in a deep hole in the river and weighted down with rocks. Choke-cherry then made a long speech in which he said he knew what was to blame for the Cheyennes' behaviour, which he promised to duly report to his brother. Having done all he could to placate his gods, he morosely led the way home.

"You talked with the Cheyenne chief?" I murmured to Flat Mouth.

"He is Red Arrow, a brave warrior. He will wait three days to go with us to the Mouse."

"Why is he willing to do that?" I curiously asked.

"He knows I will pay him. He will make a good trade," was the evasive answer.

Choke-cherry halted at the first hut and, as we rode up, he glared at me viciously and shouted something. The Pillager interpreted——

"I know what stopped me from making peace with the Cheyennes."

"What was it?" I asked.

"Bad medicine."

"What was the medicine?" I knew what he would say before he spoke.

"The hair of the white woman," he grunted, switching his malignant gaze to Miss Dearness.

I warmly replied he was a fool and some other things, and that no treaty would be made with the Minnetarees when they took the Assiniboin snakes along with them.

"My brother is a very wise man. We shall see," he replied as he rode away.

The girl had interpreted his look and had heard Flat Mouth's Chippewa translation, and her hand was cold as ice as she rode closer and placed it on mine and whispered——

"It all comes back—my fear."

"Don't you worry a bit," I soothed. "We'll get out of here flying inside of twelve hours."

In my heart, however, a deadly chill was growing.

It was now dusk, and after leaving our ponies at the corral, I escorted Miss Dearness to the hut and lighted some bark in the fire-hole to drive away the gloom. Then I told her that we had better remain where we were until morning as the ride down the river would be dangerous. Surrounding the village were innumerable pits, eight feet or more deep, which the women filled with corn and beans each fall. These were all open, and to get clear of the place at night was to risk a broken leg or neck.

"But we must get away to-night," she fiercely insisted. "Any danger but this." She waved her hand to encompass the whole village. "You heard what he said about my medicine spoiling the treaty. I care nothing for that, but there is another danger. Oh, Mr. Franklin, you've been very good and patient with me —but get me out of here to-night!"

"Very well, we'll go to-night, but we can't return to the Mandans. We must risk crossing the Missouri at the mouth of the Knife and striking north-east. If we waited until to-morrow and started from the Mandans we might find a band of Cheyennes waiting to act as escort. The chief told the Pillager he would see us to the Mouse."

"I'd rather start from here to-night and travel alone than wait any longer," she said. "Perhaps Flat Mouth could swing to one side and pick up the Cheyennes. If not, then a ride for it, and a clean, quick death at the worst."

"There must be no talk of death," I rebuked. "We'll go and get through. I was only thinking of the difficulties in getting the horses across the Missouri, but with a bull-boat we ought to be able to tow them over, one at a time. Rest easy while I go and find the Pillager and arrange for him to get the horses from the corral."

I had passed through the door, closed it, and had heard the heavy bar drop across it, when a terrific screech rang out a few huts away and in the direction of the river. The cry was caught up and repeated. I stood undecided, my thumb resting on the hammer of my gun. The door opened back of me and she was beside me, a hand resting on my shoulder, her head tilted as she sought to read my face in the darkness. The village was now in an uproar.

"The Cheyennes must be attacking in force," I muttered.

"It's something very serious," she whispered. "Do you think you can manage to get the horses up here?"

"Stay inside! Let no one in," I said, stepping out and blundering between the huts, where the path in places was only a foot in width.

I passed between two huts and bumped into an Indian. His hands struck my chest to push me aside. Then the Pillager's voice was whispering—

"So it is you. I knew the cloth."

"What is the trouble? You've been running?"

The last deduction was not because his breathing was beyond normal, but because in clutching his wrists I felt his pulse racing.

"The Assiniboin spies will not go back to tell what they saw here," he hissed in my ear.

"Good God! You've killed them?" I muttered.

"Killed both. I promised the Cheyenne chief their scalps if he would give us warriors to go with us to the Mouse. I told you he would make a good trade."

"But they'll be after you!" I softly cried.

"Choke-cherry thinks the Cheyennes crept in and did it."

"It won't do for you to be seen. It might make them suspicious. Don't tell the white woman. Stand in front of the hut. I will bring up the horses. We must cross the Missouri at the mouth of the Knife and ride for it."

"The Cheyennes will be waiting near the Mandan village," he protested.

"And it's impossible to go down the river. We would lose too much time. If the Minnetarees chase us they will take that direction."

"Ho! Eshkebugecoshe, Chief of the Pillager

Chippewas, needs no help in saving the white woman except the white woman's medicine.''

He thumped his breast and might have broken into song if I had not quieted him.

I set off, making my way toward the centre of the pandemonium which seemed to focus around the corral. Lights were now springing up in the open places, the naked children dancing and piling on fuel and looking like so many devil's whelps.

Before I reached the corral the village was well illumined. I met Choke-cherry, who bawled out something I could not have understood even if I knew his language. But as he carried a gun and had his mouth stuffed with balls, I assumed he was expecting an attack from the Cheyennes. He caught my arm and led me to the door of a hut and ordered the mob to stand one side. As the command was obeyed I looked down a narrow lane of humanity and beheld the two Assiniboins. They had been killed with a knife, and both were scalped.

I slashed my fingers across my wrist, the sign for the Cheyennes, and he nodded. He stopped to harangue the crowd and I worked clear of the shambles and hurried on to the corral.

I reached the corral and was startled to behold a line of mounted men riding down a slight rise and toward me, being well within the light of the many fires. Although they were continually descending the rise, the head of the line never reached the corral. I watched for a minute, greatly puzzled. Then a stentorian voice rose with such tremendous volume as to carry a great distance. It was repeated several times and was answered from the centre of the village. In another moment several Indians came running by the corral, one of them swinging a torch. I recognised Choke-cherry and the Pillager in the group.

I called out to him and I knew he heard me, yet he kept on with the others to find the man with the loud voice. Knowing he would return when he had finished his errand, I proceeded to pick out our animals. As

I led them out of the enclosure a warrior caught my arm and pointed interrogatively at the nags. I pointed out toward the open plain and then made the sign for Cheyenne and indicated I was taking the horses into a hut. He nodded and hurried on. I started to lead them away and a hand fell on my shoulder, and the Pillager was wrenching the halter ropes from my hands and hurriedly driving the ponies back into the corral.

"Why do you do that?" I demanded.

"Bad medicine at work," he gloomily answered. "Le Borgne comes back from the hunt. Did you not hear his voice? When he heard the noise in the village he knew something was wrong and has thrown a hundred of his hunters around the village with orders to shoot any one trying to leave it. We must stay."

Without a word I followed him back through the excited throngs. Some perverse agency seemed to be thwarting us. Something of the girl's strange fear began to assail me. It was not Le Borgne, for a ball from my double-barrel would nicely eliminate him. It was, rather, that the whole village stood for ruthless and brutal domination throught physical strength. When I came to the hut, tapped on the door, and gave my name, I was confronting the hardest task I had ever encountered.

CHAPTER X

LE BORGNE PLANS A FEAST

I HAVE met many savage chiefs, but none who ranked with Le Borgne for brutality, implacable will power and wisdom.

Despite his high quality of courage and eminent capacity for leadership, he was, from the white man's point of view, bestial with his women. They were his chattels and of no more account than his dogs. If he were so inclined he would murder them, and no one dared question the act. He had slain more than one of his wives. He went even further and appropriated any matron or maid that took his fancy, and this without protest from husband or parent, an acquiescence I never found in any other Indian community.

I knew much of his character by reputation and from the Pillager's gossip. What details of his grim history I lacked I soon learned during my stay in the village.

Choke-cherry brought the word in the morning that Flat Mouth and I were wanted by the chief. The Pillager, to make himself fit for the audience, strung his Sioux scalps round his neck and went naked except for his breech-clout. We left our weapons in the hut with Miss Dearness, except that Flat Mouth concealed a small knife in his clout. I counted the scalps on his chest and was relieved to find he carried only the Sioux's hair. I asked him in Chippewa, as we stood one side, what he had done with the Assiniboin scalps, but he smiled and said nothing.

Miss Dearness bore herself well, although she had passed a miserable night pacing the hut and making, as her woman attendant fully believed, some very powerful medicine. Flat Mouth and I had found quarters in a hut near-by and had joined the girl with the first light. Now that she knew we were to meet Le Borgne she was deeply troubled. Old Choke-cherry never would have surmised it as she paced from one side of the big hut to the other, her hair towering in a fiery mass above her proud head.

"I send good thoughts with you," she murmured after following us to the door.

"You have all of ours," I assured her. "Don't be afraid. If an American can't help an English girl he must have very weak medicine."

Flat Mouth caught the last word and gravely told her:

"The white woman's medicine makes me feel very strong. I can throw a buffalo bull when her eyes watch me."

She forced a smile and we left her.

On entering Le Borgne's hut Choke-cherry accompanied us only to the door. We found the chief seated at the left and facing the fire-hole, gravely contemplating his medicine-log. He sat on a couch raised a foot from the floor by willow mats and several heavy robes. On the cottonwood log before him stood two skulls of buffalo bulls, decorated with red earth. These were his greatest treasures, personifying his *manito*. Behind the log hung his weapons of war and the chase, and the trophies of battles, such as scalps.

He was alone, having cleared the hut of his women in anticipation of our coming. He turned his head as we entered and I was hard put to maintain my composure, for over his sightless right eye was a white patch. He continued swinging his head, and in the boring gaze of his left optic I found enough fire to more than make up for his half-sight. Like all the Minnetarees he had an extraordinary beak for a nose. His big mouth was further widened by a habitual grin, his permanent expression. When he was pleased he grinned. When he was consumed with rage he continued to grin.

That Choke-cherry stood in fear of him was shown by the fashion in which the old rascal poked his head inside the door to see if anything was wanted and then ducked back. I stood in advance of Flat Mouth. Le Borgne's first words to me were—

"Ho! I like white men."

The Pillager interpreted this over my shoulder. Le Borgne's lips writhed and twisted over his big teeth as he sought to give his smile an amiable cast. From his medicine log he took a long-stemmed, redstone pipe and filled it with Missouri tobacco. Lighting the stuff, he took a whiff and puffed it towards the heavens and passed the pipe to me and motioned for me to sit beside him. Flat Mouth squatted on his heels beside me to translate the chief's words. Our host began—

"I like white men. They bring me goods. We trade with the Spaniards through the Cheyennes and southern tribes when we are not at war with them. They say you come from a big white chief on the Assiniboin, who is to send traders here."

"We come to make the road smooth for our traders, who will bring many goods and guns," I replied.

"They say the daughter of the big chief comes with you. They say she comes to be my wife."

With an effort I controlled my voice, making it careless in tone as I responded:

"The white woman is a medicine woman. She cannot marry. If she did marry her medicine would kill her and her husband."

His brows drew down as he cogitated this, but his smile continued. Being on his right side it was necessary for him to turn his head to look at me. The effect was curious when the white patch slowly moved to one side to allow his sound eye to study me. Without commenting on my disclosure he said:

"They say your Chippewa is a very brave man and will live with my people. He has been here once before. We did not know then he was such a great warrior."

The Pillager spoke up haughtily, announcing:

"Eshkebugecoshe, the Sioux Killer, has driven all the enemies away from the land of his people and now looks round for a brave people who need him in making war. They must be very brave. They must be at war with the Sioux. I come here with the medicine woman. After I have gone with her to her father I will come back and see if the Minnetarees are good fighters."

He fingered his necklace of scalps lovingly and stared boldly into the smiling face of Le Borgne.

The Minnetaree gazed at him fixedly for some time, possibly speculating on the advantage and disadvantage of having such a pronounced fighter in his village. Shifting his gaze back to me he asked—

"You are *Bosheittochresha* (men who bring black cloth—English)?"

"*Manceechteet* (long knife—American)," I corrected.

"You work for the English?"

"I work for the big chief, father of the white medicine woman," I replied.

"Your people are cowards."

"They are the bravest of the brave. They can come out here and eat you up."

He laughed aloud and mocked—

"And yet you work for the English."

"Because they want very brave men. The chief of the Pillager Chippewas works for me. Why? Because I need a very brave man."

He ceased laughing aloud and pondered over my words, seeming to find them logical, for he nodded his head slowly as if in endorsement. Then he abruptly demanded—

"Is she your woman?"

"She is no man's woman. She can be no man's woman."

"Why is she with you if she is not your woman?"

"Her medicine helps me make good trades for her father."

"Why does she come here if not to be my woman?" he puzzled, his grin now quite ghastly.

"Her medicine made my road smooth in coming here. The northern Indians knew her and run away when she is angry. The Sioux grow blind when they see her hair."

This engaged him in thought for some minutes, for, although one of the greatest of the plains Indians, he was yet a savage and a victim of his superstitions.

"Is her medicine stronger than my *manito*?" he asked, nodding at the buffalo heads.

"Much stronger," I promptly assured. "If she wanted to become your wife your *manito* would be jealous. Your *manito* would fight with her medicine and would be killed. You would die when your *manito* died."

Again he was silent, his one eye focused on the two skulls. Then he threw up his head and said:

"Let us see this mighty white woman."

He called out and Choke-cherry bounced in, his fat face alive with fear. The chief ordered him to go and bring Miss Dearness.

I affected a composure I was far from feeling. Flat Mouth's hand rested on his hip near the little knife hidden in his clout, while the war-fires sprang up in his small eyes. While we waited, Le Borgne ended the silence by saying:

"I lost a wife while on the hunt. She was young and good to look at."

"She died of the bad cough?" I politely inquired, knowing many of the Indians were suffering from it.

He shook his head and the terrible grin widened and showed his teeth far back.

"She is not dead yet," he said. I was nonplussed, and was searching for some intelligent observation when he enlightened me a bit by adding, "She went to live with a young man."

I decided from his low chuckling that he accepted her infidelity very philosophically. He remarked:

"I look about for another woman to take her place.

They say the white woman is not like any woman ever seen in the Indian's country."

Flat Mouth's hand touched my arm, but I had already heard the sound of a light foot at the door. Choke-cherry threw the door open, and the girl entered. Her sleepless night had left an unusual pallor on her face. She wore her capote like a hood and looked like a nun as she advanced. I rose and stood beside her.

Le Borgne turned his head, tilted it and for fully a minute glared into her white face, his grin tightening and growing more wolfish. She met his gaze steadily, staring at him as though she were looking through him and not at him. With a snap of his strong teeth he muttered:

"She is very white. I never saw one like her. I never knew women like her lived. Where is her medicine hair?"

As the Pillager interpreted the girl hesitated, then catching my side glance she threw back her capote and allowed the glory of her hair to show. A shaft of sunlight from the small window opening back of the chief intensified the effect. Le Borgne dropped his redstone pipe. Although he still grinned, his big mouth was agape as he looked. Rising to his full six feet he slowly approached her. She did not wince nor move, and red and white fought the ancient battle of lust and denial for twice sixty seconds. Then the chief gingerly extended his fingers to touch her hair where the sunlight made it spun-gold. Her eyes narrowed ominously. I darted out my left foot and disturbed the balance of one of the buffalo heads. The noise caused the chief to turn in time to see the skull gently rocking. I was staring at the girl as if oblivious to the phenomenon. He drew back his hand and rubbed his chin, studying the skull. Plainly his *manito* was jealous and was warning him to keep his hands from the strange woman. He glanced from the painted skull to the blazing eyes and sun-crowned head of the girl. Then he retreated to his robes, picked up his pipe and summoned Choke-cherry. When his brother entered Le Borgne gave him an order that caused Flat Mouth to frown.

Addressing Miss Dearness in Chippewa the Pillager said:

"He says for you to go. He said something in another tongue I did not understand."

"I have my knife," she murmured.

"You are perfectly safe," I spoke up in English. "The Pillager and I are still here. We will take you away very soon. Remember, you must not show any fear."

Her head went high, and she gave me a smile as she bowed to Le Borgne and followed the waiting Choke-cherry. Le Borgne forgot his pipe in staring after her; then he asked me—

"Why do you come here and bring no presents?"

"The white woman's father will send many presents. He said it was foolish for me to bother with a few. We were told to come and ask you to tell where our trader is to live. Then we were to return very quick. The Cheyennes are better robe-makers than the Minnetarees, as they use beads and porcupine-quills, but they are south of the Missouri and the white chief does not want to go below the river."

"No trade can cross this part of the Missouri unless I say it can," informed Le Borgne. "The Cheyennes are bad. They would not put presents under the stem and make peace with us. I will carry the pipe against them soon. I will call a council of my old men and give you an answer about your trader."

He rose to terminate the interview.

"We are in great haste to go back. Can the council be held to-day?" I asked.

"Soon—to-day—another day—sometime."

It was useless to seek to improve this most unsatis-factory reply. Rugged and conscienceless, inexorable in moods; thoroughly self-dependent because of his brute strength, the man typified the muddy river which

was even now carving new channels for itself and clawing banks and cottonwoods into its swollen waters. Just
as the very country seemed to possess a savage personality unlike the Red River country, so did this savage
despot differ widely from our northern chiefs. When
he stood up to dismiss us I supposed his act was a bit
of perfunctory courtesy.   Not so, nor would it have
been in keeping with his egotism. He proposed to walk
with us and, as we set forth, he picked up a heavy war-
axe and idly swung it by its rawhide thong.

The Pillager glanced at the axe and shifted to the
man's blind side, and I noted my friend carried one
hand gracefully on his hip, near the haft of the hidden
knife. Walking thus between us he kept up a running
fire of comments upon the white men whom he said he
loved as brothers and added some mild criticism of the
absent H. B. agent, at the Mandan village, whom we
were to oppose, but never once did he refer to Miss
Dearness. I grew uneasy, thinking he intended to proceed to the guest hut. Did he do that I should look for
his savage whim to prompt him peremptorily to demand
possession of the girl. To my great relief he halted
when some distance from the hut, and, stepping aside
to a porch, informed—

"The wife I lost is in here."

He did not request us to tarry, but as we walked on
we glanced back. He stood in the doorway, loudly
calling his woman by name. She did not appear and
he entered the hut. We halted and saw him emerge,
dragging a woman after him. Wearing the same grin
and moving as deliberately as if lighting his pipe he
struck the poor creature over the head with his axe,
and she fell lifeless in front of the hut of her lover.
Then, swinging his axe by the thong, the chief calmly
walked back to his hut, with never a backward glance
at the pitiable shape he had murdered.

"—— him!" I whispered, weak and sick.

"He is very bad," grunted the Pillager, his fingers
twitching nervously at his girdle in search of the axe he

had left beside my gun. Had he found it, I have no doubt but that either the Minnetarees or the Pillager Chippewas would have lost a great warrior. In a minute he had a grip on himself and was stoically saying—

"We have the white woman to think about."

For the first time, I observed, we were left undisturbed. No children swarmed about us with their impish tricks and amateur larcenies. No dogs rushed out to mangle us. We had Le Borgne to thank for this much. Even though he murdered a woman, he was invariably hospitable to white men.

As we passed the hut where the two Assiniboins had died I asked about them, and Flat Mouth said they had been secretly buried in one of the empty corn-cellars. The village as a unit took it for granted the Cheyennes had sneaked in and killed them. It was hoped to keep the news of their death from their tribe until Le Borgne could bring about a peace with the Cheyennes, or call in a large war-party of his old allies, the Crows.

"The knife they found by the bodies was a Cheyenne knife," gravely added the Pillager.

"I saw you talk with the Cheyenne chief, but I did not see him give you the knife," I said.

"He is a very brave man. His brother is a medicine man who knows much magic. When we leave the village for the Red River I will stretch their hair on hoops."

"Throw them away!" I urged. "If they should be found we will all be killed."

"I have promised them to the Cheyennes. A Pillager chief does not keep the hair of dogs, but to throw them away now would show I was afraid. That would spoil my medicine. I will make old Tabashaw grunt when I sing my new song."

The scalps were another danger added to our list. Did the Minnetarees so much as suspect the Pillager was the slayer there would be no mercy shown him. Even a Sioux was safe if he succeeded in entering the village.

What happened to him when he started for home was another matter. However, it was useless to argue with the Pillager. As profitable to ask a fanatic to forsake his religion as to expect an Indian to do what he believed would spoil his medicine.

"We must get away to-night," I said.

"Le Borgne said something to Caltahcota in the Crow tongue. I could not understand it," mused Flat Mouth, halting and staring toward the river.

"What has that to do with our getting away to-night?"

"Who knows? My *manito*? If so he has not told me. Perhaps the Medicine Hair knows. The buffalo head in Le Borgne's hut could tell if our ears could hear."

His words made me uneasy. I pressed him to speak more literally, but he persisted in remaining silent. He had strong doubts as to our immediate departure. Le Borgne's aside to Choke-cherry, spoken in the Crow tongue, was behind his doubts, although he had not caught the war-chief's words. I decided I did not need to walk farther and turned back to the village. A group of men approached and turned aside in a desire to avoid us. One of them I recognised as being prominent in the fiasco at the Cheyenne camp. I asked Flat Mouth to name him.

"He is Aharattanamokshe, or Chief of the Wolves, the oldest son of Caltahcota."

"Speak to him Let us learn how the tribe feels toward us. If Le Borgne feels friendly, his men will show it."

Flat Mouth greeted the young man pleasantly and asked some questions. Chief of the Wolves stared enviously at the scalps on the Pillager's breast and was very respectful in his attitude as he replied to the queries. After an exchange of a few sentences the warrior turned back to his companions while we resumed our walk to the village.

"I asked him if the men went to swim," explained

Flat Mouth. "He said the Minnetarees are such great swimmers they will go to the Missouri and not to the Knife when they wish to swim. Then he told me they went to look for willows and small cottonwoods."

"You should have asked him if the people think the white woman's medicine had anything to do with the Cheyennes' refusing the treaty, and if he said 'yes,' you should have told him it was a lie. Choke-cherry has told his brother the white woman is to blame for the Cheyennes' riding away."

"They go to find willows and small cottonwoods strong enough to use in making a new hut," said Flat Mouth.

"That is stuff for women and children to listen to," I said.

"There is much to be found out when they talk of making a new hut," said the Pillager. "Who is to live in it?"

I waited and as he kept silent I was forced to ask:

"Well, what did you find out? Who is to live in it?"

"They did not say. But no new people have come to the village except a white man, a brave Pillager Chippewa and a mighty medicine woman."

"By heavens! They build the hut for us. They expect us to stay here!" I cried in English.

My emotion gave him his cue, rather than any knowledge of English, although he was able to pick up words here and there.

"They let men sleep in the big hut or where they will," he said. "A new hut means a new wife for a big chief. I have said it. Let the white woman use her medicine now if she would go back to the Red River."

His frankness left me nonplussed and frightened. I rallied finally and managed to make light of the warning. Le Borgne was a wise man. If his Indian nature would permit him to defy the medicine of the girl—and this I could scarcely believe—his astuteness would restrain him from killing what he believed was a chance for a permanent post in the village. The great advantage of having an N. W. trader constantly supplying him with arms and ammunition would greatly outweigh his lust for a woman, whether she be red or white. War came first; women next. I spoke this aloud and told it over to myself. The Pillager listened and watched me closely. Then he spoke, his words exploding all my false hopes:

"Le Borgne is not like other Indians. He has his own way more than other chiefs. He thinks his *manito* is very strong—stronger than any other *manito*, for has he not always had his own way? When he wants anything he is like a child; he wants it and can think of nothing else. He killed a woman before our eyes. Many chiefs would be afraid her people might try to wash out her death with his blood. But he wanted to kill her; he could think of only that.

"He believes the white woman's medicine is strong, but he believes his is stronger. If he takes her to a new hut as his woman he will show that his *manito* is stronger. Then he will boast he has tamed her medicine and that it will work for him. With the two medicines working for him he will believe the big white chief we have told about will be glad to build a post here."

"I'll shoot him before he shall take the woman!" I gritted.

"I am chief of the Pillagers. It is my right to wear two eagle feathers in my hair for every enemy I have scalped in battle. It is through me the white woman's medicine will work," he haughtily retorted.

We talked no more but hurried back to the guest-hut, for I was foolish enough to think my presence might protect her. The door was open, which surprised me, as Miss Dearness was quick to close it when we went out. We entered and I called her name. Our two guns and ammunition stood where we had left them but the girl was gone. That she should attempt to walk about the village was unthinkable. I snatched up the gun, made sure it was loaded, and would have dashed out had not Flat Mouth seized me by the arm and cautioned:

"Walk softly. Wait for me."

He slipped on his robe, slung his bow and arrows over his shoulder and picked up his gun. Then he circled the hut and spent some moments at the skin couch before the fire-hole.

"We kill much time," I impatiently warned.

"Is this medicine talk for you?" he called back.

I joined him and he pointed to some words scrawled with a charred stick on the rocks forming the rim of the fire-hole. The message read:

"They take me to another hut, they say. Find me, American."

I read it to Flat Mouth, who was highly pleased with this proof of the girl's power to communicate with me. But when I would have commenced a precipitate search he restrained me, saying:

"We shall get an axe stuck in our heads. The white woman will be left with her medicine to fight alone. It is no time to run like a badger after game. We must be the fox. Le Borgne will kill us if we hurry."

He stood before me, his powerful form blocking my path until I had regained an appearance of composure. Then, nodding in approval, he stepped aside for me to pass. As we reached the door I paused and filled and lighted my pipe to show my lack of concern. This was well played, as Flat Mouth quietly informed me two men, spies, were watching us from the porch of the next hut. By an effort I forced myself to laugh, and the grim features of the Pillager took on a smile. We sauntered carelessly from the hut, the Pillager murmuring:

"She is still in the village. Le Borgne would place her in his brother's hut, I think."

This was logical, and in a roundabout way we finally arrived at Choke-cherry's abode. The old villain was seated on the porch, puffing mightily to make his Missouri weed burn in his long pipe. Several of his women were removing some earthen pots and copper kettles to the next hut. I expressed concern for his difficulty in getting a smoke and generously gave him an inch of tobacco and waited for him to fill and light up. Flat Mouth touched my elbow. I turned and, under a pretext of addressing him, observed the direction of his staring gaze. He was looking intently at the wall of the hut. Taking my time, I discovered a piece of bark hanging on the wall. On it was writing.

To Choke-Cherry, through the Pillager, I said—
"Where did you get the medicine that drives evil spirits away?" And I stepped closer to the writing.

Between puffs the old reprobate proudly said:
"It is very big medicine. It will bring me many ponies. It will keep the spotted sickness (small-pox) from my hut."

I scarcely heard the Pillager's translation, for I was reading:

"I know the worst. It shall never happen. The woman tells me in the sign language there is to be a big feast in two days. Don't run any risks for me. You have done too much already. I am very brave. It will not be hard."

"A very good medicine," I said, stepping back and feeling the cold sweat standing on my forehead. "But it is the woman part of the medicine. There is a man part that makes it whole. I will give you the man part because you are the brother of the mighty chief and will open his ears to what I say about a trading post here."

While the Pillager told him this, I picked up a bit of charcoal from a dead fire and rapidly wrote:

"It shall not happen. Be ready to-night. We can do nothing in the daytime. If not to-night, then to-morrow night. Remember, it shall not happen."

Then to the deeply interested Choke-cherry I explained:

"The medicine is now whole. When the sun is overhead take it inside and hang it over the place for medicine."

As it was near noon I knew the girl would soon see it. I had not ventured to call out to the girl and address her, as her writing hinted at a command for silence from Le Borgne.

We leisurely continued our stroll until we were at the hut of the chief. Like his brother he was outside enjoying the sun, his one eye gleaming evilly. The Pillager and I stood our guns against the upright of the long platform, now loaded with driftwood, and I greeted the chief with an amiable smile and produced my tobacco. Taking his pipe I filled and lighted it and sent a puff towards the heavens. Handing it to him and recharging my own, I said—

"When the white man's post is here the greatest of all war chiefs will smoke good tobacco all the time."

He sucked in the smoke with huge content, but eyed me suspiciously for a moment. Turning his head aside so only the dead eye showed, he remarked:

"The white woman asked for a new hut. She said her medicine was cold where she was. My men will build her a new hut. Until it is ready she will live in the hut of my brother, Caltahcota, who has moved his wives and children to another hut."

"The big white chief will thank you with many presents for your kindness to his daughter," I warmly assured. "His friends told him to build his post among the Sioux, but the woman's medicine told him to build it here. The post will make the Minnetarees the greatest and strongest of all Indians so long as they do not wrong the white chief."

"I will brain the man or woman who touches his goods," declared Le Borgne, toying with the axe he had so recently used in murdering the woman.

"He will come soon with many white men and many guns," I added.

"Why does he bring many men and many guns when he comes to his friends?" asked Le Borgne, jerking his head about to bring his one eye to bear upon me.

"Because he brings many presents and much goods, and knows the Assiniboins would kill and rob a small party."

The chief smiled and frowned, his one eye glowing like a demon's.

"The Assiniboins are dogs," he softly muttered. "Two were killed by Cheyennes in this village last night. The Cheyennes are very brave men. They have fine horses. My brother was a fool not to make peace with them. He says the medicine of the white woman spoiled the peace."

"He lies. He was afraid his brother, the big war chief, would be angry with him for his foolishness. He tries to blame it on the woman."

He did not resent my blunt characterisation of his brother and continued—

"He was a fool to hold the Assiniboins when they came to the camp. They had come to the village and left it. After they left it any one could kill them. They are dogs. My brother should have taken the ten ponies for them. I have offered a wife, three horses and a hundred skins for one of their ponies, and they would not trade."

"If the white woman's medicine is not made angry, it can get you many Cheyenne ponies," I said. "I will see her and talk about it."

"She says she wants to be alone," he replied, swinging his left eye about and darting a challenge at me.

"If she says it, it is so. Those who make her medicine angry will surely follow the broad trail to the west, where stand the many huts of the dead."

"She asks to be my woman," he announced, his right hand dropping on the handle of the big axe.

"If she asks it, it is good," I managed to reply; but

only the fact that my gun was beyond my reach prevented me from blowing the devil's head off. "But if you take her for a wife and her medicine says 'No!' then the Minnetarees will name a new war-chief in your place."

"Ho!" he rumbled, rising and folding his muscular arms across his broad chest. "A medicine man tells me my *manito* is stronger than hers. It shall be a fight between them. If my *manito* is a liar, or a coward, or weak, he will be whipped. But while they fight I will have the woman, a mystery woman, a woman with hair like red fires."

As the Pillager interpreted this, it was only his bearing that sobered me and kept me from insanely jumping for my gun. His cold face showed the utmost unconcern. After he'd finished repeating the chief's boast he stepped close to Le Borgne and taunted—

"Fool! An evil spirit draws you to your death and you do not know it. I, chief of the Pillager Chippewas, wearer of many eagle feathers for the men I have scalped in battle, say it. An evil spirit, sent by the Sioux's great *manito*, tells you to take the white woman. So be it."

Le Borgne's smile twisted his lips convulsively, and for a moment I believed he was to grapple with my friend. But Flat Mouth's boldness appealed to him. The warning about the Sioux *manito* laying an ambush and baiting him with the girl also registered deeply.

"You are a brave man," he said to the Pillager, "or you would be a dead man under my axe. I love brave men even when they are my enemies."

"I am not your enemy. I tell you the truth. That makes me your friend," said Flat Mouth.

"You shall stay to the feast I give after two sleeps. Then you must go away, for the Minnetaree village is too small for two brave men. The white man may stay, but you must go."

"And be followed by your warriors who will try to

kill me after I get away from the village," sneered Flat Mouth.

"No!" passionately cried Le Borgne, and I was convinced he spoke sincerely. "Le Borgne, the Blind, will never wish to kill the Sioux Killer. Go and kill more of our enemies. After another snow come to me and smoke some of the trader's tobacco. To-day there is a little cloud over the sun. Sometime it will go away and we shall feel warm towards each other."

We left him, having learned for a certainty how much time we had to work in. On the surface the case seemed hopeless. The girl was isolated and not permitted to see us. We might kill the chief and a few others, but we could not expect to fight our way clear of the village. The Pillager would consider it an ideal exit to go to his happy hunting-grounds in defence of the girl's medicine. We were three sentenced to death, and death it must be after two sleeps, unless a miracle rescued us.

As we skirted the village and gave ourselves to thought, I found death to be very impersonal. It meant nothing to me beyond a keen disappointment. There were so many things I had intended to experiment in and to accomplish before I died. The adventure had opened up a desire to know more about the girl. Destiny had purposed that I should succeed, else why had she come into my life? Then there was my disappearance from the Pembina post. Would the truth ever be known, or would the gentlemen of the North write me down as a deserter? Would any thieving on Black Chabot's part be blamed on me? Altogether, an abrupt finish would leave many loose ends which an orderly fate would have gathered up. The grim irony of it all, that I, a Northman, should perish by the ferocious fancy of a savage chief.

"My friend's face should be filled with sunshine," grunted Flat Mouth reproachfully.

I simulated a genial expression and looked up to find the reason for his warning. Chief of the Wolves and his friends were returning from the river, and with them rode an Indian on a pony whose appearance testified to rough and fast travel. He was the centre of the group and the target for many queries. As they draw abreast of us, the horseman noticed Flat Mouth and stared at him and his string of scalps and talked hurriedly with Chief of the Wolves. Then he jumped from his pony and ran to us seizing the Pillager's hand and shaking it warmly, crying:

"They say you are the Chippewa chief who killed the Sioux. They say the scalps you wear came from Sioux heads. Your name is heard throughout the Sioux country. The Sioux chiefs call you a great warrior and make medicine to get your skull as a drinking-dish. I, White Snake, a Minnetaree and their prisoner, heard them tell these things."

"I am a mighty warrior," readily agreed Flat Mouth. "The Snake's medicine was strong to help him get away."

"I have been with them for many moons. I went to hunt buffalo with them. Then runners came with stories of what they had seen. The hunting party broke up, and I got away."

Chief of the Wolves now impatiently reminded:

"My uncle, the Blind, is waiting for you to bring him a talk. It is not good to keep him waiting."

"The White Snake brings good news?" asked Flat Mouth, as the escaped warrior turned to mount his pony.

"Strangers come. It is good or bad," retorted the Snake. "My medicine let me get away while the Sioux were riding to meet the strangers. If they are friends of the Sioux they will come here to kill us."

Chief of the Wolves ran ahead and looked back, and the Snake remembered it was not good to keep Le Borgne waiting. The Pillager and I ruminated over the man's story. There did not seem to be much to it. The Sioux were much excited over some strangers. The Snake had failed to reveal who, or what, they were. My first thought was of some formidable war-party from the far south. Flat Mouth disagreed with me, insisting the Snake had said nothing to suggest fear or warlike preparations on the part of the Sioux. If it had been a war-party the scouts would have brought word to that effect. After we had argued it back and forth without getting anywhere he dismissed it by simply stating—

"It is the medicine of the white woman working to let her go free."

Such was his faith in the girl's powers that his black eyes glittered with hope and he walked with a springy, confident step. He had thrown aside all cares and worries. Being an Indian, it was good logic, for what is the use in believing in medicine and good-luck if your faith fails to help in an emergency? Only I did not possess the Pillager's child-like trust. We two men were the chosen instruments for liberating Miss Dearness. Her medicine was as strong and resourceful as we were, and we were helpless.

"Eshkebugecoshe, there is but one way. I will go to Le Borgne's hut to-night. While I am there you must get the girl from the hut, take her to the corral, get ponies and ride north to the Missouri."

He promptly shook his head in refusal.

"Where will my white brother be if I do get the girl away?"

"I will follow you."

"The trail you will follow will lead far from the Missouri. Even if I, chief of the Pillagers, could do this thing, the Medicine Hair would not. It is poor medicine you plan to make. The white woman's *manito* is strong enough to let us all get away. We will wait. The feast is not for two sleeps. Many things can happen in two sleeps."

His optimism did not cool off the little hell in which I lived. Desperation often begets a ferocious courage. Then there is such a thing as finding great relief in learning the worst. I was impatient to have the climax over with. I wanted to take my double-barrel gun and make an end of the situation by sending a heavy buffalo charge through Le Borgne's head. A new situation would instantly bob up, but it would have the virtue of being different from the present horror. Flat Mouth slipped his arm through mine, as if fearing I might race off and do something rash. As he induced me to walk back to the village, he talked softly, saying—

"If her medicine grows weak we will go down like brave men, taking her with us. To strike now would be as foolish as to lay an ambush and then shoot at the first warrior to approach it, instead of waiting till the game was well trapped. Wait! My *manito* whispers that many things will happen if we wait. Would Le Borgne sell the white woman?"

"We have nothing to trade," I sullenly reminded. "He wants guns, but we have none. He is bad."

"He is a great warrior. He wants the white woman for his wife. Why shouldn't he? My white brother would take her as his wife if he could."

Had he struck me in the face I could not have been more startled, for his confident assertion instantly set strange fancies in motion. I pictured a home-loving woman, busy with domestic tasks, wearing the wonderful hair of Miss Dearness and glorified by the happiness of wifehood. The contrast between this picture and her probable fate was appalling. I strove in vain to dismiss it.

During all our perils no sentiment had had time to lodge with me. Each hour had brought new hardships and dangers, and we were rushed from one dilemma to another with the stage ever set with climaxes. It was grotesque that now, in the supreme peril, I should hark back to the tantalising mood which was responsible for my seeking her up the river. Her manner of caressing my hand had not encouraged soft thoughts. It was simply her way of thanking me. From the beginning it had been difficult to imagine her in the rôle of a sweetheart, although her peril accentuated her womanliness.

"Buy her from Le Borgne," continued Flat Mouth, ignorant of the turmoil he had stirred up within me.

"With what?" I angrily countered.

"The white robes. They are very big medicine with the Minnetarees. Even Le Borgne does not own five such as you have, down in the Mandan hut. The skin of the calf is worth more than the big robes to these Indians. They believe a white calf-skin is mighty medicine."

Here was the nucleus of an idea. In the white robes and calfskin I held a value equivalent to many hundreds of skins—to many ponies.

But no one could ever foresee what Le Borgne would do. His tenacity of purpose, especially in his lusts, would not stay him from murdering a kinsman, if such a homicide be necessary to his gaining the woman he fancied. Still it was an idea.

"Ride to the Mandan village and bring the robes. See they are wrapped securely so no one will know what they are," I commanded as we entered the village near the corral.

"Little birds sing in my ears and tell me our medicine is making," said the Pillager as he brought his pony from the corral.

Some Indians gathered around us, and Le Borgne strode through the group, his one eye gleaming questions, his wide mouth twisted sardonically.

"The great chief of the Chippewas goes out to kill more Sioux?" he asked.

"He is tired of staying penned up in the village," gravely replied the Pillager. "He will ride out and look for signs of an enemy war-path. The Pillager Chippewas never wait for their enemies to come to them."

Le Borgne's smile persisted, but there was murder in his eye as he caught this taunt. Speaking very low he said:

"After the big feast when I have had the white medicine-woman for a wife, I will go with the Chippewa, and we will see who will ride the farthest in search of the enemy, and who will kill the most. We shall ride so far and fight so hard that one of us must die in battle before the other can come back. My village is not big enough for two such men to return to."

"Le Borgne is a great man, but he is not a Pillager Chippewa," Flat Mouth insolently retorted, springing on his pony.

Le Borgne ever loved a brave man. If he had any religion besides the usual Indian belief in good and bad luck it consisted of a worship of courage. Therefore Flat Mouth's insult raised him in the war-chief's esteem.

"Don't get killed so you cannot go on the war-path with me," he warned.

The Pillager waved his hand and galloped towards the north. I knew he planned swinging east and crossing the Missouri at the mouth of the Knife, risking an encounter with any loitering Assiniboins as he made for the lower Mandan village. He courted grave hazards in pursuing this course, but I could appreciate his desire to leave Le Borgne in ignorance of his true purpose. Had he set forth on the road we had come over, the Minnetaree chief might have forbidden his departure, fearing some trick.

As I walked into the village Le Borgne kept beside me. We could not talk for the lack of an interpreter, yet I sensed a change in the chief. I got the impression something was troubling him. He carried his axe and swung it in short vicious circles. Knowing my success in trading white robes for the girl depended on the particular mood he might be in, I took heart enough to believe his thoughts were for war and not for women. His talk with Flat Mouth evidenced a desire to go to battle. It was possible the White Snake's news about the strangers had aroused the warrior in him.

When we came to Choke-cherry's hut he halted, and I did the same. Chief of the Wolves and his two younger brothers and the White Snake were posted at regular intervals at the front of the hut. To learn if they were sentinels, I boldly entered the porch and placed my hand on the door. Chief of the Wolves sprang forward and pushed me back. I glanced at Le Borgne and he motioned me to step back. Speaking loudly in English for the girl's benefit, I told Chief of the Wolves to keep his hands off me or I would shoot him. She heard me, and her voice called out—

"Oh, American! I'm afraid!"

Le Borgne thrust forward his head, his one eye glittering like a piece of broken glass in the sunlight. He was suspicious. He forgot I did not talk his lingo and shot out some query which I guessed to be a demand to know what the white woman had said. I made spiral lines with my index finger high above my head, the sign token for medicine and, as one overawed, softly withdrew from inside the porch. He followed me, and I called out:

"Don't be afraid. We'll get you out of this."

With a grunt of rage Le Borgne clapped his hand over my lips. With my left hand I repeated the medicine sign, and with my right I drew my gun the full stretch of my arm until the two muzzles rested under his chin. It was a language he readily understood and he stepped clear of me.

To demonstrate he was not angry he patted my shoulder and called out to his men, evidently telling them I was a brave man. I remained a while before the hut, but the girl did not attempt to address me again, nor did I speak to her. I was interested in watching Le Borgne whenever he glanced at White Snake. It was then that the hint of worry showed between his eyes. Gradually the conviction formed in my mind that he was uneasy over the Snake's budget of news, and was wondering who the strangers might be whose coming so excited his deadly enemies, the Sioux. Or perhaps White Snake had told him who they were. He was not angry at the Snake, and yet the sight of him brought the troubled lines in his forehead. It was refreshing to think something besides amorous thoughts were inside that savage brain-pan.

I turned away to go to my hut, and behind me

sounded the girl's clear voice raised in her indescribable song of the woods and the rivers. The effect on the Minnetarees was pronounced. The chief drew back his foot and with an explosive grunt hastened away. I dropped the gun to my side.

"Don't be afraid," I called out to her as she ceased her singing. This time no one attempted to stop my speaking to her.

CHAPTER XI

THE PILLAGER SHAKES THE CALF'S TAIL

THE village was quiet and I remained in my hut until near sundown, then ventured forth, anxious for the return of Flat Mouth. If he had had no mishaps with hostile Indians he should make the trip to the lower Mandan village quickly. The men of the village, as was their custom, were lounging on top of their huts, smoking and bragging. Their arrogance was almost past belief. They believed themselves infinitely superior to the white race. They had seen but few whites, and these they looked upon as partly demented because of their willingness to give guns and ammunition for such worthless things as hides and robes.

But this sleepy calm was destroyed as I strolled towards Choke-cherry's hut in hopes of getting a word of encouragement to the girl. One moment all was peace with even the cur dogs silent, the next shrill screams were splitting the air and warriors were dropping from their huts, snatching up weapons and rushing ahead to investigate. The savage's first thought was a surprise attack. I ran with the group that was making for Le Borgne's hut. We came to an abrupt halt and beheld a strange spectacle. An Indian woman with blood streaming from her arms and breast, with her hair matted over her face, stood under the porch of the chief's hut and was pouring out what I took to be a bitter tirade.

The warriors with me instantly began falling back, betraying every symptom of fear. I held my ground, curious to learn more. The woman clenched her fists and swung her arms and shrieked out her words in a steady stream until the door flew open and Le Borgne stepped out, his axe in his hand.

He was smiling, but his long mane of black hair was much dishevelled. He stood before the woman, and I fully expected to witness another murder. She ran to him and hissed and spat like a cat, even attempting to claw his face. He jumped away from her and walked towards the corral; but swift as a wild thing she was at his side, then ahead of him, screaming, clawing his face and even bringing blood to his brawny chest.

He wheeled to one side to avoid her, and her talons ripped down his arm, leaving red streaks. Undoubtedly it was the first time Le Borgne was ever blooded without striking back. His face was a study in rage and fear. Whichever way he turned she was at his side or before him, her tongue never silent, her claws ripping at his arms and chest. Knowing his people were watching him, he would not depart from his dignity and run for it.

Never once did he threaten violence, even to the extent of pushing her away. He held his head high to escape her hooked fingers, but beyond that he did not try to defend himself. Superstition was his master, and he knew the woman was demented and believed that most woeful would be his fate did he, in anger, lay the weight of a finger on one touchèd by the Great Spirit.

He began working his way back to his hut, jumping from side to side, but never increasing his pace beyond a brisk walk. Then she slipped in some filth and fell, and he seized the opportunity to gain his hut. She was at his heels when he entered, but the door slammed before she could follow him. She beat on the door with her fists and head and yelled in fury.

None of the warriors ventured to remove her. They had returned to their roofs and were eager spectators of the scene. I pitied the poor thing and finally took it upon myself to go to her. As I touched her on the shoulder she wheeled on me like a mad wolf, but the sight of a white instead of a red man seemed to calm her. She made no resistance when I took her arm and gently led her away. She went willingly enough, but the gaze she fastened on my face was not that of a sane person.

I walked with her through the village at random, taking pains to widen the distance between us and the chief's hut. At last some women furtively stole from cover and relieved me of her. It was horrible to hear her heart-broken moaning, and I lost no time in getting it out of my ears. In my haste to escape I found I had returned to Le Borgne's hut, and I waited for him to come out. He preferred, however, to be alone. Perhaps he was busy rubbing buffalo tallow on his wounds.

Feeling faint and remembering I had not eaten anything for hours, I sought out the hut where Choke-cherry was temporarily housed, gave him an inch of tobacco and motioned for food. He gave some order to his women and they began overhauling ancient meats. I insisted on fresh meat, for one end of the hut was covered with buffalo meat the hunting party had brought in. This had not had time to spoil, and, after the Minnetaree and Mandan custom, was thrown down to grow tainted. I picked out a piece and put it in a copper kettle and the women proceeded to cook it. Then, selecting a fillet, I broiled it and directed a woman to take it to Miss Dearness. On a small stick I scratched:

"Fresh meat. Cooked it myself. Keep up your courage.

"FRANKLIN."

This message I sent along with the fillet. I knew Choke-cherry and all his wives were despising me for my tastes in insisting on fresh meat, but I remained there and watched the kettle until some of it was done and I could begin eating. When I finished I had had the only satisfying meal since reaching the Missouri.

Quitting the hut I walked towards the Knife and was

rejoiced to behold Flat Mouth coming on the gallop. He dismounted, removed the pack of robes and led his pony to the corral. It was now growing dark, and all the warriors had followed their chief's example and were inside their huts for the night. As we carried the pack to our hut, I briefly narrated the actions of the demented woman.

"She is the mother of the woman Le Borgne killed," he informed. "They talk about the girl's death in the lower village as her mother was a Mandan. No matter what she says or does, neither Le Borgne nor any of his men would dare touch her so long as she is under the protection of the great *manito*. But others had better keep out of his way, for only blood will satisfy him after her talk. Now I have a big talk for you."

We entered the hut, put our guns aside, and I urged him to proceed. First he lighted his pipe and, extending it to me, held it while I took several whiffs, this little attention being the height of courtesy. Then, after puffs to sky and earth and the four wind-gods, he said—

"The strange men the Sioux talk about are white men."

"White men? Then they must be Hudson Bay men," I exclaimed, for I did not believe the N. W. or the X. Y. could be sending men to the Missouri, although the H. B. already had done so.

"Not traders. They carry a big flag. They have guns. The lower village was told about them by White Snake. Le Borgne now knows white men are coming up the river."

"What do you think about them?"

"The white woman's medicine brought them," he promptly declared. "It will be a long time before they get here——"

"Then how can they help us," I broke in, in a rude breach of etiquette with an Indian.

He smoked in silence for a good five minutes, then coldly resumed:

"A long time in getting here, but Le Borgne has his

village here and cannot change it. He will be here when they come. He fears they are friends of the Sioux. Big medicine for Medicine Hair.''

This time I waited to make sure he had finished, then asked—

"How?"

With the utmost gravity he replied:

"The white woman will say the big white chief, her father, comes with many white men. Her medicine will tell her in a dream, she shall say. She will tell it to the Minnetarees. Le Borgne thinks only he and White Snake and the Mandans in the lower village know about the white man. He will think it big medicine if she dreams it and tells him.''

"Good!" I cried, deeply pleased at the deception Flat Mouth had so adroitly suggested. "It may give us a fighting chance. Le Borgne is in a bad mind.''

"That is good! He will not have time to think of a new wife. He will be afraid bad luck is trailing him. He will be ripe for our trade.''

"Is that all Eshkebugecoshe has to tell?"

"On riding to the village I met a scout of the Cheyennes. They have crossed the river in hope of falling on some hunting party before going home. We talked in the sign-language. I sent a sign-talk to the Cheyenne chief, saying we would leave here with the medicine woman after this one sleep. I said I would bring the Assiniboin scalps and he and his warriors must be ready to go with us to the Mouse. That was the trade we made when they were putting presents under the stem.''

This would make it the following night. Well, we either would go or we wouldn't. I wrote on a strip of bark:

"There are white men far down the river. Le Borgne is much concerned. He does not know whether they are allies of the Sioux or not. You must have a dream to-night that the white men are led by your father, the big white chief, that they are coming here with many guns, that worse than death will be the fate of any one who interferes with your liberty, let alone seeking you as a wife. Flat Mouth will interpret it to Le Borgne."

I read it to Flat Mouth and he smiled appreciatively and declared my "mystery talk" was very big medicine. I asked him if he had met any Minnetarees on his return by the river road. He shook his head, and I decided that for twenty-four hours at least Le Borgne would not know he had been to the lower village. Thus the girl's announcement concerning the strangers down the river would come in the nature of a dream-revelation and make a profound impression on the savage chief. Whatever the supernatural powers had to report to their red children was revealed through the medium of dreams. You could never make Le Borgne believe that the visions seen in sleep were not veritable views of the unseen world wherein all earthly affairs were ordered and the future of every man foreseen.

Taking our guns we made our way through the darkness to Choke-cherry's hut and after much bother got him to open the door. We would have proceeded direct to the girl's hut if not for the guards on duty there. For two inches of tobacco I bribed him to make one of his women take a bowl of fresh water and bowl of corn to the girl. I explained to him that the piece of bark I placed on the corn was a medicine to make her hungry.

The Pillager and I followed the woman until we heard her explain her errand to one of the guards and the door open and close upon her. This was about all we could do and, as the morrow promised to tax our strength, we went back to our hut and turned in for a few hours' sleep.

With the first grey light the Pillager aroused me. He had procured fresh meat from some of the hunters and hurriedly broiled it over the fire. As fast as a portion was cooked enough to be edible he cut it off for me and took the next slice, practically raw, for himself. In this fashion we made a hearty meal and set out to see if Miss Dearness had complied with my directions. As we came in sight of her prison I knew she had acted promptly, for the guards, four of them, were grouped before something hanging on the outside wall and were staring at it curiously.

The savages gave way sullenly as we advanced to read her message. They were in half a mind to order us back, but Flat Mouth was too forbidding to be hustled about. His statement that I was the only one who could tell what was in the mystery talk afforded them an excuse for permitting us the freedom of the porch.

Miss Dearness had written on the reverse side of my piece of bark:

"People of the Minnetaree, and the Blind One, their chief:

"In the night dream medicine came to me. I saw many white men with many guns far down the Missouri coming to these villages of the Mandans and the Minnetarees. I saw the big white chief, the greatest of all traders, leading the white men. I saw the Sioux begging him to stop with them. He is too strong for them to rob or kill. I heard him tell the Sioux he was coming here to build a post because the white woman, Medicine Hair, is here. I heard him tell the Sioux he would return and build a post in their country if he was not treated well by the Minnetarees, or if the white woman had not been treated well. The Sioux begged him to give them some of his many guns, and he told them they should have them if the white woman was troubled in any way by Le Borgne or his people. Le Borgne, the Blind One, the dream means you will bring the Sioux against you, every warrior carrying a gun, if you do not let the white woman come and go as she wishes, and if you do not tell your people there will be no feast, no new hut."

I translated it hastily to the Pillager, and his eyes glistened as he pronounced it good. I noticed in the writing what, perhaps, he did not. She did not refer to herself as being the daughter of the mythical big white chief. I had made much of the relationship, taking my cue from Flat Mouth. She had acquiesced in it. Now, apparently, she could not do it, though Red Dearness would be the last to object to his daughter using any subterfuge to cheat an Indian.

Flat Mouth was for bringing out the robes and placing them on sale at once. I advised waiting until we could learn the chief's mood. Flat Mouth then asked if we should take the writing to the chief now. Again I was for delay. To my way of thinking the girl's "dream" should be announced to Le Borgne at a psychological moment, at some time during the sale of the robes. I knew the fellow well enough to realise that he could not be forced into any decision. The pressure must be applied gradually; the effect must be accumulative then, if we could bring him to a pitch where he wavered, the girl's revelation should be used as the last straw. The Pillager was good enough to proclaim my reasoning sound, only he destroyed all compliment in his speech by adding that it was the white woman's medicine working through my tongue.

We stepped clear of the porch and were about to return to the hut and our pack of robes, when again I heard that fearful screaming. The guards scurried to less exposed positions; even the Pillager betrayed concern. The screaming grew louder and the Pillager, too proud to run and hide, flattened himself against the wall of the hut and stared uneasily at the pitiable figure now appearing from between two huts.

Le Borgne's demented mother-in-law was a sorry sight as she passed us, tossing her hands and tearing at her hair. Since her last appearance she had slashed herself with a knife, for she was bleeding from several fresh wounds. She walked with her head thrown far back, yet she neither stumbled nor fell nor wandered from the middle of the narrow way. This to the Pillager was simply another proof that she was under the direct control of the great *manito*. She was making straight to Le Borgne's hut. As soon as she passed a hut the inmates would emerge and climb to the roof, none daring to follow her. I followed her, however, and for this reason the Pillager followed too.

We halted on coming in sight of Le Borgne's porch and were just in time to see the war-chief duck inside. The woman, with her head still flung back and her gaze directed to the heavens, gave an ear-splitting shriek and ran forward. How she saw him, or knew he had retreated into the hut was a mystery to me. Nevertheless she did know and, with a maniacal cry, ran on to the porch and attempted to open the door.

After several minutes of furious efforts she backed away and began cursing him:

"Oh, one-eyed killer of women! May your medicine turn to water! May the Sioux tear out your heart and give it to the dogs!" she screamed.

The Pillager was so deeply impressed by her terrible prayer that he interpreted only patches of it. For some minutes she carried on in this violent fashion, then, with a despairing shriek, she turned and fled swiftly between the huts.

"It is bad to have such words spoken against you," gravely said the Pillager. "Le Borgne may say he doesn't care, but inside he is very much afraid."

The more frightened the Minnetaree became, the better the day looked for us, and, feeling almost optimistic, I led the way to Choke-cherry's hut and cooked some meat and sent it to Miss Dearness. Despite his hearty meal at our hut the Pillager broiled for himself several slices of meat and devoured them voraciously. When he had finished I said I was ready to offer the robes. To my surprise he objected.

"The white woman's medicine is working through the mad woman," he insisted. "Let the medicine work. We will wait. We have until the sun goes down. My blood tells me something is in the air that will make this day remembered among the Minnetaree.''

"Do you think the woman's people—she being a Mandan—will make trouble for Le Borgne?"

He smiled grimly.

"They are dogs. They do not dare lift their heads when he looks at them. They will say she took a Minnetaree man and now belongs to that tribe; that the daughter, the dead woman, is a Minnetaree. We will climb on a hut and watch what comes next.''

This we did, selecting the hut we were in. Some thirty warriors were already there. They respectfully made way for the Pillager, and we took a position facing Le Borgne's hut.

We sat there but a few minutes, smoking our pipes and watching the curious groups dotting the surrounding roofs, when we observed, off to our left, a commotion among the spectators. They were swarming to the south side of the roofs, craning their necks and keeping very quiet.

"She is coming again," whispered Flat Mouth, putting up his pipe. "She is like a ghost that cannot find sleep."

As the guttural chatter on the roofs subsided, I heard her voice wailing in a low-pitched key as she once more was impelled to make the rounds of the village. We could trace her progress by watching the people on the roofs. Then the moaning undertone leaped high like heat-lightning as she flayed Le Borgne, using terms that would bring death to any other in the five villages.

She denounced him as a stealer of women, as a killer of women. These accusations, especially the first, might be easily overlooked, even accepted as something complimentary. But when she added he was a coward, that the sight of a man's blood made him sick, that he dared not leave his hut unless surrounded by many braves, the effect was quickly registered inside the hut. He began bellowing in terrible rage, and the warriors on the roofs began shifting their positions so they might not be so prominent when he showed himself. Those remaining on the ground scurried to climb up on the huts, or ran for the outskirts of the village.

Flat Mouth breathed with a hissing sound, as he read these signs of fear, and whispered——

"They are afraid to meet their chief when he comes out!"

For fully ten minutes the woman kept up her vilification, her tongue never ceasing, her bitterness never losing its acid edge; then, as she had done before, she turned and ran swiftly away. Some women darted from a hut, seized her and induced her to go with them. Chief of the Wolves dropped from a roof and ran to his uncle's hut announcing her departure. The door flew open with a smash, and the chief jumped out. Chief of the Wolves disappeared between two huts after one glance at the man's face.

Le Borgne was frightful to behold. To me he seemed to be as insane as the woman. He had thrown aside his cloak and wore only his breech-clout, his long coarse hair enveloping him like a shaggy cloak. His gigantic body trembled and shook. Standing before his porch, he crouched low and began jerking his axe up and down by the wrist-thong, all the time twisting his head back and forth to rake the village with his baleful glance. Then straightening and lifting his arms above his head, he emitted a bull-like roar and smashed his axe against the long platform filled with driftwood. He was praying for an enemy to appear—some one he could vent his blood-lust upon.

"He goes mad like the woman," murmured the Pillager, his hands twitching as he crouched on the edge of the hut and glared down at the chief. He reminded me of a Red River lynx on a bough about to leap on its prey.

"He asks his *manito* to send him something he can fight and kill. It would be a good coup to take his scalp!"

"It would mean death for the white woman and for

us," I sternly rebuked, fearing lest he seek to test his strength against Le Borgne's.

"Not if it is her medicine working through him as it is working through the woman," he muttered, licking his lips wolfishly and craning his neck to watch the movements of the chief.

Le Borgne roared even more loudly and without cessation. It was just a bestial cry with no words in it. As he howled his horrible yearning for battle his arms kept up a violent gesticulation, and the men on the huts crept to the opposite sides so as to remain unseen. The Pillager and I remained where we were.

"Ho!" grunted the Pillager, smiling savagely. "Very soon I must fight that man because he will have it so. They say he can fight good. I will wear a painted hand on my arm after we get back to the Red River to show I dodged under his axe and struck him with my empty hand on the arm before killing him."

"Are you going mad? Are you a foolish man?" I cried. "You say it is the woman's medicine working; then let it work. It has not asked you to do anything."

"Watch!" hissed the Pillager, balancing on the edge of the roof. What I saw gave me hope that the grim pantomime was ended, for Le Borgne suddenly darted back into his hut.

"He will stay hidden until the woman comes and makes him a madman again," I said.

But the Pillager seemed abnormally contented as he kept his eyes fastened on the closed door; his hands no longer twitched. Before I had time to wonder at this marked change in his demeanour, the door of the hut flew open again and now Le Borgne was wearing his robe. The Pillager gathered his heels under him and slipped his hand through the noosed thong of his war-axe. He said——

"Watch!"

Stalking a few rods from his hut, Le Borgne raised his mighty voice in a war-cry and, catching the robe with his left arm, he swung it round his head and hurled it aside. It opened and caught the wind and fluttered like some monster moth to the ground.

"He has cast his robe! The white woman's medicine has made him cast his robe," softly rejoiced the Pillager. "Now he is under vow to his *manito* to kill the first person he meets, man, woman, or child, that doesn't belong to his tribe. All the village knows it, and the Minnetarees will stay in hiding, although his vow does not mean he will kill any of them. You and the chief of the Pillager Chippewas are not of his tribe."

Now the muscles of his arms and legs were knotting in bunches, then relaxing and rippling smoothly as he prepared to leap to the ground and have at the brute.

I grasped his arm and warned:

"You must not do it. The white woman's medicine does not call you to fight him."

Le Borgne raised his war-cry and began stalking the empty spaces between the huts in search of a victim to satisfy his vow. Doors slammed throughout the village and the men on the roofs lay flat and hidden from view, although a Minnetaree should have had no cause for fear. Le Borgne doubled over and shook out his hair and danced from side to side, the silence of the people permitting the *thud-thud* of his stamping moccasins to be plainly audible.

"He has said it! He cries for blood! He dances for death! The Medicine Hair's *manito* makes him do it. Her *manito* pushes me to him. I will go and kill him!" snarled the Pillager, striving to cast off my grip.

"You will kill us all," I cried, feeling my hold breaking.

"I'll kill Le Borgne who has cast his robe," panted the Pillager. Then he raised the war-cry of his tribe and, wrenching loose, dropped to the ground.

I stood up intending to follow him and make sure with my gun that Le Borgne died did he fight with my friend, when I observed the Minnetaree chief had shifted his course so as to place our hut between him and the Pillager. I looked down on the Pillager, and he, thinking Le Borgne was all but upon him, was shaking out his Sioux scalps and engaging in a little ceremonial dance of his own, brandishing his axe most adeptly. I looked back after Le Borgne and saw the mad woman running towards him.

It was a tense situation. Le Borgne, bowed low and intent on his grotesque steps, did not see the fury approaching him. The Pillager, with a segment of the hut between him and his man, was conducting his advance with close attention to ritual, never dreaming of the woman's presence. The first that Le Borgne knew of the woman was when she grabbed him by the hair. With a roar he straightened, swinging her feet off the ground and raising his axe. She screamed vituperations and fell back to the ground with both hands filled with hair. Le Borgne recognised her in time to save himself from a hideous crime—the killing of one under the Great Spirit's protection.

With a shout of rage and fear he leaped back. She was at his face again, and, for a second, I believed he would brain her. Then his arms dropped to his side and he turned his back on her. She caught his long hair and began tearing it out, making terrible animal cries as she did so. He paid no attention to her and did not seem to sense her presence, but swung his axe and hurled it high over the nearest hut, and then strode rapidly to his own hut with the woman worrying his neck and hair. She released him as he reached his porch. He went inside and closed the door.

I looked about for the Pillager and beheld him standing with folded arms, disgustedly watching the anti-climax. I dropped down beside him and exclaimed——

"He didn't kill her!"

"He could not kill her," he growled. "She has been touched by the big *manito*. No one can hurt her, no matter what she does. Her coming was bad medicine for my coup. Had I seen her, I would have reached him first; then his heart would have been glad and his axe would have sang a song as it hissed against mine.

Yet it could not kill her, although she is not of his people"—and he made the spiral sign with his finger—"so his vow is broken. He cast his robe for nothing, and that is very bad medicine for him, but not so bad as if he stuck his axe in the woman's head. A strong medicine has shown him he cannot always do as he promises. But it is very bad not to keep a vow. It will hurt him with his people unless he can get some good-luck medicine. The medicine of the white woman works against him all the time."

"He must have seen you, yet he did not offer to fight you," I said.

"Why should he fight me?" asked the Pillager in surprise. "He had no fight with me except as my coming let him make good his promise. When the woman reached him first his vow was spoiled; he had no promise left, so he threw away his axe to tell every one the vow was dead. But it is very bad for him." There was almost a touch of sympathy in the Pillager's voice as he said the last.

"How long must we wait before we show the robes and offer to trade?" I asked.

"Now is a good time. Le Borgne knows bad luck is biting his heels. He is afraid that everything is against him. He needs a strong medicine. He is not thinking of feasts and a new wife."

It was pleasant to get into action again. As we passed the girl's hut I called out to her, and she opened the door a crack and spoke—

"Can we do it to-night?"

Owing to the fear and confusion over Le Borgne's behaviour we could have done it then if we had had her at the corral. The guards about her hut were still in hiding.

"It must be to-night if I fail in what I'm about to try. I am going to offer to buy you first."

"Buy me?" she faintly repeated. "But you have no goods."

"If I fail we will get away to-night," I comforted.

"When I call your name step to the door and touch the writing on the bark, then get back out of sight."

At this point Chief of the Wolves ran up and reminded that we were not to talk with the white woman. However, he was very civil about it and displayed no arrogance. His gaze rested on the Pillager with a sort of worshipful admiration, and he added:

"I saw the Chippewa chief drop to the ground. I thought he was about to drop into Le Borgne's arms. What a battle that would have been!"

"Not a long battle—just a cracked skull and the Minnetarees would have to look for a new war-chief," calmly retorted the Pillager.

Now old Choke-cherry came trotting up, his broad face picturing deep trouble.

"I have been to see my brother," he whispered. "Bad spirits are around him. Never before has a Minnetaree chief cast his robe and not done as he said."

"He needs new medicine," I advised.

"He will give many ponies for a new medicine," eagerly cried Choke-cherry. "Has the white man some magic he will trade for ponies?"

"I have some medicine I will trade," I replied. "I don't know whether I will trade for ponies, or robes, or something else. It is a very strong medicine and will kill all bad luck, but I will not trade it for poor ponies. I want ponies such as the Cheyennes have."

Choke-cherry's face showed great fear. If he told this to his brother, the chief would bitterly upbraid him for not turning over the two Assiniboins to the Cheyennes for the ten ponies offered.

"We have many good robes," he cried. "Let the white man bring out his medicine. I will tell the village to be ready to trade. If the medicine is new and strong and will help the heart of Le Borgne to grow stout again, and his head to grow clear again, we will give every robe in the five villages."

"We will see," I carelessly answered, walking away.

"Now is the time," muttered Flat Mouth as I hurried to get the pack.

"The best of times," I rejoiced. "Le Borgne is afraid his buffalo *manito* has lost its strength. He cast his robe and made himself a foolish man. The villages will think his war medicine is spoiled. He must get good-luck medicine, or else there will be a new war-chief."

The Pillager well understood the method of offering a white robe for sale and undertook charge of the arrangements. Two upright stakes were placed before the door of the hut facing Miss Dearness's prison. Across these supports he placed a third stake. The open space before the hut was packed. The roofs of the surrounding huts were covered with the curious. The Pillager took advantage of the opportunity to indulge in oratory. By his touching his axe and the Sioux scalps I knew he was declaiming his greatness, and, as all must have known of his willingness to fight Le Borgne, he was heard with the deepest respect and attention. But when he reached behind him and fumbled with the cords of the pack and continued his talk his audience smiled sceptically.

He paused and said to me in Chippewa:

"I have told them we never bother to trade in anything but white robes. I have said we carry a pack of them with us wherever we go but never offer to trade unless we see something we want very much. These dogs think my tongue is crooked." Then, picking up the robe, he flung it over the cross-piece.

A shout of amazement greeted the appearance of the robe. Choke-cherry exclaimed—

"The Sioux-killer spoke with a straight tongue!"

Flat Mouth angrily cried out—

"Did you think a chief of the Pillager Chippewas, wearer of many eagle feathers, would come to the Missouri to tell lies to hut Indians?"

"It is a fine robe. We will buy it," declared Chief of the Wolves.

Ignoring him, Flat Mouth reached into the pack and

drew out another robe and threw it over the first. Choke-cherry was inarticulate for several minutes. Admiration, awe, and covetousness were reflected in the disjointed outcries of the Minnetarees. When Choke-cherry recovered speech it was to proclaim hoarsely:

"Better medicine was never brought to a Minnetaree village in my day. Chippewa, Sioux-killer, set your price. We will buy the robes."

"They are not mine to sell," informed Flat Mouth, dragging forth the third robe and draping it over the others so the three tails hung in a row.

"They are common robes coloured with white earth," accused Chief of the Wolves, crowding forward and clutching roughly at the top robe. But as his fingers encountered the fleece and his suspicious gaze failed to find any trace of a deception, his jaw grew slack and he stared stupidly at the treasure. "My uncle speaks true," he faltered. "We will buy them if it takes all the robes in all the villages."

Through the Chippewa I repeated what I already had said to Choke-cherry; namely, that while I did not care to take the white robes with me on leaving the village, I had seen nothing yet for which I would trade. Whatever it was it must be of the best. I was not even prepared to say I would take robes, ponies, dressed leather, or a combination of such goods in payment. I would display the robes and see what the Minnetarees had to offer. If I found something to my liking I would trade.

"So be it!" howled old Choke-cherry. "Take what you will. We can get more. But never was such a chance to get medicine robes. I will give my medicine-pipe. It is a great mystery—very strong medicine."

"Yet it could not make the Cheyennes lead their ponies under the stem," sneered Flat Mouth.

"The village shall buy them and give them to our chief, so his bad luck may grow red again," said Chief of the Wolves.

"The Blind needs much medicine to make him open his one eye," ironically remarked Flat Mouth.

No one heeded this derisive speech, for a mighty trade had come to the Missouri and must be completed. Grunts and yelps arose when the Pillager produced the fourth and last of the robes and hung it in place.

"It is magic!" faltered Choke-cherry, edging backward. "The white man can make the Sioux-killer find white robes all day."

"If it is magic then the robes will turn brown after they have gone away," said Chief of the Wolves.

The Pillager smiled scornfully, saying—

"You talk like foolish men."

Raising a hand for silence and attention, he dipped into the pack for the last time and reverently lifted up the small calfskin, all white but for the black border round the right eye. This he exhibited to the astounded mob and then gently laid it on the robes. The calfskin was much more valuable than the robes.

The deep silence which followed this climax was broken by the Pillager announcing—

"This is all we bring this time."

"You said you had nothing to trade," gasped Choke-cherry.

"I always have something to trade when I think there is something worth trading for," I corrected. "My medicine has told me in my sleep that I could make a good trade here. I am waiting to see what my medicine meant."

Men darted away to inform Le Borgne of the powerful medicine. Others scoured the village to round up property. A scene of amazing activity followed. In a short time seven horses were brought up, each loaded with robes, dressed leather, moccasins and embroidered leggings. Without bothering to glance at this, the first bid, the Pillager shook the calf's tail as a sign of refusal.

Choke-cherry dashed frantically among the men and hooted long-winded speeches to which no one seemed to pay any attention. He was exhorting them to greater efforts in syndicating their goods. As proof of his own desire to help win the miracle for the good of the village, he brought out his medicine-pipe, newly decorated with feathers and hairs. The horses and truck were left at one side, and the warriors separated to round up more collateral.

A warrior returned from Le Borgne's hut saying the chief wished the robes to be bought in with no delay and delivered to him. After receiving them he would come out and see his people. I fancied that in each mind was the fear that unless the robes were delivered, per request, he would come out anyway, to see his people, and would come with his wrist thrust through the loop of his war-axe. Seven more horses were brought forward, this time the pick of the herd, and in addition to the robes were many of their copper kettles. As their superstition forbade them cooking meat in their earthen pots, the offer of the kettles was conclusive proof of their determination to procure the robes.

Again Flat Mouth shook the tail. Again the Minnetarees scattered for more goods. Chief of the Wolves, I noted, darted away toward his uncle's hut, and with my gun in my lap I thereafter kept an eye out. It was while the savages were collecting their third batch of goods that Le Borgne came hurrying toward us, his nephew walking behind him. The chief carried his axe. He had been told the robes were not to be bought in a hurry and he was very angry, a sullen rage that burned on top of his former wrath when he was compelled to violate his vow. He wore his robe.

The Pillager gave me a quick look, and I patted my gun and smiled grimly. If Le Borgne attempted to get the robes by casting his robe again and slaying the first alien he met, he would never more than get started in lifting his axe. The Pillager, who was naked to his clout, picked up his robe and threw it over his shoulder. I followed his example, borrowing one hanging inside the porch where I sat.

Le Borgne grasped the significance of our action and surveyed us in silence for several moments through his smouldering eye, his ghastly grin making him look like a death's head.

"The day is warm," he boomed, slipping off his robe and giving it to Chief of the Wolves to hold.

"It is very warm in the sun," agreed the Pillager, dropping his robe to the ground. I was glad to throw mine off.

With this unspoken agreement that there should be no casting of robes, the chief took time to sweep his eye over the horses and goods and the white robes and, more precious than all, the calfskin. His voice was unsteady as he asked—

"Where did the white man get these medicine robes and the hide?"

"Far from here," I briefly replied.

Le Borgne turned on his people and warned:

"This is no time to bring a few ponies. This is a big medicine sale. It must end quickly. Mighty medicine does not like to be hung out in the sun waiting for a buyer——" Then to me, the Pillager interpreting —"Go to all the Minnetaree huts and take all you find, save only that one hut." And he pointed to where the girl was imprisoned.

He was practically offering all movable property in the village. I have no doubt but that he would have thrown in the huts if we had had a way to take them with us. I shook my head. The Pillager reached down and wagged the tail.

My refusal threw the chief into a paroxysm of rage, yet he restrained himself and said:

"Go to all the Minnetaree huts! Go to all the Mandan huts on the Missouri! Take what you will—all the ponies you will. If any Mandan tries to stop you, tell him I sent you!"

"My medicine tells me it is not robes and kettles and ponies I want," I replied. "I can get kettles among the white people. I can get better ponies and robes among the Cheyennes."

"What do you want?" he fiercely demanded.

"Miss Dearness!" I called. The words meant nothing to him, but at the sound of her name, the girl began singing, and the door of her hut opened. She stood there, wrapped in her capote, long enough to touch the piece of bark hanging on the wall. Then she retired and closed the door.

"My medicine tells me that is what I will buy with my robes," I said to Le Borgne.

Le Borgne swung his axe and roared a refusal.

The Pillager spoke to Choke-cherry, who timidly procured the piece of bark containing the girl's writing and brought it to me. I motioned for Le Borgne to give heed, and proceeded to read the message very slowly, the Pillager interpreting and, of course, embellishing it somewhat. Le Borgne listened attentively, after the first few words, and his strong face grew uneasy as he heard the girl's "dream."

She had seen the white men, many of them, with many guns, coming up the Missouri to the Mandans and the Minnetarees. The whites were too strong for the Sioux to trouble. It jolted him when he was told the leader of the whites was the big white chief we had talked so much about since reaching the river. His face lighted when he was told the white chief would build a post in the village because Medicine Hair, the white woman, was there. And it grew dark as night when he was warned what would happen if he troubled the white woman, or limited her coming and going.

"I have never wanted a woman I did not take," he roared.

"If her father, the big chief, is coming with many guns and men I do not need to buy her," I carelessly said, shifting the position of the calfskin so Le Borgne would observe the black markings round the right eye.

He had not noticed this peculiarity before, and for the moment it drove all thoughts of the woman out of his head. It was his right eye that was dead. The right eye of the medicine calf was circled with black,

denoting death. If ever a *manito* sent a particular medicine to a great warrior, surely this was the skin sent
to Le Borgne.

"You want this woman for your woman?" he demanded. Of course the girl heard the Pillager repeat it
in Chippewa, as he talked loudly.

"I do. That is why I offer to make a trade for her."

"You can go back and get other white women. There
are some more?" he asked.

"Many of them—more than there are Indian
women."

He laughed aloud at such an exaggeration.

"Why do you want this one when you can get so
many? I want her. She is the only white woman I
have seen. If there were many of them here I would
sell her for a pony."

"If there were many of them here you could not get
the medicine robes," I retorted, forced to play the game
according to his savage viewpoint and hold it strictly
to the level of barter and trade.

"I will not sell her," he growled. His brother made
to implore him to change his mind, but did not dare go
beyond a few faltering words. The warriors looked
glum, and more than one angry glance was cast at Miss
Dearness's hut. They wanted to see their chief in
possession of the robes. To murder us and appropriate
the robes would be a violation of their etiquette besides
being sure to bring down retribution upon them in some
way, such as the loss of a trading-post. Afraid as they
were of their leader, I could see some of them thought
he was paying too high a price for his whim. If his
medicine suffered, then the whole tribe suffered.

I spoke to the Pillager. He gathered up the robes
and the skin and repacked them, with the calfskin on
top, the black eye showing. While Le Borgne had
refused the trade, I had not lost hopes of buying the
girl. His refusal was to prove his independence, and,
perhaps, had been incited by a glimpse of the girl's
white face.

Le Borgne stood and glared at us, his hands fingering his big axe, his eye observing the double-barrelled gun across my left arm.

Deep in the village rose a dismal chanting. The mother of the murdered girl was abroad again. The effect on Le Borgne was immediate. His eye flickered with fear. The woman was getting on his nerves. He wished himself back in his hut with the door barred, as shown by his instinctive glance in that direction. Yet he could not spend the rest of his life in a hut. It was intolerable to anticipate months and perhaps years of the woman's nagging—her accusations of cowardice. Let even a mad woman repeat a thing long enough, and he would lose something of his standing in the tribe. While he must not touch her, he should be protected by his medicine. If his medicine was spoiled he must renew it. The chanting grew louder and clearer. Miss Dearness also heard it, for she now sang out to me:

"Choke-cherry's wife, when bringing me meat, said the crazy Mandan woman is going back to her people in the lower village."

I picked up the calfskin and said to Le Borgne:

"I think you are a foolish man, but I am not to blame for that. I am angry because Chief of the Wolves spoke evil of my medicine robes and skin. I will prove to you that the medicine is strong in this skin. You shall hold it in your hands until the crazy woman comes and goes. Then you shall give it back to me, and I will take my pack elsewhere and trade."

He seized it greedily and I stood aside and waited. I smoked and tried to show the unconcern I did not feel. I had acted on an impulse set in motion by Miss Dearness's words. I also believed I could detect a new tone in the poor woman's lament, the quality of sadness and resignation. The people stood very quietly, all eyes turned to where the Mandan woman would emerge from among the huts. If the sight of the chief should inflame her mad rage, the trade value of the white calfskin would greatly depreciate. In that event we would make a good fight of it that night.

Now the woman appeared, her head bowed low, her chanting weirdly depressing. The stage was well set for her coming. The Minnetarees fell back to give her clear passage and no one spoke nor moved. The chief and I stood a little in advance of the people, he standing like an image, holding the white calfskin in his two hands, his axe dangling from his wrist, his one eye fixed on the woman.

She drew close and I believed she was to pass by without lifting her head, but the steady impact of Le Borgne's gaze caused her to look up. For a moment I believed she was going to fly at him, for she halted and stared in his face. Still, there was a sane light in her eyes now. She recognised the powerful medicine he was holding. The silence of the people was impressive. The whole affair smacked of the ritualistic. Perhaps she realised she had a leading part in it, and must not destroy the symmetry of the whole. Or the poor thing may have been just heartbroken and only anxious to get back to her people in the lower village. Whatever the influence that kept her subdued, she gazed for a moment into the brute's face, then dropped her head, resumed her chanting and walked on toward the river road.

I plucked the skin from Le Borgne's hand rather briskly and tossed it to the Pillager to replace in the pack.

"White man, wait!" hoarsely cried Le Borgne. "Give it back to me!"

"You will trade?"

"Take the white woman! Give me the robes and the skin!"

"Miss Dearness!" I called out. "Don't come to the door till I give the word. Then be ready to ride. I've bought you!"

I nodded to the expressionless-faced Pillager and he

handed the pack over to Le Borgne, who started hurriedly for his hut, hugging his new medicine close. Old Choke-cherry yowled in joy, and assured me such a medicine feast would be given that night as never was before enjoyed by the Willow Indians, as the Minnetarees call themselves. I did not seek to discourage him, but so soon as the Pillager brought the horses I purposed to start for the Mouse River. Already the Pillager was making for the corral.

Now the Minnetarees had a despicable custom in trade of agreeing to a bargain, exchanging goods, pronouncing themselves perfectly well satisfied, and, after an hour or so, coming back and demanding that their property be returned to them, leaving the purchase price "on the ground" as they say. Flat Mouth had told me about these trade tricks by which they hoped to induce the trader to increase the price first agreed upon. Not once, but as often as the victim will endure this insolent disregard of the bargain, will they come back and ask for their property or an increase in goods.

Whether Le Borgne would act in this fashion in an ordinary trade I did not know. I was inclined to believe he would trade fair, but, with the girl as the stake, the temptation would be great, once he got over his first enthusiasm in owning the robes. He might be cunning enough to believe that the white skin had already sent the Mandan woman from his village, and that she had seemed to be the source of his annoyance and trouble. That his murder of the younger woman was back of it all would never appeal to him.

Soon the Pillager came back with the horses, riding one with his gun held high, his bow and quiver of arrows over his shoulder, and his other hand clutching the two halter ropes. He was closely followed by a crowd of men, women and children. Chief of the Wolves was very active in getting in front of his horse and causing the chief to rein in. I stepped to Miss Dearness's hut and spoke her name. She opened the door and came out, her head closely muffled, her face very pale, and her blue eyes blinking at the sun.

"I saw it all," she whispered. "I cut a hole through the hide-door. It was brave of you, wise of you. I'm so glad you—bought me!"

A commotion in the crowd attracted my attention. Chief of the Wolves, sensing our purpose and seeking to delay us, had crossed in front of the Pillager's mount once too often. Struck by the horse's shoulder, he had been hurled to one side. An angry murmur arose. Flat Mouth brought the two horses to the porch and, as I took charge of them, he backed his horse violently, splitting the mob into two sections. Then he brought his animal about, faced the savages and, with his axe held out to one side, he leaned forward and cried——

"Do you want to see a Pillager Chippewa cast his robe?"

Old Choke-cherry urged the men to give us room and not to crowd round us like foolish children. Chief of the Wolves crawled to his feet and glared murder at the Pillager's back. Then he glimpsed me with the double-barrel, and slunk aside.

"Make a hole through them, Eshkebugecoshe!" I called out, slapping the girl's mount and sending her after the chief.

Flat Mouth's horse commenced prancing and bolting from side to side as though unmanageable, and the crowd broke and scattered, some diving into doorways, some running in between huts, and, as the way cleared, the Pillager advanced with the girl close behind him. I came last with my gun half raised, watching the tops of the huts as well as the ground. No one, however, made any active demonstration against us. We avoided Le Borgne's hut and struck north for the Missouri. In my last glimpse of the Minnetarees I beheld Chief of the Wolves running towards Le Borgne's hut with old Choke-cherry bobbing after him.

We soon made the Missouri, and Flat Mouth quickly found a bull-boat. I paddled Miss Dearness across, and he swam over with her horse in tow. Leaving my gun with her, the Indian and I went back. I remained in the boat and towed my mount over, while my friend repeated his feat of swimming.

Flat Mouth said three days of ordinary travel would take us to the Côteau du Missouri, the high ridge separating the waters of the Missouri and the Mouse, but believed we should make it easily in a bit less than that as we had no pack animals and were sacrificing everything for speed.

He set the course for Miss Dearness and me to follow while he rode down the river to pick up the Cheyennes. The girl and I had not gone far before he came after us with twenty warriors. They would go with us to the Côteau, he said, but no farther, as our line of flight was along the western edge of the Sioux territory. When I asked him where the rest of the Cheyennes were, he said they had crossed the river to go home, being afraid of the Sioux.

Before sundown our escort abruptly bid us goodbye and galloped madly back to the Missouri. Perhaps it was better that way, for while the twenty horsemen gave us a brave appearance, they also furnished a large target for a Sioux eye. It would be necessary for them to delay and kill meat, and our pace would be much slower than when we rode alone. That night Flat Mouth used his bow and arrows with good effect, and we had fresh meat.

For two days more we pushed on, watching for the Assiniboins on the west and ahead of us, for the Sioux on the east and ahead of us. Then we struck the ridge and beheld a high hill which Flat Mouth called the Dog's House. What was most encouraging was to behold the banks of the Mouse.

That night as we sat in the smoke of a smudge to protect ourselves from the mosquitoes and wearing dressed-leather hoods over our heads as an additional protection, Miss Dearness coughed and choked and at last managed to say—

"The X. Y. will pay you for the robes and skin you paid for me."

"Never," I imperilled my lungs by replying. "It's the only trade I ever made I was satisfied with. I've only one thing to regret."

She nodded for me to explain, and I said—

"Since we started from the Missouri you've been so wrapped and bundled up I've forgotten what the colour of your hair is."

Instantly the hood flew off, the capote fell back, and, in defiance to the millions of mosquitoes, the red glory of her hair was revealed. With a yelp of protest I leaned forward to aid in adjusting the hood and the capote and, losing my balance, would have made clumsy work of it had she not caught my elbow and steadied me for a second.

Flat Mouth, who had been with the horses to see that the torture inflicted by the mosquitoes did not stampede the animals, now drew up to our fire, the horses crowding in behind him to get into the smoke. I wanted to talk with the girl—to have her talk to me, and yet I was glad he came. I fired questions at him to keep my mind from her.

We learned our course now would be down grade and over a pleasant country with no obstacles to speak of. The land was dotted with small hillocks and these usually were covered with buffaloes. If it had not been for the mosquitoes, the trip would have been very comfortable. Of course we must forever be on the watch against the Assiniboins and Sioux—and also against a pursuing party of the Minnetarees. The latter we expected to discover at any time, swarming down on us to give back our robes and reclaim the girl. Not until we reached the ridge did we cast them out of our fears.

The first night after quitting the ridge, when a fresh wind had blown the mosquitoes away and we were bowing our heads over our cooking, some uncontrollable impulse seized me and mastered me, and shortly I awoke to the astounding fact that I had kissed the girl.

She made no move of resentment, nor said any word, but put on her dressed-leather hood and glanced at me reproachfully. I jumped to my feet and strode off in the darkness, cursing myself. She was under my protection, and I had not supposed my three years in the wilds had so entirely wiped out my training. I can see now I was unnecessarily harsh with myself, that I was young and meant no harm. Still I took myself to task seriously enough that night. When I went back and found her, still hooded, a pathetic and lonely little figure, I had no fine words. I kicked the turf and did manage to blurt out:

"That won't happen again. Don't bake your face with that hood." With that I went over by the horses and threw myself down.

Her cold voice cut like a knife as it followed me, saying—

"Having bought me, I suppose you believed you owned me."

I groaned and dug my fingers into my ears. Before I slept that night I knew I loved her and had spoiled everything by my unpardonable action.

The Mouse was conquered and we passed down the Assiniboin in two canoes obtained from Fort Assiniboin. I paddled one, and she and Flat Mouth paddled the other. I had attempted to renew our old footing as though nothing had happened, but the glance she gave me told me how hopeless it was. After that I met her only as we landed to make a camp at night, and then only as we ate our fish and meat. She no longer eyed me coldly, but stared at me without seeming to see me.

At the Forks we passed the camp of some H. B. men from the Albany factory. I waved my hand but did not turn in to join them. I had no heart for companionship. It was not until I was some miles up the Red that I observed the absence of the girl's canoe. It came in sight just as I had finished cooking and eating a fish and was resuming my journey. I knew she and the Pillager had turned in at the H. B. fire.

I forced myself to think of old Tabashaw and to wonder if the old rascal had succeeded in bullying and coaxing all the rum from Probos. I repeatedly framed my report to the Gentlemen of the North, trying to excuse my absence from my post and explain why the spring hunt had resulted in a failure.

Then it came over me and nauseated me—homesickness. To remain there through the summer, fall and winter, and to see no white man's smoke until the next summer, seemed to be more than I could endure. All the way up the river I fought it over with myself. Then I realised how silly it was to try to keep the girl from my thoughts. I loved her. I would tell her so. At least she should know that much of the truth, even though she laughed at me. I believed I would feel better if I humiliated myself to her.

So, when I reached the stretch below the X. Y. post on the Scratching, where poles must be used instead of paddles, I stayed in camp and killed time until she and the Pillager came up. I thought she wanted him to go on, but seeing me, he was eager to land. I greeted her and she eyed me blankly. I fidgeted and waited. Then I could not endure it longer. The Indian was some rods away, roasting some meat. I made sure of my position in my canoe, then turned to her and said:

"That time—back there—I wouldn't have done it if I hadn't loved you."

"Don't mention it," she politely replied, turning and walking to the fire.

"I won't again," I called after her, cursing myself for an addle-headed lout.

I sent my canoe into the stream and pitted my strength and sleepless mood against the river and the hours. More of a ghost than a man, I at last crawled ashore at the Pembina post at the edge of evening.

The old familiar drunken howls saluted me from the fort. I picked up two oak axe-helves, where some of the drunken beggars had thrown them, and tucked them under my arm. When I reached the stockade gate I heard old Tabashaw making a drunken speech and exhorting his tribesmen to enter the fort, find Probos and drag him from his hiding place and cut his throat. I glanced up at the fort windows and saw Probos's fat, greasy face flabby with terror. Leaning my gun against the stockade, I took an oak helve in each hand and quietly stole upon the gathering.

Then did I put the fear of the *manito* into their souls. I waded back and forth cracking heads and upbraiding them for worthless dogs and concluded by getting old Tabashaw by the neck and kicking him outside the stockade. Probos, with tears running down his flaccid face, told me the Indians had grown to be very insolent; that his life was threatened every day. No trade had been brought in, as none of the hunters had gone out. It was believed the Sioux had killed me and the girl and the Pillager. On the morrow Tabashaw had proposed to raid the X. Y. post down the river and secure the supply of liquor. Then he proposed to burn all posts on the river.

Next morning I sent Probos back to the Reed River and had the Indian women clean up the fort. I assessed every hunter in the camp with a debt of fifty skins to pay for the rum he had consumed, and told them they would not get any more until they squared their debts. For two weeks I worked with the devil riding me. I hated the thought of night and invented excuses to keep up and busy. The gardens had been sadly neglected and the women were kept at work tending these. The hunters were gradually cleared from the fort and the grounds until I had nothing to do but sit down and hate myself and the country. The Pillager had been but a poor companion after he joined me. He spent most of his time hunting buffaloes, and when we met he made no reference to Miss Dearness. I wouldn't ask him about her or affairs at the X. Y. post for anything, and he had no talk except concerning how fat the cows were and the like.

One day I walked down to the river, thinking to take my canoe and paddle upstream and kill time. As I stood, trying to decide whether I really would go or not, a canoe rounded the bend down stream and I could scarcely believe my eyes as I beheld the flaming torch of hair. I would not go upstream as she was going in the same direction. She continued in the middle of the river, fighting the full force of the current. I stared straight ahead. She came abreast of me but did not appear to see me. Then, with a vicious cut of the paddle, she turned inshore, and before I knew it was pulling her canoe up on the beach.

"You're not very neighbourly," she quietly remarked, looking up into my face.

"I'm poor company," I replied.

"Well, I'm going away. I've brought you the keys to the post. Angus will stay there till you come to take over things."

"You going——" I whispered, feeling this was the end of the world.

"Going back east," she pleasantly explained. "The coalition doesn't seem to interest you."

I must have looked my stupidity, for she patiently explained:

"The N. W. and the X. Y. have joined forces. I'm to turn over everything to you."

"When did you learn this?" I cried.

"When I stopped at the H. B. camp at the Forks and found an X. Y. express there. He was on his way to me with a message from the X. Y. headquarters. Simon McTavish is dead. Sir Alexander MacKenzie is now willing to combine. There is no X. Y. company. It's the Northwest company now."

This was astounding and most welcome news. It would make it possible for N. W. Northmen to bring the Indians back to their senses. I said—"When do you go?"

"Soon. In a day or so. There's a summer brigade coming down the Assiniboin. The Pillager is to paddle me to the Forks."

I rubbed my head and forced myself to reason a bit. Then I knew what had puzzled me and I asked——

"If you knew about the coalition when you reached the Forks, why did you keep on to the X. Y. post and wait two weeks before telling me?"

She turned away abruptly, with more of her aloofness, I assumed. I stepped out on the strip of sand and picked up the paddle she had dropped. Then, turning, I surprised her stealing a glance at me. Never could a Sioux knife in grating through my ribs give me such a pang as did sight of the two tears rolling down her cheeks.

I gaped, then seized her hand and waited a second to make sure my medicine was right. She did not offer to draw away. Very slowly I drew her to me.

"What made it wrong the other time was because you hadn't first told me that you loved me," she whispered.

A brown river rushed over the southern horizon, dotted with the brown carcasses of its shaggy victims, bringing the breath of menace from the country of the Sioux where the opportune coming of the Lewis and Clark expedition up the Missouri gave me my chance to help the English girl. She always held it was not right—the way the fur trade was conducted. And I always sat silent and let her have her own way of thinking. As I grew older I realised it was a beautiful way she had of thinking. Being a Northman, I didn't agree with her in my thoughts. But now, since she's gone away on the river that is always calling, I wonder.

*Printed in Great Britain at the
Press of the Publishers*